Julie Shackman is a feel-
journalist.

She lives in Scotland with her husband, two sons and their little Romanian rescue pup, Cooper.

julieshackman.co.uk

x.com/G13Julie
instagram.com/juliegeorginashackman
facebook.com/julie.shackman
bookbub.com/authors/julie-shackman

Also by Julie Shackman

A Secret Scottish Escape

A Scottish Highland Surprise

The Cottage in the Highlands

A Scottish Country Escape

The Highland Lodge Getaway

The Bookshop by the Loch

A Scottish Island Summer

A SCOTTISH HIGHLAND HIDEAWAY

Scottish Escapes

JULIE SHACKMAN

One More Chapter
a division of HarperCollins*Publishers* Ltd
1 London Bridge Street
London SE1 9GF
www.harpercollins.co.uk

HarperCollins*Publishers*
Macken House, 39/40 Mayor Street Upper,
Dublin 1, D01 C9W8, Ireland

This paperback edition 2024
1
First published in Great Britain in ebook format
by HarperCollins*Publishers* 2024

A catalogue record of this book is available from the British Library

ISBN: 978-0-00-861433-1

Printed and bound in the UK using 100% Renewable Electricity
by CPI Group (UK) Ltd

This book is dedicated to all the very special people who make up our precious National Health Service.

Prologue

Alistair materialised at the passenger side door of the toffee-and-black Rolls-Royce and reached for the handle. He had been our family's chauffeur for many years and today would not have been the same without him.

In the backseats, I shot a big grin at my dad beside me.

"You look stunning," he said with a sigh, the crow's feet around his hazel eyes fanning out with pride. "Right. Let's get this show on the road, shall we?"

I took a big breath, before gathering up the hem of my wedding dress. It was a slim, elegant affair, with Italian vine embroidery on the high, stiff collar and three-quarter-length sleeves. A long train, edged with the same vine motif, fanned out from my ice-blonde chignon.

September sunshine splashed everywhere.

Alistair assisted me out of the car, as a bank of press photographers and journalists spilled their way out onto the road. "Och, you look a real bobby-dazzler, Miss Anastasia."

I planted a kiss on Alistair's freshly shaven cheek and he blushed hot pink under his smart peaked cap. "Thank you."

I'd chosen to get married at the medieval church, which sat only a stone's throw from our family home, Bannock House, in a village on the outskirts of Edinburgh. The stained-glass windows of the church glinted down like precious jewels and its spires shot up into the denim-blue sky.

I tightened my grip on my bouquet of blush roses and amber gerbera, interspersed with thistles and ferns.

Everything was perfect.

I appreciated the frothy arrangement of flowers entwined around the high wrought-iron church gate, which matched the blooms of my bouquet. Being a florist, I'd put the most thought and planning into the flowers I wanted for my own wedding day.

More shouts and appeals from the press pack rose into the afternoon air.

"Miss! You look gorgeous. Could you just turn this way please?"

"Miss, could we get a shot of you with your father please?"

My dad rolled his eyes up to his sandy hair. "Don't that lot ever give up?" he hissed to me under his breath.

We both turned around outside the church. "Just let them have a few pics, Dad. Much easier that way." I squeezed his hand. "The party girl's finally settling down. I bet they can't believe it."

"Neither can I," quipped my dad. "You should've had a loyalty card for all those nightclubs and after-parties."

I laughed and waved at the press pack. "Right. Thank you, ladies and gentlemen," I called out. "I think I ought to go and get married now!"

More crackles and whirrs from cameras followed me and my father as we made our way closer to the church entrance.

On hearing the organist launch into one of our musical selections – Vivaldi's *Four Seasons* – my stomach erupted into a series of manic flutters.

Dad's arm slid through mine. "Ready, poppet?"

"Stop. Hold on!"

My older brother, Marcus, erupted out of the church entrance, his partner, Jacob, hot on his heels. They both looked like a pair of sharp, cheek-boned models, all louche and handsome in their pale grey morning suits and waistcoats.

"What is it?"

Marcus and Jacob exchanged strange glances.

My smile died. "What's going on?" My imagination started to go into free-fall. "Oh God. Is it Declan? Has something happened?"

My attention shot past my brother's shoulder and into the cool, elegant interior of the church, where there was a sea of angled hats and fascinators. A few of the guests were turning around in the pews to observe the commotion.

It was like a who's who of British entertainment and society. My floristry business, Majestic Petals, mainly supplied the events and private homes of prominent clients, which meant I had an address book overflowing with impressive and high-profile individuals, some of whom had, over the years, become friends.

Marcus shifted uneasily.

I blinked at my brother, confused.

"Has Declan had an accident?" asked Dad.

"No, not an accident," managed Marcus in his familiar Scottish rumble. He was struggling to look at me. His dark brown floppy fringe lifted a little in the breeze.

"Then what?" I pushed. My tastefully manicured fingers gripped my bouquet tighter.

"He's not coming," said my mother. She had emerged out of the church and was hurrying towards me, immaculate in her aqua fitted suit and wide-brimmed hat.

I stared at her. "What are you talking about?"

From outside the church grounds, I could sense the press had caught wind of a story. A fresh volley of camera clicks went off, competing with the sound of excited chatter.

Mum reached up one hand and stroked my face. Her navy eyes expressed sadness and … was that pity?

Icy fingers tore at my heart. "What do you mean, he's not coming? We're about to get married."

My parents, my brother and Jacob all swapped strained looks.

Mum slipped one arm around my waist. "Come on, darling. Let's get you home."

Chapter One

Fourteen months later

Oh no. Why was he looking across at me?

I attempted to conceal my face behind the thrusting arrangement of oriental lilies, white roses and alstroemeria I was pulling together for Mr McColl's wife's sixtieth birthday. I tried to reassure myself by keeping my fingers busy lacing the blooms in and around one another.

Once I'd finished this bouquet, I would turn my thoughts to how to make the next window themed display of my shop, Flower Power, feel special. It seemed like only yesterday that I'd removed the pumpkins, bats and broomsticks from the Halloween arrangement. Now, I was working towards transitioning from the ambers and russets currently in the window to the festive theme I'd been planning. I loved Christmas and as this would be my first one here in Heather Moore, I wanted to create winter window scenes with extra sparkle.

It would soon be upon us. It was mid-November already!

It was almost four o'clock now though, so perhaps I would make a start on that tomorrow when my two trainee florists, Amber and Rowan, were back.

I waited for a few seconds before risking another peek through the slim stems of the flowers I was arranging. The stranger was still there, lurking beside one of the shelves, from which dangled several of the heart-shaped door decorations I'd constructed from acorns, figs, pine cones, and tartan ribbon.

The man was sporting a large pair of dark sunglasses, despite the hailstorm that had raged just ten minutes ago. More appropriately, he also wore a chunky grey woolly hat and he'd swathed a paisley scarf up around the bottom half of his face. He kept jerking his head round, as if checking the door of my shop.

I refocused on the flower arrangement I was creating and breathed in its heady perfume. This was what I'd been hoping for: the chance to begin a new chapter of my life in which no one knew me.

I loved the colours and shapes of flowers and plants, their assorted scents and the feel of the petals against my fingertips. They were like solid, dependable friends, bringing light and joy into the every day.

I didn't even mind the crazy early starts, when I had to jump in the van at five o'clock in the morning and head to the nearest flower market in Muir Port, which was a forty-five-minute drive away. The canvas stalls would flap in the breeze, sheltering tubs of flowers erupting in every shade and hue.

Under the slumbering tangerine sky, the smell of fresh coffee kept the wholesalers awake and the quiet buzz from car radios danced around the space. The contentment I experienced as I wandered around, selecting what I wanted to buy for Flower Power, was something I hadn't felt for a long time.

Memories of Declan flickered before my eyes. What a humiliation my wedding day had been. The guests staring at me out of the church door, like I was a museum exhibit. The sharp pap and clap of the cameras, the journalists like eager bloodhounds, smelling a story. *Oh, look! The society girl's been dumped at the altar.*

My insides twisted themselves up again into a fierce knot at the memory of it. Mum and Dad had escorted me back to Bannock House, while Marcus and Jacob had announced to the stunned guests that the wedding would not be going ahead and the reverend had dealt with everything else.

As if jilting me on our wedding day hadn't been enough of a slap in the face, it transpired that the money I'd given Declan as an investment for his Making Music Foundation, a charity for underprivileged kids, had vanished with him. The police were still unable to track him down. He'd melted into the night with my heart and my money.

Our relationship had been one enormous lie from the

start. His proclamations of love, the proposal, the "charity" – it had all been contrived like some sort of cold-hearted military operation.

The realisation that he'd been a conman, a mercenary bastard only after me for my money, still festered like an open wound.

I had been taken in by a pale-eyed, fair-haired, charming Irish Adonis. I'd let Declan Rooney play me for a fool. I was determined that would never happen again.

I slunk off straight afterwards for a six-month trip around Europe to recover. I soaked up the sun as I sat outside sweet little cafes in Venice and savoured the atmosphere and bonhomie in Barcelona. It didn't take away my humiliation and heartbreak, but it helped put some much-needed distance between me and the pain.

I swallowed down a growing, choking ball of emotion and fiddled with some ribbon. *Come on,* I chided myself. *Don't stay stuck in the past. Forget about what happened.*

When the name for my new floristry business came to me six months ago, I thought Flower Power was perfect. It made me feel like I was taking control of my life and my future. I reclaimed my love of flowers, started over and put Declan and what he did behind me. My much-loved Uncle James passed away suddenly last year and left a substantial amount of money in his will to both me and to Marcus. Thanks to him, I'd been able to recover from a lot of the financial difficulty Declan had dropped me in and buy the cute little former teashop that was up for sale and transform it into Flower Power. At least flowers were a bright, fragrant, beautiful constant in my life.

I shuffled further to the right from behind the pale pink wooden counter and angled my head around the edge of the display I was working on. I could see Mrs Vardy in her woollen beret examining some new potted gardenia I'd bought from the flower market in town a few days ago. Their leaves were speared and glossy green while their stunning frilly flowers were white and lacy, and I took pleasure in surrounding myself with such treasures.

My attention flew back to the loitering man who seemed oddly fascinated by the vases of lilies I had put at the front to draw customers into the shop.

Panicky thoughts started to leap around in my head. *Hold on. Has he recognised me? Is he preparing to confront me?*

No, that's just not possible. I forced myself to relax.

I'd changed my appearance since my partying days and since the aborted wedding. Gone was my pale, straight blonde hair – I'd reverted back to my natural, light brown waves. I'd also put a few pounds back on, after slavishly dieting and exercising in the run-up to the big day. I was curvier and healthier and I felt better, so that was one good thing. At least I didn't look like a starved twiglet anymore.

I snapped my attention back to the man again.

He did seem more interested in my stock than in me. Or was that just an act to hide his intentions? Was he a journalist, trying to make me think he wasn't?

Memories of the sneering headlines about the "Uptown Girl" being stood up at the altar by a struggling Irish musician zipped through my mind at one hundred miles an hour.

No. Stop it. I was being stupid. That was all in the past. It was society-column fodder. Wasn't it? I was getting irritated with myself. I had to stop surmising that every new face in Heather Moore was here for an ulterior motive.

Declan had done a wonderful job of destroying my trust in people. Apart from my family, since being jilted by him and having gone through such a heart-breaking deception, I found myself building an imaginary wall between me and everyone else. It was safer that way. No risk of being let down or hurt. I eyed the man again. Perhaps he was a shoplifter? Or he was planning to rob the till?

He might have seen my baby-pink-and-white shop as an easy target. But why focus on my business when there were others strung along beside mine that did more cash transactions?

Bolts of worry shot through me. Perhaps I was being naïve. It might only be a matter of time before someone did recognise me and then my quiet life here would be over before it had begun. "Oh, there's that rich girl who was publicly humiliated by that mercenary rogue."

My heart began to gallop against my ribcage.

Shit!

I don't need this.

Oh, this is ridiculous! I can't just stand here and watch him for the rest of the day.

Maybe the police were pursuing him? No. I was letting my imagination go wild.

I couldn't hide behind this half-completed bouquet any longer. I had to stop being afraid and face the situation head-on. I could also close up for the day and go home; the prospect of lounging in a hot bath was delightful.

My curiosity piqued, I set my shoulders. I had to ask him what he was doing and what he wanted, otherwise he was going to become part of the fixtures and fittings.

I pushed my mouth into what I hoped was a polite smile and made my way towards him. Mrs Vardy brushed past me with a friendly nod and left the shop without buying anything. Again.

I turned my attention back to the man.

I had to be brave, otherwise I could be hovering there, carrying out surveillance, for another hour. I cleared my throat.

"Excuse me, sir. Is there anything I can help you with? It's just—"

He didn't give me the opportunity to finish my sentence.

"Oh, no. No. I'm fine." His accent was educated English. "I spotted your shop the other day and just had to come in."

I expected him to remove his sunglasses and swipe off his hat, but he did neither. He dug his chin even deeper into his scarf.

"Oh, thank you."

He gestured towards a selection of my potted plants for sale. "Paperwhite narcissi. I always think they're like mini white daffodils." Then he turned. "And the daphne. Isn't that beautiful?"

I smiled at him. "It is. I always think its reds light up beds and borders, particularly at this time of year."

"Indeed, they do."

I studied him – well, what I could see of him, which wasn't much. "You seem to know your plants."

"I'm a plant lover," he confessed after a few moments' pause. "And flower obsessed."

"Then you've come to the right place."

It was then that the man shot out one hand to his forehead. His voice became thin. "Oh, I'm terribly sorry." He faltered a little on his feet.

I rushed closer to him. "Are you all right?" I reached for his arm.

"I've just come across a little dizzy."

I led him behind the counter, to where there were a couple of chairs. "You sit down. I'll get you a glass of water."

I went into the kitchen area beside my office and filled a glass from the tap.

When I returned, the man had thankfully remained seated, but he still hadn't removed his hat, sunglasses or scarf. He thanked me for the water and took a grateful sip.

"Would you like me to call an ambulance?"

"Oh goodness me, no. I'm beginning to feel better already."

I frowned down at him. "Are you sure?"

I lowered myself into the chair opposite him. "How did you get here? Did you drive?"

He nodded and took another mouthful of water. "I've

taken up too much of your time already, miss." He stood up and placed the glass on the counter, swaying a little.

I jumped up and angled him back down into his chair. "I think you should get checked out by a doctor."

"Absolutely not," he scoffed, his voice growing stronger. "I've just been dashing about rather a lot, overdoing it."

"Well, I don't think you should drive."

I could tell he was looking at me from behind his smoky sunglasses. "Perhaps you're right. Better to be safe than sorry."

At that moment, a lady in a thick cream coat came in and asked about our potted hesperantha. While I attended to her and rang up the purchase at the till, I could hear the mysterious man having a brief conversation behind me on his mobile. I was relieved to hear that it sounded like he was asking someone to come and collect him.

I thanked the woman and waved her off. I'd just turned the shop door sign to *closed* when there was a discreet knock on the door.

"Oh, that will be my lift home," the man rushed, sounding relieved. He sprang up from his seat. "I'll get that."

"It's all right," I assured him. "I'll answer it."

I unlocked the door and opened it to find a tall, distinguished, middle-aged man decked out in full chauffeur regalia. "Sorry to trouble you, madam, but I've come to collect Mr King."

From behind me, there came a resigned sigh.

The driver looked awkward, as though he'd said

something he shouldn't. He shuffled from foot to foot. "Oh hell! I'm sorry, sir."

I turned around. "I take it you're Mr King?"

My voice died.

The mysterious man had removed his hat and sunglasses and was in the process of loosening his scarf.

I took in his features, from the shock of centre-parted silver hair falling onto his shoulders, to the cleft in his chin. My brain was trying to catch up. Mr King. Ezra King.

My brain shuffled through snapshots of him on TV playing William Shakespeare, a playboy sleuth in a romantic comedy, and a dodgy barrister in a recent crime drama.

My eyebrows rocketed to my hairline. *Bloody hell!*

My mouth flopped open.

Oh my God!

My voice squeaked with excitement. "You're Ezra King."

He had just accepted a BAFTA lifetime achievement award in front of an applauding, star-studded throng a few months back. I had seen clips of it online.

This was ridiculous, and I did wonder for a few seconds if I was hallucinating.

Why would Ezra King be here, in Heather Moore? It was such a quiet little part of the Scottish Highlands, welcoming but sleepy. The locals meant well and always gave the impression that although they wanted to know every detail of your life, they would be there without question if you found yourself in any sort of difficulty. So far, I'd been able to fly beneath the radar and just live under my new persona – Bailey McArthur, the florist, and that's the way I liked it. I was determined to make my new life matter here. I would do everything I could to protect the new me. I'd fight to keep my new future that I was carving out for myself. Good grief. If my mother knew Ezra King was only a few feet away from me right now, she would be drenching herself in Coco Chanel and charging over from Tweed Muir like Wonder Woman on steroids.

I thought of my mum, dad and brother co-existing beneath the regal towers, crenelations and flower-studded gardens of Bannock House. Declan had even managed to taint the memories of my childhood home for me, and I had avoided going home as much as possible since the wedding. That was where I had met him, at one of Mum's fundraising events a couple of years ago. His ceilidh band, Reeling, had been performing and he was the fiddler. Quite apt.

I dreaded the whispers and the pitying looks from the Tweed Muir locals after my car-crash of a non-wedding.

Guilt pulled at me again. I knew my parents missed me visiting, but it was still an open wound. Until my pain and embarrassment had subsided, I would rely on keeping in touch with Mum and Dad by Zoom, text, and phone calls.

I made myself refocus.

Ezra King straightened himself up and gifted me with a grateful smile that made his eyes crinkle. A flash of red stole over his cheeks. "I'm so sorry for disrupting your business like this."

I hoped I didn't appear too starstruck. I'd had a stream

of prominent clients when I was running my previous business, but this felt different somehow.

I realised I was staring at him. "Well, it's not every day I have an award-winning actor dropping by."

He pulled a face as he fiddled with his hat in his hands. "I'm sorry if my get-up seemed a little over the top, but I just want to live here in peace and enjoy some anonymity for a change."

He smiled ruefully over at his chauffeur. "Jackson here normally takes me where I want to go, but I was going stir-crazy at home and just wanted to get out and be a regular person for a bit. Does that make sense?"

You have no idea, I thought to myself. "Yes, it makes perfect sense."

Ezra King paused to drink in his surroundings. He gestured around with a sweep of one theatrical hand towards the explosion of plants and flowers on the shop floor. "So, what was this place before?"

"It used to be a tearoom."

"It's lovely. Your displays are beautiful."

I glowed with satisfaction. "Thank you. I only opened a few months ago, so I'm still trying to build up a client base."

He took a few steps to appreciate my wooden shelving and cabinets that were slicked with glossy white paint, and which ran the length of the shop. I'd had the old bottle-green carpet removed and, in its place, lay a cherry wood floor. I'd chosen a shade of pale silver paint for the walls and ceiling, which I thought complemented the bright, cheery pink of my counter and the shop entrance. Warm spotlights cast a golden glow onto the array of plants and flowers billowing from every shelf and corner.

Flower Power was situated at the end of the small high street, which was comprised of a newsagent, an expensive gift shop, a deli, and a glassware business. When I took over the shop, I retained the lovely original bow windows and had the sad grey pebble dash replaced with bright white paint, and the black door renovated into a stylish deep rose-pink panelled affair.

On the other side of the tree-lined road was a dense woodland which attracted many tourists because of its rumoured connections to an old Scottish king. It was said that King Angus had concealed himself from the marauding English army by hiding in the woods and even scaling one of the trees.

I forced my attention back to the star of stage and screen standing across from me. I couldn't believe it. This was surreal!

I gave him an admiring glance. "I loved your portrayal of Shakespeare in that TV show."

His eyes, under his pensive, dark brows, twinkled with appreciation. "Thank you, my dear. That's very kind of you."

He fell quiet as if debating whether to say something else.

"So, you've moved nearby?" I asked in a tentative voice.

"Yes," he blurted out. "To Heather Moore."

I blinked at him in surprise, flattered he was confiding in

me. "Wow! Well, you'll no doubt notice a difference between living here and city life."

His long mouth curled up. "Good God! I bloody hope so!"

Jackson, who was leaning by the shop door, grinned at his boss but remained discreet.

Ezra let his hands rise and fall. "My manager holidayed here once a couple of years ago and raved about the place. She said it was the prettiest Scottish town she'd ever seen and mentioned something about the history of one of the trees you have around here. And the hillsides … well, she loved it." He gestured towards the shop window, explaining that his manager was "a real fuss-pot with very high expectations", and so he had decided to check out the place that had enchanted her so much.

"And so, you decided to escape the rat race and move here?"

"In a nutshell."

Ezra King glanced over his shoulder, even though it was only the three of us. "Look, Miss…"

"Bailey McArthur," I answered quickly, "but please call me Bailey."

Ezra nodded. "Look Bailey, I'd very much appreciate it if you didn't tell anyone about me. I just want some peace."

I rushed to reassure him. "There's no need to explain, Mr King. You have my word." I understood his situation far better than he knew.

Ezra's light grey hooded eyes shimmered with relief. "Call me Ezra. And thank you." He performed a resigned shrug. "I wanted a bolthole, I suppose. Somewhere I could breathe and appreciate the simple things." A wry smile enveloped his face. "Sorry again to crash land in your shop like this on a Monday afternoon. I'd planned to come in and browse, not put you to so much trouble."

"You didn't," I assured him. "As long as you're feeling better now."

Jackson looked at me quizzically.

"Ezra felt a little faint," I said.

Jackson frowned. "You told me you just felt a bit tired. Perhaps we should get you checked over, Mr Ezra."

Ezra shook his head. "Thank you for your concern but no. I'm feeling top notch again now. No fuss required."

Jackson glanced over at me and rolled his eyes.

"Well," I began, trying to unscramble my head. "I'm not Heather Moore born and bred either. I only moved here earlier this year, but I do love it and I'm sure you will too." I allowed my thoughts to drift for a few moments. "My brother and I had great family holidays here with our parents when we were younger. I feel like this town has let me start over again."

Whispers of Declan loomed over me once more like a black cloud. The realisation that he'd only loved my family's bank balance and not me, gripped me like a cold chill.

I bit my lip. "I hope you enjoy living here."

"I'm sure I will," he beamed. He looked around at my plants and bouquets again. "So, what did you do before?" he asked.

I floundered for something to say. "Oh, I've always been a florist. I just fancied a change of scene."

Ezra's considered gaze raked over my face. "I sometimes think we're all trying to escape from something – or someone – even if we don't realise it at the time."

His words struck me in the chest. I managed to force a smile, keen to change the subject.

His expression shifted, before righting itself again. "Does floristry run in your family?"

I shook my head. "No, not at all." I bit back the information that it was dear old Ernie Saunders, our late gardener at Bannock House, who nurtured my love of plants and flowers from an early age.

I would watch him turn over the warm, rich, dark earth of the flower beds, pat the rainbow-coloured blooms in place and plant out our herb garden.

Ernie was very much into his Scottish history and persuaded my parents to grow flowering medicinal plants in the gardens, just like at Holyrood Abbey. Housed beside crocuses, tulips and dusky roses were daisies for coughs and wounds, sorrel for ulcers, and fennel for eye conditions, snake bites, and mad dogs (don't ask). Ernie would arrange them in a geometric pattern to reflect the style and fashion of a seventeenth-century garden.

The myriad scents, from sweet, tangy lemon balm to dense, musky lavender, enchanted me, and when Ernie offered to show me how to plant seeds and deadhead roses, I was smitten.

"And you seem to have a real talent for it, going by your stunning displays." Ezra cut into my thoughts and chuckled. "Oh, that reminds me of the time Jack Nicholson asked me to help him choose a bouquet for Angelica Houston."

"Gosh." I blinked away memories of Ernie's kind, leathery face watching nine-year-old me dancing under the cherry blossom trees, spinning and whirling amongst the soft pink confetti. I focused back on Ezra.

He glanced at his chunky watch. "I'd better go. I've taken up far too much of your time already and I've got a decorator due to give me a quote. Thank you again."

I smiled back at him and extended my hand.

He shook it warmly. "Thank you, Bailey.'

"Not at all,' I said. 'And your secret is safe with me."

"I'm sure it is."

Jackson pushed himself away from the wall. "I'll arrange for your car to be collected later," he said to Ezra.

"Thank you. It's parked round the back of this shop."

As he got ready to slip away through the shop door, Ezra put his disguise back on – hat tugged over his brow, sunglasses, and the scarf covering the bottom half of his face.

"I promise to return as a proper paying customer next time."

"Thanks for taking care of him," whispered Jackson to me, as he hung back to allow Ezra to move ahead. "He's a stubborn old bugger at the best of times."

I laughed, locked the shop door behind them and made

my way back to the counter, my mind still trying to reconcile the events of that afternoon.

It was rather ironic. There was me, panicking that Ezra might know who I was. Another wave of relief flooded through me because he hadn't seemed to recognise me. I'm sure he would've said if he had. Perhaps he wasn't a fan of the gossip magazines.

I grinned to myself. It felt odd to find myself rubbing shoulders with a celebrity again after all I had done to leave that life behind.

Chapter Two

I spent the next couple of evenings throwing around ideas for Christmas promotions I could introduce into the shop.

Business had been good, but it could be even better. At least the locals seemed to be slowly embracing my new business, but there was always room for improvement. Even Joan Webber, a local farm owner and renowned recluse, had briefly dropped by to purchase some potted heather. I knew it would take time to build up a reputation, but there was no way I was about to rest on my laurels. I had to keep going and come up with bigger and brighter ideas.

Perhaps with the approach of the festive season, trade might pick up. I'd been very careful with expenditure and only recruited a couple of local girls as trainee florists. Amber McCabe and Rowan Moffat were studying floristry at college and their shifts helped me out when it was busy as well as providing them with the hands-on experience they needed.

If things picked up, I would advertise for another full-time florist, but I didn't want to get ahead of myself.

The weather had been sunny but icy cold the last couple of days, which meant the surrounding hills were peppered with frost. I looked up for a minute and sighed with pleasure at the view from the shop windows over the King Angus woodland. It looked like it had been draped in spun sugar.

While I served customers, my mind replayed the phone conversation I'd had with my brother on Monday evening.

"You can't hide away in the back of beyond forever, little sister."

"I'm not hiding."

"Yeah, right."

My brother had sighed down the line. "Declan Rooney's a hateful bastard who'll get his comeuppance. You shouldn't punish yourself for what he did to you."

I had rolled my eyes and gazed around my flat.

Declan had had something of the air of River Phoenix about him – the same pretty boy features, the same petulant mouth and intense gaze. When we met, he'd been flirting with Lizzie McKinnon, the daughter of my mum's personal stylist. I'd glowed when he switched his attentions to me, which at the time felt immensely flattering. Only in retrospect was I able to admit that his interest had shifted when he found out whose daughter I was.

It was because I had loved Declan with all my heart that

my dreams had crashed and burned. Along with it went any notion of trusting another man, let alone starting a serious relationship. That was something I didn't need – putting my feelings and emotions out there, to be deceived and trampled over again.

Whatever my brother said, I felt like I was striking out on my own, trying to put the past behind me, and let go of the betrayal and public humiliation Declan had inflicted on me. Ok, so my trust issues still festered like an open wound but at least I was making something of my future.

Still, it was a relief that Wednesday evening to climb the rear staircase to my flat above the shop. The couple who'd run it as a tearoom had also lived above it for many years, so when I bought it, the place had been clean but dated. I had done a complete renovation and it now boasted a sitting room in warm butterscotch, and was teamed with flashes of sunshine-yellow cushions on the toffee-coloured leather sofa and chairs. The shelves were decorated with wooden ornaments of cute foxes and dogs I'd thrifted from various charity shops.

The chintzy rose wallpaper in my bedroom was gone, replaced by muted lavender walls with blonde wood furniture and simple white cotton bedding.

The kitchen was the one room which hadn't required as much attention, so I retained the cream cupboards and had a local tradesman freshen up the space with poppy-red and white tiles and a black marble breakfast bar.

It was a small two-bedroom flat, but it was cosy, it was

above my new business, and it was mine. The perfect home for my fresh start.

I tapped my pen against my teeth as I mulled over possible ways to improve Flower Power's fortunes. This would be the first Christmas for my new business and I was determined to make a splash. Marcus's comments about me hiding away here in Heather Moore had fired me up to make sure I was doing everything I could to make a success of Flower Power. No one would be able to accuse me of not actively promoting my work.

As well as bouquets, I was planning to offer Christmas table centrepieces, festive wreaths and decorated boughs. There were a couple of hotels in the area; perhaps I could offer my festive floristry services to them.

And I still had to decide what I was going to do about decorating the shop window. Perhaps an ice palace theme with white tea roses, lilies, frosted cones, fake snow, and silver decorations might be a little more original than robins and reindeer.

I'd just finished scribbling down more actions on my to-do list, which now included contacting the local hotels as well as some of the restaurants and other businesses in the surrounding areas, when I shot up straighter in my seat in surprise. The landline telephone was ringing.

It was part of the fixtures and fittings and had belonged to Mr and Mrs Rankin, the tearoom couple who lived here before me. I never gave the number to anyone, because I never used it. Anyone who wanted to get hold of me either used my mobile number or rang me on the phone in the shop. It was only because the landline phone in the flat was such a gorgeous vintage treasure that I was loathe to part with it. It was an opal affair in a cream finish, with rotary dialling and a brass cradle for the receiver. It looked like something out of *Downton Abbey*, and I loved it.

Its ringtone, however, was sharp and insistent. I padded over and stared down at it for a few seconds. *Ok, Bailey, looking at it isn't going to help!*

I lifted the receiver, as though it was about to burst into flames at any moment.

"Hello?"

There was a pause.

"Who's that?" barked a deep male voice.

My spine stiffened. I had to stop leaping to conclusions, but the sound of a strange, questioning voice made my shutters clang down. The doubting whispers were back, insisting that it was only a matter of time before someone realised who I was. Had the moment finally arrived when I would be torn from the peace and quiet I was creating for myself here? Could this be it? My stomach pirouetted at the thought.

I tried to find a level of calm. *Stop it,* I told myself. *Stop thinking the worst. This could be an innocent case of a wrong number.* I took a breath. "Who are you looking for?"

I heard a sound like paper being crumpled at the end of the line, as though he were reading something. "I'm looking for Archibald and Hazel Rankin." His accent was a cultivated English one.

A kernel of relief bloomed in me. "I'm sorry. They don't

live here anymore. They moved down to London to be near family."

The male caller's irritation was evident. "But what about this tearoom business of theirs? The Tea Cup…?"

"You mean The Little Teapot—"

His gruff vocals interrupted me. "Yes. Well. Whatever. What's happened to that?"

I blinked, taken aback at how abrupt he was. I clutched the receiver. "I'm the new owner of the business. It's a florist's now."

"A florist?" he repeated, incredulous.

"That's right." I could feel my defensive hackles rising under my fleecy pyjamas. Anyone would think I'd just told him I was money laundering.

There was a series of growls down the line. "The Rankins are no longer around," the rude voice relayed to someone else in the background. "This girl says she owns the place and it's now a florist."

Girl?! This man certainly hadn't graduated from Charm School or, if he had, they needed to conduct an urgent review of their teaching practices.

I overheard another even gruffer male voice rear up in the background. This one was Scottish and fast-paced. "Och, well then, you'd better think of something else, hadn't you? I'm not prepared to let this one slip through our fingers."

Which one? What were they talking about?

I frowned. "Would you like me to try to find the contact details for the Rankins? I have them around somewhere."

But I was talking to thin air. The caller had hung up.

I stood there, stunned, looking incredulously at the telephone receiver.

Talk about rude!

With my curiosity swirling, I dialled 1471 to see if I could retrieve the number of the man who'd just called me. No luck. The message, "The caller withheld their number" echoed in my right ear.

I replaced the receiver on its cradle and studied the phone. What on earth was that about? I gave the silent phone another frown. It was all very odd.

I forgot all about the call by Friday morning as I wrestled with updating the Flower Power website. I listed some new arrivals, boasted about our current discounts on offer and hoped to encourage people to think about their poinsettias, Christmas wreaths, and festive centrepiece decorations by advising customers that they could begin submitting their orders from the start of next week. I uploaded some new images of my latest handiwork to reiterate the point.

I also posted an advert for autumnal door wreaths. They were actually the leftover Halloween ones consisting of orange, tangerine and amber flowers, interwoven with black ribbon and studded with tiny bat and cat silhouettes. I'd decided to recycle them by removing the black ribbon, bats and cats and reinvigorating them with some berries and cones. I asked Amber to take a few pictures of them and upload them to social media sites. Waste not, want not!

Then I gave Amber some revision questions ahead of a theory test on her course. We went over everything, from the preferred size and shape of vase for an arrangement to how to trim stems in three varying heights like football stadium tiers to create more volume.

We also discussed what was currently trending – tropical flowers in a geometric vase without a lot of greenery; mounded arrangements of just one type of flower; and woody branches with fruit or berries – when the shop doorbell tinkled.

Out of the corner of my eye, I noticed a figure entering huddled in an ankle-length, dove-grey coat with a flash of red scarf at the neck. It took me a moment to realise it was Ezra's chauffeur, Jackson.

"Good morning," I said, closing the lid of my laptop.

Jackson's features were open and friendly as his eyes shifted from left to right, checking out who was around.

Amber afforded Jackson a brief, disinterested glance, before turning her attention to a young couple who were admiring the potted heather.

Jackson strode over and dropped his voice. "Ezra's out back. Would it be too much to ask for you to let him in through the fire door please?"

"Of course."

I hurried to the back of the shop and clanged open the heavy door. Blimey. This was unexpected. Why was Ezra back again so soon?

Ezra stood facing me with a cheerful smile plastered across his face. He swiped off his hat and jammed it into his coat pocket.

"Good morning, Bailey. How are you? Sorry about the cloak-and-dagger stuff, but I've got to be careful."

I smiled. "I'm well, thank you, Ezra. How are you?"

"I'm quite chipper."

Jackson emerged, told Ezra he would wait in the car, and then slipped out of the fire door as Ezra made his way in.

I snuck a peek over the shop floor. Amber was striding around, all Cleopatra eye make-up and Doc Martin boots, as she guided the couple over to where we housed some hanging baskets.

"I don't suppose you have a minute?" he whispered.

"Oh. Yes. Of course." I made sure Ezra was safely ensconced in my office with the door closed. "Amber, can you keep an eye on things here for a few moments please?"

"Sure."

I slipped into the office and closed the door behind me. Ezra was appreciating the potted orchid on my desk and the framed pictures of artistically photographed flowers on the walls.

He sat himself down. "I wanted to thank you again for the other day." His wide mouth slid into a lopsided smile. "You were so kind and understanding."

"You're welcome. How are you feeling now?"

Ezra dismissed my concern with a wink. "Like I'm twenty-five again."

He leaned forward in his chair. "The reason I've

dropped by is because there's something I wanted to talk to you about."

I couldn't imagine what he was going to say and my eyes grew wider as Ezra explained. "I mentioned to you the other day that I'm a huge flower and gardening fan. Always have been." He threw me a coy look. "I love to be surrounded by fresh flowers and I used a charming young gentleman when I lived in Knightsbridge. But now that I'm here, I'm looking for a new florist to supply me with stunning floral displays for my new home."

He paused again for effect. *Ever the actor*, I thought.

"I wondered whether you would be interested in supplying regular flower arrangements for my home here. I envisaged every couple of weeks?" Ezra steepled his tanned hands together on top of my desk. "Your displays are gorgeous and I suppose it's also my way of thanking you properly for what you did for me the other day."

Although this felt a little close to my old celebrity business for comfort, I found myself agreeing. "But I didn't really do anything."

"In a way, that's right. Some people would've gone straight to the papers and capitalised on having me in their shop like that. You didn't. You kept your word, and for that I'm very grateful."

Empathy for his situation radiated out of me; he was trying to get some peace and equilibrium in his life, just like I was. He had no idea how easily I could relate to his predicament. "I would never do something like that," I assured him.

My hand flapped to my chest and rested there. Since I'd gone to ground after what happened with Declan and closed down my former floristry business, my previous clients had understandably gone elsewhere for their decadent floral displays.

Flower Power was a fresh start – and a whole new type of client and business model.

But the opportunity presenting itself now with Ezra to get my creative skills noticed again in a new market was priceless. I did worry that perhaps one of his friends might ask for my details and recognise me, since word-of-mouth was how I had grown my old business, but it seemed unlikely and the risk felt small. I was old news, after all, and his Scottish retreat was miles from the social hub of London where famous friends might drop by and ask for local recommendations. How many celebrities needed a Highland florist?

I'd changed my name too and my appearance. In my mind, I had done and would continue to do everything I could, to move on from the mess of my past.

I was aware I still hadn't said anything. I was delighted, but conflicted. This was such an amazing opportunity for the business. I couldn't say no. I didn't want to.

The more I thought about it, the more I wanted to take on this commission – and do Ezra's new home in Heather Moore proud. I'd just have to hope that any of the visitors to his home weren't keen readers of the society columns, or interested in floral arrangements.

Ezra was appraising me from his chair. "And Bailey, I'm

not expecting … what is it you call it? Mates' rates? You've only been open a matter of months, so I insist on paying you the full whack for your services."

I knew it would be a lot of hard work, but it would be worth it.

Ezra's brows arched, expecting an answer.

Come on, Bailey! Say something!

Dismissing any more debate with myself, I managed a huge, silly grin.

Ezra's laughter lines feathered. "Is that delightful smile a yes? Can I rely on you to furnish my house with the most extravagant and dazzling flowers?"

I jumped to my feet, almost knocking over my potted orchid. "You bet you can! Thank you, Ezra! Thank you so much!"

I couldn't contain the fizzing in my chest. This was such a coup and meant so much for my fledging business.

I darted round my desk, shook his hand and, forgetting myself for a moment, delivered a grateful kiss to his cheek. "Thank you so much, Ezra. I'll make sure your flowers are something special." Crikey. My voice sounded like Minnie Mouse.

Ezra's craggy complexion popped pink as he hitched up the collar of his coat. "I've no doubt about that, young lady."

He plonked his hat back on his head as I escorted him out of the office and towards the fire door, where Jackson was waiting in a big black car. Ezra slipped his sunglasses and scarf back on and glanced up and down the quiet car park. He dug his hands into his coat pockets. "Right. I'd better go. I'm expecting a new sofa delivery at three o'clock."

My curiosity was piqued. I couldn't envisage him moving into one of those new-build houses on the estate out towards the farmland. Ezra didn't seem like a "new build" type of guy.

"Erm... I probably need your address, if that's ok?"

He rolled his eyes melodramatically. "Oh, I'm a stupid old sod. Of course." He chuckled to himself. "I've bought that old property towards the reservoir. It needed quite a bit of work." He shifted from foot to foot to keep warm. "You must come over and see inside the house, of course. You'll need to see what I've done with the place so you can design appropriate arrangements."

"You live at Duxbury Hall?" I said. "Oh wow. I'm sure it's looking fantastic."

Situated a couple of miles away, Duxbury Hall was a secluded property – a mix of dry-stone walls, sash windows and stacked chimney pots on a considerable plot of land. I'd heard stories about a flurry of activity in the area since last autumn and the Heather Moore gossips had wagered that a person of note was planning on taking up residence there.

I remembered hearing it had once been owned in the 1900s by a silent movie actress who'd taken refuge there after her fiancé had gone off and married someone else. It seemed fitting, therefore, that Ezra should take ownership of it now. No doubt he'd turned it into something special.

Ezra smiled. "It's not too shabby."

As he turned towards his waiting car, he called over his shoulder. "I'll drop by again in a day or two."

A thought struck me. "Oh, Ezra, I have two part-time students who will be helping with the arrangements. What do you want me to tell them?"

Jackson leapt out of the car and opened the back door for Ezra to clamber inside. "I'd rather you didn't say anything for now. I just think the fewer people that know about me being in the area, the better."

"Of course." I nodded. "I understand."

I watched him wave and Jackson gave me a nod as the car glided away.

I'd just have to be discreet where Amber and Rowan were concerned. Ezra was trusting me and I wouldn't betray that trust. Both of the girls were lovely, but Amber could talk for Scotland and one word in the wrong direction and Ezra could find himself under siege from fans and reporters. I'd just have to come up with something to explain this new influx of work.

With my stomach still tumbling over with excitement, I burst back into the shop. Amber was unpacking a box of new satin ribbons in a kaleidoscope of colours. "I love this one," she commented, holding up a sheaf of the deepest blue.

"It's very pretty," I agreed, struggling to pay proper attention to what she was saying. I checked my watch and tried to unscramble my thoughts. "You should be heading home now."

"Thanks, Bailey. I will do once I've finished unpacking

these ribbons and draping them over the hooks in the store room."

I swallowed hard, my adrenalin pumping.

Amber frowned at me. "What did that old guy want?"

It took me a moment to realise who she was referring to. Shit. She must've caught sight of Ezra leaving the office.

One of Britain's most revered actors and she was referring to him as an "old guy". I'm sure Ezra would've been delighted to hear himself described as such. "He's not old," I replied, avoiding her question.

Amber arched one brow as if to say, "That's your opinion." She returned to pulling swathes of ribbon out of the box.

Chapter Three

Later that day, I heaved a contented sigh as I swivelled the shop sign to read *closed*. I removed some leaves from the stems of some of the pastel-coloured carnations. If they tumbled into the vase, they could cause bacteria in the water.

The thought of retreating upstairs to pamper my feet with peppermint lotion and pour myself a glass of crisp white wine was delicious.

I moved around the shop, clicking off the spotlights and plunging the plants and flowers into darkness, so they sat like graceful, still silhouettes.

A sudden flicker of movement outside the shop door made me draw up.

Was there someone out there?

I squinted. Sure enough, a tall shimmering figure had appeared through the frosted glass of the shop door. I wondered if they might move on, but they hovered there.

Recalling that I'd already locked it, I raised my voice. "Sorry, we're closed."

I moved back towards the counter to collect my bag, but a thud and a rattle of the door handle made me whirl around.

Was someone trying to get in?

The door handle let out another fierce crank.

I tilted my chin in an effort to conjure up some confidence. "We're closed. We reopen tomorrow morning at 9am."

I hoped whoever it was would evaporate into the dark, but instead they remained a smudged apparition through the glass.

They jiggled the door handle again.

"I'm sorry," I repeated louder. "We're closed. You'll have to come back tomorrow."

The door handle jerked up and down once more.

Right! That was it!

Remembering I had a small bottle of hairspray in my bag, I lunged towards the counter to retrieve it. A good squirt of that right between the eyes would disable them for a while.

My knuckles turned white as I gripped the can of hairspray in my right hand, my finger on the button, ready to spray. My heart thumped against my chest. "How many times do I have to tell you? We're closed."

There was yet another defiant jerk of the door handle. My heart took off into an even faster gallop.

I rummaged inside my bag again, sending its contents

spewing and clattering out on top of the shop counter. "Oh shit!"

I snatched up my mobile. My fingers were tumbling over themselves. "Don't get any ideas! I'll ring the police."

"Please don't do that," insisted a male voice through the door, making me jump. "I need to speak to you."

With my can of hairspray held in mid-air, I hesitated. An echo of recognition rang around my head. What was it about his voice? I was sure I'd heard it before.

There was a tap of feet from the other side of the door. His silhouette was black and broad against the pinpricks of streetlights. "I think it might have been you I spoke to on the phone. About the Rankins?"

I focused again on his voice. It took a few seconds for my frightened brain to catch up and recall the details.

That was it. It was him. It was the arrogant man who'd rung the flat, looking for Archibald and Hazel Rankin.

I hovered behind the safety of the closed shop door, my container of hairspray still gripped in one hand and my mobile glowing in the other. My worry increased. "What do you want? Who are you?"

"I'm Zach Stern. I'm a journalist."

Dread clutched the insides of my stomach. *A journalist?* What did he want? Was it to do with me? Had he found out I'd moved to Heather Moore and that was why he rang the Rankins? Had Declan discovered I'd moved here and been shouting his mouth off from whatever stone he'd crawled under, wanting to twist the knife? But how would he have discovered me here? I'd been so careful. Or had someone local recognised me and tipped off the press? How likely was that?

My rambling thoughts whirled around my head like a carousel.

I knew I had to try and calm down.

I couldn't legislate for other people's behaviour, but then another thought bounded into my head. It was one I found myself starting to scramble for. I clung onto it, like a lifebuoy in stormy seas. Maybe someone had told this journalist about Ezra? Maybe he wasn't here about me at all.

Then a pang of guilt hit me in the chest. Thinking that way didn't make me feel any better. In fact, I felt worse. I didn't want Ezra to be hounded by reporters. He'd just moved here and was starting to get settled.

I edged a little closer to my shop door, my ankle boots clicking on the wooden floor. *Now what should I do?* If I didn't let him in, I could make matters so much worse and the chances were that he'd return again anyway. If he was like most of the journalists I'd come across in the past, he would persevere until he got whatever story he was after. They didn't tend to give up, if they believed they had a lead.

And if he was here to snoop around about Ezra, there was no way I was prepared to give him any information. Even though we'd only just met, Ezra trusted me and I wasn't prepared to betray that trust. He was giving me the floristry commission for his home, for pity's sake!

"Hello? Are you still there?"

His voice cut across my thoughts from the other side of the locked shop door.

"Please can I come in? It's bloody Baltic out here."

The stiff winter evening – this part of the Highlands was famous for its bone-rattlingly cold weather, especially in the weeks before Christmas – was clearly having an effect on his manners as, other than the swearing, he was more polite than he had been when talking to me over the phone.

I chewed my bottom lip. I'd no intention of allowing this man in until I knew for certain what he wanted – or who. My brain searched for stalling tactics. "How do I know you are who you say you are?"

There was the sound of fumbling, before a business card hissed its way under the door.

I set my phone and hairspray down on top of the counter, before moving back towards the shop door and the rectangular white card now lying face-down in front of me. I snatched it up and turned it around. Sure enough, the name **Zach Stern** leapt out in bold, black lettering. Underneath his name was printed **Journalist – *Stargazer Magazine***, followed by his contact details.

My breath stuck in my throat.

Stargazer Magazine. A glossy weekly publication that featured gossip and revelations about celebrities. *Oh, no.*

"I really would appreciate a few minutes of your time," came Zach Stern's deep English drawl through the door.

My thoughts refused to calm.

This was ridiculous. I was going to give myself a migraine.

"What about?"

"Hi? Hello? Are you still there?" His agitated voice interrupted me again. "Look, I don't mean to sound rude, but can't you let me in for a few minutes so we can talk? I can't feel my toes out here."

I crouched down and pushed the business card back under the door, still scrambling around in my head for an idea of how to throw this man off the scent. "What is it you want?"

There was a frustrated sigh, then, "All right, if I tell you, will you please let me inside?"

I wrapped my arms around myself. "Maybe."

"Oh, for Christ's sake!"

I glowered at his silhouette, even though he couldn't see me through my closed shop door. "Sorry? I didn't quite catch that?"

There was an agitated growl from outside. "I hope you're satisfied. I think I've just lost all circulation in my hands."

I rolled my eyes, but didn't make a move to open the shop door.

Zach Stern let out a defeated grunt. "Nice to see such warm hospitality around these parts."

I cocked one brow and still didn't move to open the door.

There was a deep sigh. "All right. I'll tell you. It's Ezra King."

Shit. I was right. Had someone local ratted on Ezra? Had someone spotted him at Duxbury Hall or here and decided to make some easy money? The prospect filled me with dismay. If this was what had happened to Ezra, might I be next?

I rubbed at my face. "Ezra King?" I repeated, my voice sounding brittle. "As in, the actor?"

"No, Ezra King the refuse collector. Of course, the actor! I just told you that!"

I folded my arms and sniffed. "There's no need for sarcasm."

"Sorry," mumbled Zach Stern from the other side of the door. "But it's perishing out here."

I continued to assess the mysterious shape of this journalist.

I saw him push an agitated hand through his hair. His features were obscured and shifting behind the frosted glass as he shuffled from foot to foot.

Then he moved even closer to the other side of the door, sending me retreating a few steps backwards.

"Look, Miss…?"

"Bailey," I murmured. "Bailey McArthur."

"Right, Ms McArthur. I won't take up too much of your time. I promise. But I'm at risk of hypothermia out here and I hoped you might be able to help."

I fiddled with one of my dangly earrings and decided to play dumb. "Help with what?"

"Help doing a crossword. Help with finding Ezra King!"

There it was, the brittle sarcasm again.

I fiddled with the strap of my watch. All I wanted to do was escape upstairs to my dinky little flat and put a safe distance between me and this journalist. "So why did you say you wanted to speak to Mr and Mrs Rankin the other night?"

I heard Zach Stern blow out a cloud of air. "I did some investigating after we received the tip-off about Ezra King being seen around here. I took a look at Heather Moore online and I found a website giving details of Mrs Rankin being involved in local amateur dramatics."

"And you wondered whether she might know anything or have come across Ezra King?" I supplied. "Well, like I told you, the Rankins sold me this place and moved to London to be near family."

There came another frustrated grunt from the other side of the shop door. "I suggest the local amateur dramatics society update their website then. Hazel Rankin is still listed as one of their major players."

There was a charged silence for a few moments before I put out my hand and let it hover over the door latch. If I let him in, perhaps I could control the situation more. I had no intention of misleading a journalist, but I wasn't prepared to tell him anything about Ezra either.

I just hoped he wouldn't realise who I was. I was beginning to like the new me. I was toughing it out after being conned and jilted and I refused to lose the lovely, quiet life I was building for myself here in Heather Moore.

The life I lived before, falling out of nightclubs with celebrity friends all seemed so pointless now, when I surveyed Flower Power.

I had to try and be composed. I didn't want to put this

journalist on high alert about Ezra or myself. Refusing to debate the matter a moment longer, my hand shot out and unlocked the shop door.

A snap of brisk, November chill shot through the open door, as did the athletic, tall figure of a handsome man. He possessed thick, wavy, blueberry-black hair, pushed back from his angular face. He wasn't what I was expecting.

Zach Stern appraised me through intense, dark brown eyes. He extended a gloved hand. "Good to meet you. Apologies if I don't maintain eye contact. My eyelids are frozen."

I shook his hand in return and allowed my long hair to fall over my face in an attempt to obscure it. I didn't want to take any chances, just in case I did seem familiar to him. "I'm sure you can appreciate me being careful."

He cocked one brow and turned his attention to his surroundings. "So, this is yours?"

I nodded, watching his broad shoulders swing this way and that under his long charcoal wool overcoat.

"I've only been open since late spring, but business is improving."

I battled to ignore the warning voice yelling in my head. *What the hell do you think you're doing? You're sharing idle chit chat with a journalist. You need to get rid of him. Fast. You'll be discussing the weather and last night's TV next.*

Deciding that I should get this unnerving situation over with as soon as possible, I suggested we talk in my office. The light wouldn't be great in there either at this time of day, which would be an added advantage.

He glanced around while following me across the shop floor. I clicked on a couple of the low lights, which bathed my sleepy flowers and plants in a golden hue. I could hear his boots thudding along behind me.

I indicated for him to sit down opposite me at my desk. I clicked on my desk lamp and angled it away from my face. He didn't waste any time exchanging pleasantries. Even his voice didn't marry with the image I'd conjured of him in my head. He seemed more like the type of journalist who should be writing in-depth political analysis for the likes of *The Times*.

"So, Ezra King," he announced, pinning me with his burning, dark gaze from across the desk.

I hoped I could maintain an aura of calm and that my neck wasn't a sea of red blotches, like it always was when I got nervous. "What about him?"

"Like I said, we've been told he's been seen here in Heather Moore."

I performed an indifferent shrug. "Are you sure? I very much doubt it. Maybe it's a lookalike. They say we all have a doppelganger."

Zach Stern frowned at me. "So, you haven't seen him? He hasn't been in here?"

I fought to maintain a level of calm in my voice. "Nope. I think I'd recognise him if I saw him."

He suddenly leant forward. "You're certain of that, are you?"

I swallowed. "Yes. Of course."

"It's just we were told that someone who looked very

much like him may have come in here."

I forced out a bark of laughter. "Well, he didn't."

He lounged back in his swivel chair, as though my office belonged to him. A bolt of irritation fired through me. He wasn't lacking in confidence. "It's just that someone contacted the magazine to say she and her friend were driving through Heather Moore on their way to Inverness recently." He tilted his dark head to one side as he continued to speak. "She said they were sure they saw him in his car and they thought he may have come in here."

Great. Just bloody great! Annoyance on Ezra's behalf stirred up inside of me. I knew what it was like to be betrayed; for people to let you down. I pushed Declan out of my head and made myself refocus on what Zach Stern was saying. Why was this anyone's business? Couldn't they leave him alone?

The tips of my cheeks sizzled. I hoped he wouldn't notice. I let my hands flail around. "What would someone like Ezra King be doing round here?" I offered Zach a pointed look. "So, are you planning on writing a story about it? About Ezra King living here now, which he isn't."

"You sound very sure of that." Zach Stern eyed me.

I straightened my shoulders and said nothing.

"So, you can't tell me anything?"

"I wish I could help," I said with a sigh. "Sorry."

"Yes. I'm sure you are." His black brows fenced. "Well, if you can't help, can you suggest anyone else around here who I can speak to?"

I toyed with my ring. A jagged edge of worry nicked me.

I'd been deluding myself if I thought he would just accept what I told him and move on. "So, you're hanging around then?"

"Oh, I'm not planning on going anywhere. I have my editor breathing down my neck and this is an exclusive I'm not going to pass up."

My smile was tight. "An exclusive? What? 'Actor spotted in Scotland'? Hardly front-page news."

Zach forced a hand through his hair and it fell back from his face. "No, you're right. It isn't."

My irritation was rising. "Well, what are you talking about then? Why are you so keen to speak to him?"

Zach gave me a measured look. "It seems our Mr King isn't as lily-white as he portrays."

A sliver of worry shot through me. "In what way?"

But Zach Stern just offered a withering look. It was a stupid question. As if he would tell me.

Instead, he moved the conversation on. "I've checked into one of the local hotels."

My stomach plummeted. Oh goody. I'd been naïve enough to think that he might decide his Ezra King hunt was a wild goose chase and he would take himself and his posh coat back to the city. But talk of Ezra possibly being involved in something shady and Zach Stern's determination to stay around had put paid to that optimism.

"Which one?" I asked, a rising dread growing. "I mean, which hotel are you staying at?"

"The Cedar Loch." He studied me across my desk. "So,

no suggestions of who I could talk to around here about Ezra King, then?"

I sat there, conscious that a magazine journalist was still in town and pursuing Ezra. And he was clearly determined to stay around until he found something. Anything.

Hang on! An idea skipped into my brain. Zach was staying at The Cedar Loch, where Moira Telford worked as a receptionist. Moira was a lovely woman, but she was also infamous for flirting with her more attractive male hotel guests. She should keep our friendly neighbourhood journo occupied for a while.

If my idea worked, it could buy some more time and if Zach Stern got irritated or frustrated enough, he might just decide to drop his search for Ezra. Right now, anything was worth a try. I didn't want him hanging around Heather Moore. I wasn't prepared to risk him identifying me, and I felt very protective of Ezra too.

I switched on a smile. "Come to think of it, when you get back to your hotel, ask to speak to Moira Telford. Have you met Moira yet?"

"No."

"She's one of the hotel receptionists. I'm sure she'll be very happy to speak with you." I drank in Zach Stern's enviable lashes and sweep of dark hair. Moria would think Christmas had come early. Sure, there was a chance she'd have seen Ezra, too, but the main thing was that *I* didn't betray him.

I dropped my voice, even though it was only the two of us. "What Moira knows about Heather Moore is legendary."

I fought to conceal a smile. "She'll be very helpful, I'm sure."

"All right. I'll speak to her. Thank you." He rose to his feet and I hurried to bundle him out of my shop as soon as possible.

It was as I was clicking open the door that he drew up and examined me again from under his thick brows. "I hope you don't mind me saying but have I seen you somewhere before, Ms McArthur? You seem familiar."

A deep chill, like ice cold water, shot down my spine. I struggled to arrange my mouth into a cool smile. "No. Don't think so. I have one of those faces." *Ugh! Stop with the clichés, Bailey!*

After a few seconds' consideration, Zach pulled his attention away. "Well, thanks for speaking to me – finally."

I poked my tongue out at his retreating back.

Chapter Four

That evening, I pulled together my dinner, which ended up consisting of plaice, mashed potato, broccoli and sweetcorn.

Once I'd cleared up, I nestled onto my sofa, arranged my laptop on the occasional table in front of me and found myself typing *Zach Stern* into the search engine.

The events from earlier had rattled me. What had Zach Stern been talking about? What was Ezra supposed to have done?

I waited and the screen rippled.

A couple of images of Zach appeared. One was a moody, black-and-white head and shoulders shot of him in a fitted white shirt that was straining across his broad chest. He was staring down into the camera.

Another was of him looking like James Bond in a dinner suit, clasping an impressive, spikey designed journalism award.

I scrolled down further.

There was a biography of staff on the *Stargazer* magazine website, which included Zach's.

Under the heading, *Zach Stern, Senior Investigative Reporter*, was his profile:

Stargazer *is delighted to welcome acclaimed journalist Zach Stern to our team.*

Zach, who has worked for such prestigious titles as the New York Daily, *the* London Informer *and the* Daily Herald, *will bring you all the sensational exclusives, in his own inimitable style.*

Zach, who was born in the St John's Wood area of London and studied journalism at Kingston University, says he always wanted to be a reporter, because he wanted to give people who didn't have a voice a chance to be heard.

When not reporting for Stargazer, *Zach enjoys running, working out, reading James Patterson novels, and listening to rock music.*

I examined the accompanying photo of Zach again, all arched dark brows and a serious, set mouth.

I clicked away from the magazine website and returned to trawling through a few more articles about him. Phrases like *"Recognised for his tireless dedication to investigative journalism; Lauded reporter; Respected journalist with a thirst for a good story; Zach Stern's relentless fight to get to the truth, earnt him the prestigious Investigative Journalist of the Year Award in 2021"* tumbled past my eyes.

My frown deepened as I read on. That was strange. What was an accomplished journalist like Zach Stern doing working for a gossip magazine like *Stargazer*? He had a glut of journalistic accolades and had netted so many scoops and yet, here he was, on one of the country's most sensationalist celebrity gossip magazines. It didn't seem to make sense.

It would be like seeing King Charles at a Slayer concert.

I scanned some other random articles about Zach. He'd covered everything from political wrongdoings with MPs' expenses to the American elections. I then returned to the *Stargazer* website, which was bragging on the front cover of their latest issue that they had an exclusive on a reality TV star who'd undergone her fourth boob job in so many months. They were also boasting about their double-page spread on the new home of a famous premier footballer and his girlfriend, which included shots of their lavish zebra-print carpet and gold kitchen taps.

Having seen enough, I switched off my laptop and closed the lid.

Well, whatever his reasons for going to work at *Stargazer*, I knew I had to be careful. Zach had already remarked that I looked familiar. I swallowed hard at the memory.

Those bloody society columns!

My thoughts shifted to Ezra.

I would have to warn him that a journalist was lurking around in search of him. It was the least I could do.

In the meantime, I would just have to ensure I stayed one step ahead of Zach Stern – my settled life here in Heather Moore and the future of Flower Power could depend on it.

I was about to return my laptop to the kitchen table, but my fingers refused to budge. They hovered on the closed lid. It was thinking about *Stargazer* that had dragged everything back up again.

I watched as my hands rested on the charcoal laptop lid, before flipping it back up and daring me to switch it on again.

I always said I wouldn't and that I didn't want to. Yet the urge to look back and see how far I'd come was irresistible. It felt as though the tips of my fingers were itching.

I knew it wouldn't achieve much. In fact, it wouldn't achieve anything. It would just stir up moments and memories that I'd pushed away; recollections that filled me with burning regret.

But looking at that magazine online had triggered morbid curiosity in me again.

My fingers shifted to the keyboard until I found myself pulling up newspaper images of Declan and me announcing our engagement. I was gazing up at him like a rescued puppy, flashing my sapphire engagement ring, but he was too busy exposing his canines to the press photographer.

There were also photos of me at various parties and nightclubs. In some, my then-blonde hair was plastered to my face as I negotiated my way out of some exclusive venue in the early hours. They rippled up onto the screen, one after the other, as though they were taunting me.

I shrank back and stared at my unrecognisable self: the

heavy make-up, fake tan, my starved frame, the long, platinum-blonde hair extensions, the brash attitude, and pointed, needle-thin high heels.

I was used to the odd sycophant and occasional hanger-on doing their best to inveigle themselves with me, so they might gain a crumb of fame for themselves, but I never envisaged Declan would be the same. In many ways, he'd proved himself to be far worse. At least with the hangers-on, they were obvious and didn't try to hide it.

I blinked away the beginning of tears and scrolled down a few more images. There were a few shots of Marcus, me and Jacob together, taken at a couple of charity events organised by our mother.

When we were kids, Marcus was always the protective big brother and was somehow able to calm Mum down if she got worked up at me for staying out until all hours, when I walked on the wilder side of life. It was impressive to watch, rather like a lion tamer with a ferocious beast.

I peered at my laptop screen, fighting to process the fact that this young woman and I were one and the same. She was like a ghost from my past, with her flash clothes and dripping in extortionate jewellery and designer handbags.

And to think I would be out, throwing shapes on exclusive dance floors, before heading to work at Majestic Blooms a matter of hours later, to spruce up the flower arrangements of the likes of musical theatre stars, rock singers and well-known authors.

The memory of me sporting sunglasses to shield my fragile eyes, as I gingerly stepped into the marbled hallways of the great and the good, to create fresh flower displays for them, came back to haunt me.

Had I really been able to exorcise that former version of myself from my life? Perhaps Heather Moore could finally help me do that.

My fingers stumbled over the laptop keys, before switching it off and retreating to bed.

I decided I'd seen enough of who I used to be.

Lady Anastasia McLaren-Kerr.

Chapter Five

The next morning – Saturday – saw a steady stream of customers, keen to avail themselves of the re-invented, former Halloween door wreaths and bouquets that Amber, Rowan, and I had been working on.

There were also a few Christmas wreath and festive table decoration enquiries.

I arrived at Flower Power just after 7am, but the Heather Moore woodland across the way looked so inviting in the rose-gold morning that I decided to delay entering the shop for a few minutes and take a meander before I got started for the day.

The bare tree branches twisted and knotted overhead like intricate, Italian Renaissance artwork and the twigs crackled under my feet.

I breathed in the fresh, zingy scent of damp grass and earth.

It was so dense and quiet, I could almost imagine King

Angus racing through here and clutching his crown, as he attempted to scale one of the trees to escape his enemies.

I turned and started to make my way back when I heard the thudding of footsteps behind me.

It was that bloody journalist, Zach Stern, out for an early morning run.

He was dressed in a black-and-white tracksuit; dark trainers and his sweaty hair was falling forward.

Looking around wildly, I jumped behind a nearby, gnarly tree, pressing my back against the trunk. I held my breath. Yes, this would be fine. I'd been quick, so I was sure he hadn't seen me….

"Ms McArthur?"

Oh shit.

I wished the tree would open up its trunk and let me crawl inside for the next ten years.

Grinding my teeth together, I hoped I looked like I always threw myself against trees early in the morning and jutted my chin out. "Oh, Mr Stern. Good morning. I didn't see you there."

Zach's mouth twitched. "Too busy examining the rings?"

"Sorry?"

He pointed at the tree.

"Oh, right. Yes. Er… I mean, no." I cleared my throat and struggled to keep eye contact with him. "Just taking a little walk before starting my day." I spotted his broad shoulders under his tracksuit top and averted my eyes. "Anyway, better be off. Have a good day."

Zach's dark chocolate eyes shone back at me from under his flopping hair. "Oh, I'm sure I'll catch you later. Stories to investigate and people to speak to."

I struggled to deliver a polite smile. Bugger. That meant he was planning on interrogating me again.

He forced a hand through his hair as he steadied his breath. His attention stayed locked on me, like a heat-seeking missile.

I moved off, setting my shoulders.

Arrogant prick!

As soon as I unlocked the shop door, I whisked on my pink-and-white apron, so I could water the plants, administer their feed and get a head start with tweaking a couple of the birthday orders that were due to be collected. I also intended to jump in my car and head straight over to Duxbury Hall to see Ezra as soon as there was a bit of a lull in the shop. Bumping into Zach like that just now had made me even more determined to alert Ezra. He needed to know that Zach Stern and *Stargazer* magazine were on his tail. My indignation fired up. If that journalist thought for one second, he could breeze into Heather Moore and upend Ezra's life – and possibly mine – he'd better think again!

Amber and Rowan were more than capable of holding the fort in my absence, but I didn't want them to feel like I was taking advantage.

I stood behind the counter, snipping some nerine stems

at an angle so the blooms would absorb more water. They also looked better with angled stems when arranged in a display as it meant they tended not to lie flat at the bottom of vases. I paused to admire their rosy lipstick shades.

As soon as it hit ten-thirty, Flower Power seemed to exhale a sigh of relief as the last couple of shoppers clattered the doorbell on their way out, armed with their burnished seasonal bouquets and berry-studded potted plants.

A couple of stray copper leaves tumbled along the pavement outside the shop door. Christmas was getting ready to land its sparkly, gorgeous, hectic self on us all.

"I'm just popping out for half an hour or so," I announced, darting out from behind the counter with my coat and bag. "Will you both be ok? Any problems, just ring my mobile."

Amber saluted and Rowan gave a fervent shake of her red ponytail. "We'll be fine, Bailey."

I hugged my quilted jacket tighter around myself and headed for my hatchback car at the rear of Flower Power. I had no contact details for Ezra, so I couldn't ring him. If he wasn't there, perhaps I could leave a note? All I knew was that I had to alert him about Zach Stern and his magazine.

Zach's reference to a "scandal" kept flitting through my head.

I got in and shut the door. The interior smelled like the perfumery counter of a department store and a spare pair of scissors, gardening gloves, and a few packets of flower food were sticking out of the glove compartment.

The November sky was a churning gun-metal grey, promising an imminent downpour.

I set off, driving away from the cluster of shops, which were now sporting festive window displays, and past the moody patchwork fields towards the country lanes that would take me to Duxbury Hall.

I tried not to dwell on Zach's presence in Heather Moore. I hoped Moira had kept him so occupied with her own lurid tales that he wouldn't feel much like doing more investigating. Something told me, however, that I was being a little too optimistic on that front.

The sooner Zach Stern took himself back to *Stargazer*'s offices in Glasgow, the better.

I negotiated my way past a field of curious cows huddled together for warmth by a wooden fence and turned down a side lane, banks of grass rising up on either side.

I pulled my car to a halt and murmured, "Wow," at the sight that greeted me.

Duxbury Hall now carried just faint echoes of what it used to look like before.

Imposing black and gold gates were now in situ, together with security cameras, at the bottom of the private tree-lined drive.

Ezra had converted Duxbury Hall into a gleaming white turreted affair, with two Grecian-style pillars at the grand entrance.

The gardens had also been transformed, and where there had been rampant weeds and daisies roaming everywhere, there was now a swathe of manicured lawns, together with cultivated flower beds running down either side and freshly planted trees. I could just imagine the fluttering blooms that would erupt out of the earth in the coming spring.

There was even a tinkling Grecian-style water feature further down the garden.

I got out of the car at the gates and pressed a buzzer. There was the faint smell of putty and cement in the air, intermingled with the zing of damp moss. Towards the other side of the house, there was a stillness in the spiky bare branches of the woodland.

A brisk male voice asked me who I was and once they were satisfied, the gates swished open to allow me entry.

I drew up at the entrance and parked. Jackson was there waiting for me on the grand steps. A sliver of gold light shone out behind him.

Part of me expected Zach Stern to stride out, brandishing his notebook, after tailing me here.

I gave my head a mental wobble. Bloody hell. I hoped not!

"Bailey," beamed Ezra's distinguished expression, appearing behind Jackson.

"Ezra. Hi. I'm sorry to disturb you."

He beckoned me in with one generous sweep of his hand. "No apology needed. I was just on the phone to my manager." He grinned at me. "It's a pleasure to see you. Please do come in."

I stepped into the tiled hallway to find myself confronted by an ornate pearlized staircase which surely even Cinderella would have envied, a floor-to-ceiling mirror edged with gold leaf to my left, and a polished chequered floor in champagne and white tiles under my feet.

An appreciative smile enveloped my face. "I know this is going to sound like a cliché, but I really do love what you've done with the place."

Jackson smiled. "Not too shabby, is it?" Then he evaporated.

Ezra stood with his hands clasped together behind his back. "I wish I could take the credit, my dear, but that belongs to my interior designer, Gaston, and a squad of talented builders and interior design people."

He gestured to the left. "Would you like a coffee or tea? Mrs Watson, my housekeeper, has rustled up one of my favourites – pecan shortbread."

"Thank you, but I'd better not. At any other time, I would, but I've left Amber and Rowan manning the fort back at Flower Power and as it's Saturday, I don't want to leave them alone too long."

"That's all right. I understand. So, to what do I owe the pleasure?" he asked. "Have you come round to discuss your design ideas?" He offered me a delighted grin. "I hope so, because I also wanted to speak to you about my plans to throw a little, private soirée. I was thinking about having it on New Year's Eve."

"Oh?"

"I wondered if you'd be interested in providing the floral arrangements for that too?"

I let out a delighted gasp. "That would be wonderful. I'm… I'm honoured. Thank you." My face split into a grateful grin. "I'm more than happy to chat things over with you while I'm here." Then I remembered the real reason for my visit and my smile faltered. I flicked him an awkward look. "In all honesty, I wish flowers were the main reason why I've come to see you." I paused. "There's something I have to tell you."

Ezra angled his head to one side. "What is it?" He performed a small smile as he eyed me. "I thought you seemed rather preoccupied, if you don't mind me saying."

I let out a sigh and plucked my mobile out of my bag, which was dangling from my shoulder. "Have you heard of *Stargazer* magazine?" The house smelled of warm vanilla potpourri and the scent wrapped itself around me.

One of Ezra's thick salt-and-pepper brows arched. "Yes, I have. Something tells me I'm not going to like this."

He beckoned me to turn and follow him into his sitting room, which was just past the staircase.

It was very grand, as I thought it might be, with an eclectic mix of polished maple furniture, two sumptuous sofas in bitter-chocolate leather scattered with lemon-yellow cushions, and silky, Chinese print drapes in pale gold pooling down the patio doors at the rear of the room. They led out onto the lawns that seemed to stretch on forever, taking the eye right down to another bank of thick trees.

Ezra sat down on one sofa, I seated myself on the other one opposite him. His swathes of thick white carpet made me nervous. Thank goodness I'd declined a cup of tea. I also prayed I didn't have mud on my boots.

I pulled up the *Stargazer* magazine website on my phone and scrolled down to Zach's bio. His handsome, angular features shone out of his photo. I thrust the phone towards Ezra.

He gave me a wary look and stared down at my phone.

"This reporter, Zach Stern, turned up at Flower Power last night, just as I was closing up," I said. "He was asking about you, Ezra."

Ezra's looked up abruptly from examining Zach's photograph. "Me?"

"Yes. Apparently, two women travelling through Heather Moore thought they saw you in your car and decided to tip off the magazine Zach works for."

Ezra's breath sounded like a balloon deflating. His shoulders sank under his navy jumper. "Oh dear. Maybe I shouldn't have ventured out like I did."

"It's ridiculous that you feel you can't go out," I protested.

He cast Zach's bio another cool glance and handed my phone back to me.

I readied myself. "I also bumped into the journalist, Zach, this morning in Heather Moore woods. He was out running and made some comment about hoping to catch up with me again later." I buried images of Zach's muscular legs. "And there's something else."

"What, my dear?"

"Last night, he said something about a scandal."

Ezra's expression paled.

"He didn't elaborate..."

Ezra tried to push out a disinterested smile. "Oh, poppycock!" he rushed. "Probably some made-up nonsense. Happens all the time, unfortunately."

He fell quiet for a few moments.

I couldn't ask him anything else about it. How could I? I'd only known the man five minutes. "I didn't tell this Zach Stern anything. I denied you'd been in Flower Power, let alone that I'd met you or spoken to you."

"And did he believe you?"

I shrugged my shoulders under my quilted jacket. "I'm not sure. I just wanted him out of my shop, to be honest." I hesitated. "He's staying at a local hotel. From what I've read about him online, he's the sort of character that once he gets the bit between his teeth about a story, he doesn't give up."

Ezra sank his head back against his oversized lemon-yellow cushions. "So much for me enjoying a life of tranquillity in the Scottish Highlands." Frustration gripped his face.

Resentment about Ezra's situation piled up inside of me.

Who the hell did this Zach Stern think he was turning up in Heather Moore in order to make Ezra's new life implode, just so he could get a column out of it? And his sheer presence around here was making me nervous, too. If he was as dogged as his reputation suggested, my new life here could be under threat as well. Was it only a matter of time before he worked out who I was?

My stomach lurched. I thought of how happy Flower

Power had made me, and the fresh start I was trying to build here.

Why should Ezra and I have to worry so much about our future here? How was it fair that people trying to get away from media attention were constantly hounded?

Well, I wasn't about to give up my new life here without a fight! Zach would have a battle on his hands if he thought he could dismantle my new life and everything I'd worked so hard for. "We need to think of something to throw him off the scent," I suggested, shuffling forward on Ezra's sofa. "Something to get rid of him."

Ezra's serious, long mouth flickered at the edges. "I hope you aren't suggesting we have him assassinated? Having said that, I do know of a couple of shady but influential London gentlemen who possess certain connections."

I let out a snort. "No, tempting though that is, Ezra. Nothing illegal." I let my hands rise and fall again into my lap. "We need to let him think that there's no story up here. We have to convince Zach Stern he's been sent on a wild goose chase. Then he'll bugger off back to Glasgow. Fingers crossed."

Ezra twitched his sharp nose. "How? I mean, how are we going to get shot of him?"

I could feel my shoulders sinking again. "I don't know. I haven't thought of anything yet."

"Then try not to worry about it just now. I'm not."

I offered Ezra a small smile of support. I could see his eyes had tensed, though. He was trying to reassure himself.

He may well be an accomplished actor, but he wasn't fooling me.

Ezra clapped his hands together. "Now, seeing as you're here, why don't I give you a tour of the rest of the house? It might give you some more ideas for the floral displays." He stood up and stuffed his hands into the pockets of his dark jeans. "I'm very much a fan of Christmas, so I'm more than open to any festive themes you may have up your sleeve."

"That sounds like a plan. Thank you."

I followed him out of the sitting room.

Ezra guided me through to his study across the hall. It looked out onto another section of the garden and a set of wavy hills in the distance.

A semi-circular oak desk was facing the window, dotted with various acting awards and papers. "I have to decide where I'm going to put these," he grimaced, patting one gleaming gold award.

"A nice problem to have."

Ezra grinned.

As we made our way past his desk, I noticed a copy of his recently released autobiography, *King of the World*. The book cover consisted of swirly gold type, with his name running underneath the title and a colour portrait photograph of him leaning nonchalantly with one hand placed on top of a world globe. He was wearing a sharp, black suit, bright blue shirt, and dark tie.

Ezra noticed me appreciating it. "I worried that the world globe idea might look a bit odd, but it actually works rather well."

"It does," I agreed. "And you look very dashing."

Ezra's cheeks hinted at a blush. "I suppose I don't scrub up too badly. I remember the time Meryl Streep told me I was every bit as good-looking as George Clooney."

I tried to hide a smile.

He scrutinised himself on the cover again. "No doubt you've heard the contents of my book have caused somewhat of a rumpus?"

I stepped back out into the hallway, taking in the shades of cream and gold. "I did read something about that in the papers."

Following behind me, Ezra dragged a hand through his thick hair. "And I'm sure that won't be the end of it." He fell silent for a few moments, looking pensive.

I decided to change the subject for a few moments. I didn't like to see Ezra so preoccupied. Bloody Zach Stern!

"How would you feel about using gold in the floral displays?" I pointed to his gold-leaf mirror and the soft hues on the walls. "At this time of year, it'd be warm and comforting as well as stunning."

Ezra folded his arms. "That sounds lovely. What did you have in mind?"

I grabbed my phone back out of my bag and pulled up some images. "I was thinking of having rustic colours down here, inspired by the surrounding forestry. It'd also compliment your interior." I pointed to the images on my phone. "I was going to suggest preserved eucalyptus, baby's breath and ferns, as well as pinecones, golden ears of wheat and dried flowers."

Ezra studied the pictures I was showing him. "Sounds perfect."

"I'm glad you think so. We could have tatarica, lagurus and setaria, with oats and hill flowers." I gestured to my phone again. "The whole effect would be a sumptuous, wintery display featuring golds, silvers, bronzes, and crisp white."

I glanced up at Ezra's dramatic staircase. The banister would look stunning wreathed in a festive garland of holly and ivy for Christmas. There were also a couple of eye-catching abstract paintings of what looked like pastel-blue cubes balanced on an upended triangle.

Ezra spotted me studying them. "They're by a young French artist. Please don't ask me what they're supposed to represent, but I spotted them in Paris last year and I loved the colours."

"I can understand why they caught your eye." More ideas trotted through my head. "How about using an electric-blue in the upstairs floral arrangements? I could tweak the downstairs suggestions and incorporate sea holly in blue, together with witch hazel, thistles, and forsythia for the upper part of the house." I could feel my face beaming with enthusiasm. "Witch hazel looks like fireworks exploding and forsythia has a gorgeous, spicy scent."

I showed more images of the flowers on my phone to Ezra, who nodded. "That sounds wonderful and very seasonal. Perfect."

"And if you did want something extra special in the run-up to Christmas, I can add some bright blue ribbon for an extra splash of colour and also create a matching wreath in the same rustic colours to put at the entrance. I could interweave that one with streams of gold satin ribbon?"

I knew my endless stream of ideas was beginning to run away with me but I couldn't help it.

Ezra however, didn't seem to mind. In fact, he looked very impressed. "Ideal. Thank you, Bailey."

It was great to be able to distract myself with something other than nosy magazine journalists. A creak from somewhere towards the kitchen made me jerk my head up.

I turned around to see a tall, wiry man, not dissimilar to Ezra in stature and hair colour, loping towards us.

Ezra encouraged the older man over, who introduced himself as Joshua McColl, Ezra's new gardener.

We exchanged pleasantries and handshakes.

"I was just speaking to Bailey about the floral heaven she's going to create for me every couple of weeks," explained Ezra, then put his hand on Joshua's shoulder. "And Joshua can turn a weed into a flower just by looking at it."

Joshua rolled his dark hooded eyes. "I think you're exaggerating a bit there, sir."

"Oh, stop with the *sir* nonsense," insisted Ezra. "I've told you before."

I took in Joshua's features again. "You could be related," I joked to Joshua, smiling over at him. "Like brothers—"

My words vanished as an idea screamed inside my head. No. We couldn't do that. What if it didn't work? We could end up looking total idiots.

Nonetheless, I studied Joshua's profile, so similar in its hawkish way to Ezra's. No, it was a crazy idea. Use a decoy? Dupe Zach Stern and make him think the sighting of Ezra had been a case of mistaken identity? That the two women hadn't seen Ezra King in his car after all but Joshua instead?

I'm sure my mouth was hanging open as I mulled over the idea. Was I losing my mind? It was mad. But then, desperate times do call for desperate measures.

"Bailey?" asked Ezra. "Is everything all right?" He and Joshua were looking at me, bemused.

'Fine, thank you,' I said, the cogs in my brain still turning. It could work. Well, it might work. There was still this mysterious scandal thing that Zach had mentioned and which Ezra had speedily brushed off, but we couldn't just let Zach Stern blow up our lives and plans.

Surely, it was worth a try?

Colour illuminated my cheeks. We had to do something. Zach Stern was already sniffing around the area in search of Ezra and I could be next. I recalled him staring at me in my office and commenting that I seemed familiar. The situation was becoming too risky. A journalist like Zach Stern wasn't just going to shrug his shoulders and vanish. If I could throw him off Ezra's scent, then maybe I could be as resourceful when it came to protecting my own identity. I'd already had one man ruin my life and I wasn't about to let a second one do the same. Zach Stern had to leave. There was too much at stake, for Ezra and for me.

I took my phone back out of my bag and rang Flower

Power, telling Amber that I'd be half an hour late coming back. Then I turned to Ezra and gave him what I hoped was my most winning smile. He and Joshua looked unnerved and exchanged puzzled glances.

"I don't suppose I could change my mind about that cup of tea, could I?"

Over a cup of tea for me and two cups of tar-like Brazilian coffee for them, together with Mrs Watson's mouthwatering pecan shortbread, the two men looked at me like I'd sprouted another head.

"But Joshua doesn't look like me at close quarters," spluttered Ezra.

"Maybe, but from a few feet away he does," I said. "I had to do a double-take when I saw him. And from the back you're identical," I insisted. "You both have similar hair colour and hairstyles. Joshua's tall, too, and slim … distinguished."

Joshua cradled his cup in his hands. "Och, flattery will get you everywhere, lass."

I smiled.

"But he doesn't sound like me," pointed out Ezra. "I'm a classically trained actor, darling. I can do accents. He can't."

"But that's irrelevant. The point is, it will explain how those two women mistook a random stranger for somebody famous as they drove by. They wouldn't have heard you speak or seen you close up." Warming to the idea, I took a sip of my tea and carried on. "If Zach Stern persists in his search for you, Ezra, we give him Joshua."

Joshua's brow creased in worry at the thought of being handed over to Zach, so I clarified. "Metaphorically speaking, of course." My enthusiasm ramped up a notch. "Zach Stern will feel like such a prat for following such a flimsy so-called sighting."

I hoped my crazy suggestion might be infectious, but Ezra and Joshua didn't appear convinced. They both bore concerned glances over the top of their coffee cups.

"Och, I'm not an actor, Bailey," blushed Joshua, shuffling around on Ezra's leather sofa in his grass-stained rugby shirt and combats. "I'm at my happiest when I'm knee-high in my breeches in earth and heather."

I moved to speak again, in the hope of encouraging Joshua to change his mind, but Ezra clanked down his coffee cup on its saucer. "We'll think about it," he said without much enthusiasm. "I do appreciate you trying to help, Bailey. Really, I do."

I nodded my understanding. "Well, like I say, hopefully some other juicy story will draw Zach Stern's attention and he'll forget about trying to locate you."

Deep down, I doubted that very much, but I felt like I needed to be positive.

Amber was serving an elderly lady in a crocheted beige bonnet, who was armed with a pot of skimmia japonica, fringed with shiny berries.

I held the shop door open for her and she nodded her head, clamped her hat down tighter and disappeared up the pavement.

A sudden burst of rain made its presence felt on the windows, the raindrops chasing each other down the panes.

"Everything been ok?" I asked, shrugging off my quilted coat and hanging it up on a peg in the corner. "Sorry I was a bit longer than I expected to be."

"No worries," replied Amber, clattering some spare change in the till. "It's been a bit busier than we thought, but nothing we couldn't cope with. We've taken a few more orders for Christmas wreaths."

"Good. Thank you, girls. I appreciate it."

Amber flicked me a curious look from out of her hazel eyes, winged today with green eyeliner. "Everything ok?"

I thought again about Ezra's house, with its regal pillars and shiny, pearly staircase.

I chewed my lip, deep in thought. Judging by the distinct lack of enthusiasm shown by Ezra and Joshua, I was thinking it less and less likely they'd agree to it. But what were we supposed to do?

I was open to suggestions.

Rowan finished watering some of the herbs and offered to make the three of us a brew, while interrogating Amber about a pair of long, high-heeled, velvet boots she'd spotted online. "How easy do you reckon they are to walk in? How are you supposed to keep them clean?"

I smiled to myself and decided to stick with my jewelled pumps and ankle boots for comfort. Being on your feet all day demanded comfortable shoes.

Rowan handed out steaming mugs of tea to Amber and me and then cradled hers in her hands. "I was thinking about getting a pair of those lace-up suede boots for winter that Taylor Swift was wearing on TV the other night."

Our conversation was interrupted, however, by the shop door clattering open, sending the bell into a frenzy. It was Zach Stern.

My cheeks fizzed. Oh, no.

The collar of his black tweed coat was up and there was a knotted, charcoal scarf around his neck.

He gave his black floppy hair a shake, trying to dislodge the rain that drizzled through it. He reminded me of a big bad wolf.

Amber and Rowan did a double-take at the tall, dark stranger.

He shifted his dark gaze around, before resting it on me. "Good morning, Ms McArthur. Long time no see," he said with a glitter in his eyes. "I don't suppose you've got a spare moment?"

I wanted to apologise and say I was too busy, but the shop was currently experiencing a brief lull in customers. Amber and Rowan swapped looks. "We can manage, Bailey," insisted Rowan, drinking Zach in.

Oh great. Sure, you can.

I flicked on a smile. "Ok. Thanks girls." I turned to Zach. "Let's go into the office."

I strode past the plants and flowers, wafts of their heady perfume in a travelling cloud around me. *Keep your cool, Bailey. Tell him nothing. Everything will be ok.*

I tried to ignore the rippling nerves in my stomach as I closed my office door with a decisive click. I gestured to the other chair, but Zach didn't sit down. One of his black brows rocketed up to his hairline as he stood on the other side of my desk. His generous mouth was in a tight line. "I meant to say to you this morning, but you dashed off. Thank you so much for suggesting I speak to Moira Telford last night. I spent half the evening attempting to ignore her flirting and the other half bored to tears about the affairs and jealousies raging behind the scenes of the local drama group."

Relief swam through me. I fought the urge to smile. Good old Moira. "What do you mean? She knows everyone, and I thought she might be able to help you."

Zach's irritated stare bore into me. "Oh, come on, you knew I wouldn't get any information from Moira last night, only a severe case of earache."

I jammed my lips together to stop myself from laughing. "I don't know what you're talking about, Mr Stern."

Zach continued to glower down at me. "I'm glad you find this so amusing. But I believe Ezra King has moved to the area."

He straightened his broad shoulders under his heavy coat. "You lot round here might stick together like two coats of paint, but I didn't get where I am by giving up on a story."

You lot?!

I jumped to my feet, indignant. Heather Moore had been good to me. As children, Marcus and I had spent many happy holidays here, rooting around in the woods, tumbling through the grass and nagging Mum and Dad to treat us to Mr Conte's moreish clotted cream ice cream cones.

Mum hadn't been quite so enthusiastic about us holidaying in the area. She was far happier floating around in one of her kaftans under baking hot Mediterranean sunshine, but she and Dad compromised with the promise of a trip to Venice each autumn.

Living here and running Flower Power, I was finding myself becoming more and more attached to the place. I was seeing it through fresh, adult eyes. The locals were spending their hard-earned cash on my flowers and I was striking out on my own, carving a future which a year ago, I never would have thought possible.

I experienced a burning sense of irritation at Zach Stern's condescending tone. How dare he sweep in here, intent on destroying the life of someone like Ezra King, who just wanted to escape from the microscopic world of London's oppressive media attention?

I flashed Zach an icy stare, the words fighting to get out of my mouth. "Well, seeing as you're flinging insults around! If you're the pinnacle of modern, serious journalism, why the hell are you working for a gossip magazine?"

Zach's square jaw tightened. "Excuse me?"

"You've won a ton of awards and yet you're reporting on such pressing issues as what sort of avocados Madonna buys during her weekly shop and why Robbie Williams has decided to sport a fringe. Are these things really so very important to you?"

Zach's mouth flatlined. He looked discomfited all of a sudden. "My career choices are none of your business."

"And neither is it any of your business who may or who may not be living here!" I tried to rein in my emotions, but they were in free-fall. "What gives you the right to rock up here and try to lob a grenade into people's lives?"

A chilly atmosphere descended.

Zach reached for the handle of the office door and yanked it open.

"Don't you have any scruples?"

An odd look washed across his face. He straightened his back. "You'd be surprised." He pushed out his chin. "But I should warn you I don't give up easily, Ms McArthur. That's why I'm so good at what I do."

He pinned me with his unwavering gaze. "You're not telling me everything. I know it."

My stomach lurched. "Psychic now, are we?"

He ignored my barbed comment. "I find in my line of work that the truth always surfaces in the end."

"The truth? About celebrity gossip? Very noble of you."

He angled his head at me as he was about to leave my

office. His eyes narrowed. "Nothing like making wild assumptions about people."

I shifted uncomfortably.

"You know, I'm sure I do recognise you from somewhere."

A sickening dread pooled inside me. I pushed my chin out and fought to keep my voice calm. "I thought you were leaving. Don't let me stop you," I said. Then, unable to resist it, I added, "Oh, and be careful where you're running. There's lots of rabbit and fox holes in the woods."

He shot me a hot gaze, before whirling away in his coat and out of my shop.

Chapter Six

I spent the remainder of Saturday afternoon chewing over what Zach had said, before taking decisive action.

As soon as the clock struck five, I ushered Rowan and Amber out, insisting I would clear up, sweep the floor and water the plants that needed it.

Both girls were delighted, seeing as they'd agreed to meet up with some mutual friends to go clubbing in Glasgow.

Once they'd vanished in a typhoon of plaits and perfume, I locked the shop door, picked up my phone and brought Ezra's mobile number up, which he'd given me when I called round.

He picked up after a few rings. "Bailey! How are you?"

"I'm all right, thanks." I let out a worried sigh. "He's been back here, Ezra. The journalist. Zach Stern."

"What?!"

I took a breath. "Look, I know my suggestion sounded crazy, but we might just have to give this a shot – using Joshua as a decoy."

Ezra let out an unconvinced grunt into my ear.

"Isn't it worth giving this a try? It's up to you, but if Zach Stern finds out you really have moved here, you're going to end up splashed across that wretched magazine of his."

I tried not to think about the mounting worry I had about my own life here. All it would take was one loose tongue or him digging around in my past and then my life would start tumbling down around me, like a pack of playing cards. The press would be salivating to be able to reveal how the so-called party-mad Bollinger Babe who was jilted at the altar and swindled by the man she loved was now running a little florists in the Scottish Highlands.

"I thought you were enjoying living here," I murmured, as the pale light danced through the shop windows.

"I do," Ezra assured me. "I feel settled for the first time in a very long time." He hesitated. "But even if poor Josh were to agree to act as me, how on earth would it work?"

"I would speak to Zach and say I'd been thinking about his Ezra King search and that those two women who claimed they had a sighting of you were wrong. I'll say it was a case of mistaken identity."

"Dear God. A sighting? You make me sound like the Loch Ness Monster."

I let out a bark of laughter. "I'll say there's somebody

locally who I've realised looks like you and I'm certain that Joshua was the person the two women saw that day – not you."

Ezra let out a long, low, dramatic breath of air. Then he laughed. "I've performed at the RSC and on the west end stage, sweetie, so being me would take some acting skill."

I twitched my nose as I turned it all over in my head. "Ezra, Joshua won't need to put on an acting performance. Those two ladies who saw you that day; they never spoke to you and I'm certain they didn't take any photos of you. Zach Stern would've said."

Ezra hesitated. I could hear the wheels turning in his head.

"It sounds like they don't have any concrete proof it was the real Ezra King they saw."

Ezra made a murmuring sound.

"So … what do you think?" I began to pace up and down the shop floor. Outside, in the Heather Moore sky, shards of stars were beginning to pop. "I know it sounds ludicrous, but it could work."

"*Sounds* ludicrous?!"

"Do you have a better suggestion for getting rid of this journalist, Ezra? Because I'm all ears."

There was the crackle of phone connection.

"All right," he agreed after a few seconds of deliberation. "Under the circumstances, I don't think we have any other option."

At least we were trying to do something. "Great. It's not as if Joshua has to stalk around the town being you." I paced again. "We just have to convince Zach Stern that it's Joshua, and not you, who those women spotted."

This mysterious scandal issue was sitting between us, but I couldn't bring myself to mention it. How could I? It was none of my business, just like it was none of Zach Stern's business. And Ezra didn't seem to want to refer to it either.

Ezra made a clicking noise with his tongue down the line. "I have my doubts about your cunning plan, but all right." He sucked in some air. "I'll give Joshua a call now and use my persuasive charm on him. It worked with Sharon Stone back in 1986."

I bit down a smile. "I'm sure it did."

"Give me five minutes and I'll call you back and let you know what he says. I'll also offer him some extra renumeration for his efforts."

"I'll wait to hear from you."

He ended the call and I popped my mobile down on the counter and faffed around watering and tending to the amaryllis. Its blood-red petals added a burst of vivid colour into the descending darkness of the shop.

I tilted my head to admire the flowers as I adjusted their stems in the vase. The amaryllis was said to symbolise strength, determination, and success. I stroked the petals, their velvety texture brushing against my fingertips.

No arrogant journalist, even if he did have spectacular dark eyes, was going to take my new life away from me. I wasn't prepared to risk it.

My mind conjured up images of Zach Stern's penetrating gaze again.

I found myself clearing my throat and drilled my attention back to the amaryllis.

I flinched as my mobile trilled on top of the counter.

It was Ezra. "I've just spoken to Joshua and after assuring him that this will all be a case of smoke and mirrors, he agreed, albeit rather hesitantly." Ezra made a small chuckle. "I think the extra money I offered him did help to swing it in the end."

"That's wonderful," I breathed. "Thank you, Ezra. Thank you so much. And please also thank Joshua from me too. I'm very grateful."

Ezra hesitated down my ear. "Shouldn't *I* be the one thanking *you*? You sound even more delighted about this than I do. Why are you so grateful?"

"I—" I winced and wanted to chew my own tongue off. Even though Ezra couldn't see me, I shrugged, then reached out and toyed with the glossy bottle-green leaves of a nearby Yucca plant. "Oh, you know, I'm … pleased we can protect your privacy," I said quickly. "Anyway, I'll give Zach a call tomorrow, say I've thought of something and arrange to meet up with him. Then I'll tell him about Josh looking like you." I gathered myself. "He might think I'm bluffing, but I'll do my utmost to throw him off. It has to work."

Ezra chuckled. "That sounds like a plan. Anything is worth a try." He paused. "Thank you, Bailey. For helping me, I mean."

"No, thank *you*. And I promise you your flowers will make Glasgow Botanic Gardens look modest!"

Chapter Seven

The next morning, Sunday, dawned with me turning over in my head what I was going to say to Zach Stern about Ezra/Joshua.

Oh God. All this had sounded far better yesterday but now that I was giving it much greater thought, my confidence in my "plan" was beginning to droop like my tea roses if I forgot to water them.

I gave my head a mental shake. No. This could work. It had to. It would. We just had to convince ourselves it would and then Zach would believe it as well … wouldn't he?

I showered, washed my hair, slipped on my dark brown polo neck and dark brown jeans and popped two slices of bread into my toaster for breakfast.

I had to sound convincing when I told him about what I believed was "mistaken identity" where Ezra was concerned. Zach didn't strike me as gullible, so it was imperative I make this convincing.

I poured some milk into my tea and glanced out of my kitchen window at the wind-whipped hills over in the distance. Talk about playing with fire.

Monday zoomed up to greet me.

I'd tried to call Zach yesterday, but his phone was switched off. Desperation had raced through me. Although Zach hadn't rumbled who I really was, the longer he was here in Heather Moore, the greater his chances of making that discovery. The sooner we could get shot of him, the better. Frustration swelled inside me when he didn't answer. So much for putting my cunning plan into action.

I'd set off earlier this morning for the flower market and was back, armed with an array of shiny new plants and flowers in a festive array of rubies, pillar-box reds and oranges.

I opened up the shop and was just sipping a mug of tea when I heard two murmuring female voices outside the shop door.

Wow. Some people were keen for a Monday morning in November!

Curious as to who they might be, I stole a look out of one of the shop windows.

Two young women, who both looked around my age, were huddled in their winter coats. They kept staring into Flower Power and shuffling from foot to foot as they talked to each other. One had a blocky fringe and waist-length straight brown hair, while the other was a shoulder-skimming strawberry blonde.

I angled my head as I drank my tea. Were they anxious brides, keen to book my floristry services? Or perhaps they were hospitality employees, here to talk to me about an upcoming event?

I tried not to dwell on the suspicious voice in my head. I couldn't keep hiding every time a new face appeared in Heather Moore. Bloody Zach Stern! He was making me jump at shadows.

I examined the two young women again.

Refusing to think more negative thoughts, I returned to the counter, just as the bell on the shop door rattled to warn me they were on their way in. An icy blast of air shot in from the hillsides as they entered.

"Can I help you?"

The strawberry blonde gave her companion a sideways glance. "Sorry to bother you, but we're looking for Bailey McArthur."

I hesitated. Who were they and what did they want?

Well, I wouldn't find out standing here, gazing at them. "Can I ask why?"

It was the turn of the dark-haired woman to speak. She glanced around herself. "It's a bit, well, delicate."

I frowned.

"Are you Ms McArthur?" asked the blonde woman, squinting at me. They both possessed cut-glass English accents.

I could feel myself hurriedly erecting that wall of protection again. "Are you journalists?"

They swapped confused looks. "No. Why?"

I hesitated before I answered. "I'm Bailey." I pursed my lips in thought. "What's this about?"

The strawberry blonde was apologetic and glanced around her. "Is there somewhere we could talk more privately?"

"We won't take up much of your time," assured her friend. "Please, Ms McArthur."

"More privately than this?" I gestured to the empty shop.

They shuffled awkwardly, still looking frozen by the chill wind and I was glad my parents had insisted I have a panic button installed under the shop counter, just in case of armed robbery.

Even so, I'd have been surprised if they'd suddenly morphed into raging criminals.

The women drank in the sight of the frilly petals, sprouting leaves and trumpeting blooms.

"This is lovely," said the dark-haired woman appreciatively. "Have you been open long?"

"Thank you. Only since May."

Neither of them had yet introduced themselves. They just stood there in their stylish coats and boots. Going by the way they were appraising me, they weren't interested in flowers, though. I knew I couldn't spend my life wondering about every person who came in or happened to pass me in the street or I'd end up an anxious wreck, but I couldn't deny that these two young women were acting rather weird and exchanging odd glances.

"Sorry, but who are you and why did you want to speak to me?" I hoped I didn't sound abrupt or rude, but I was becoming unnerved.

The dark-haired woman wrung her hands together in front of her and shot her friend another, somewhat knowing, glance. "It's all a bit awkward."

I could feel my eyebrows rising. "Oh?"

"We're hoping to find someone."

I blinked back at her and forced a polite smile. "Who is it that you're looking for?" I asked with apprehension.

"We understand someone high profile was seen coming into your shop recently."

My senses screeched onto high alert. Ezra. They must be talking about Ezra. Oh no. Not again!

The brunette, dressed in a ruby-coloured belted coat, took a few steps forward in a pair of pointed, black boots. "We're looking for a gentleman called Ezra King."

I felt my jaw tighten. I gave a dismissive shrug. "What, the actor? What about him?"

The strawberry-blonde woman hopped from foot to foot.

"I don't mean to sound rude, but you're mistaken," I said, adding a light-hearted smile for good measure.

The delicate-featured strawberry blonde's hand fluttered up to the burgundy scarf knotted at her throat. "But we were told he'd been seen in Heather Moore, and in this shop in particular?"

"Told by who?"

Her dark-haired companion's freckly complexion zinged with two spots of colour. "My mother."

"Your mother?" I repeated, confused.

The blonde hitched her leather bag higher up her shoulder, a smear of embarrassed colour appearing in her cheeks and reached out to squeeze the brunette's fingers, as though in an act of solidarity.

There was an electrified silence while I tried to work out what was going on.

"This is just as big a shock to both of us as I'm sure it will be for him…," said the brunette. She straightened her shoulders and took a steadying breath. "But we've just discovered we might be Ezra King's daughters."

The two women seemed to morph from well-groomed young women into self-conscious adolescents as they stood there.

I blinked at them. Ezra possibly had a family? I didn't recall ever reading about him having kids in interviews and he'd never mentioned children to me, but I supposed I didn't know everything about him.

The dark-haired girl gathered herself. "We wondered if you had an address for him or knew where he was staying? We wanted to speak to him."

If they were telling the truth then Ezra obviously didn't know about them, otherwise they would have a way of contacting him.

I studied both of their pleading expressions.

But were they genuine? I only had their word for it.

If they were, my heart went out to both of them, standing there in front of a total stranger and speaking about something so life-altering.

I paused. My sympathy was ramping up. It couldn't have been easy coming here and my curiosity was alight. The dark-haired one said her mother had told them Ezra was here in Heather Moore.

They both looked cold and a little lost. Should I at least hear them out? Give them the benefit of the doubt for the time being? "Come on. Come and have a seat here."

They both broke into grateful smiles. The strawberry-blonde woman tightened her scarf. "Thanks."

They trailed along behind me, as I arranged three chairs behind the counter.

They took up seats beside each other and I offered them tea or coffee, but they both declined. I got the impression they were just anxious to get the information they came here for.

I sat down too. I decided to introduce myself again, to break the silence. The dark-haired woman said her name was Caroline Rushmore and indicated to her half-sister. "And I'm Laura Maddox."

"I'm so sorry we didn't say who we were before now," said Caroline in a rush. "It's all come as such a shock." She gestured to herself with an elegant hand, adorned with two silver rings. "My mother is Toni Rushmore, the 60s model and actress."

"And my mum is the author, Jules Maddox." Laura sat forward a little, planting her hands on her knees.

I watched as Caroline fished about in her bag on her lap and handed me two cream envelopes. Inside, were their birth certificates. They insisted I take a look at them. "Our father isn't named on them but our mothers are."

I looked from one to the other. I was no expert but their birth certificates looked genuine. "Yes, I've heard of both of your mothers. Of course, I have."

I folded the certificates back up, slid them into their respective envelopes and handed them back to Caroline. She delivered a hesitant smile. "I'm sorry if we're putting you in an awkward position, but we just needed somewhere to start."

I thought of the recognisable images of Toni Rushmore in her heyday, her raven-black bob and panda eyes make-up and the impressive, engrossing moral dilemma novels of the flaxen-haired writer Jules Maddox.

I studied them both. They could still be trying to con me, in the hope of extracting information about Ezra. "So how did you two find one another?"

Laura gave an eyeroll. "That was thanks to social media. I don't know if you know much about Ezra King's recent autobiography, but he revealed in it, that he had affairs with both our mothers almost thirty years ago."

My eyes popped. "Really?"

Laura nodded. "And that was when my mother told me who my real father was. I couldn't take it in at first." She gave a small glance at Caroline. "After the initial shock of finding out, I read up about Ezra and stumbled across an Ezra King Appreciation Page on Instagram."

Caroline chipped in, explaining that she'd made the same discovery after her mum found out she'd been named in Ezra's autobiography too. "For years, I'd heard rumours that a former MP was being pin-pointed as my real father. Everyone knew Lionel Cavendish was gay and once I got older and heard the same stories, I kept asking her to tell me the truth but she wouldn't talk about it. I think I knew all along that Lionel wasn't my dad."

Her fingers tumbled over each other in her lap. "Lionel was a good friend of my mum's. He still is. He's been like an uncle to me, but he isn't my biological father."

She scooped a lock of hair back behind her ear. "Laura and I became friends on Insta. We started chatting and then when Laura told me why she was also searching for information on Ezra King, I couldn't believe it. But it's such a relief to find someone else in my position…"

Laura nodded in agreement. "I felt so conflicted when I first found out about him, but when Caroline told me she was his daughter too, we both agreed we had to do this."

Laura shot an encouraging smile of support to her sister beside her. "We've both said that we'll undertake DNA tests to prove for certain that we are his daughters. We've nothing to hide."

I listened to them. They sounded genuine but I couldn't be sure.

I pushed around thoughts in my head I couldn't tell them anything. For one thing, I couldn't betray Ezra and if I did, what would happen if Zach found out? Also, it might not be true – either because Ezra was not their biological father or because they were part of a ploy to get me to reveal where Ezra was.

"So, you're convinced here's here in Heather Moore?" I said playing for time. "Because your mum said—"

"Yes,' Caroline cut in. 'And one of her friends also said that a while ago he'd been making enquiries about houses in this area. She's an estate agent to some high-profile people. We put two and two together and..."

Now it was Laura's turn to speak again. "What with those two women on the Insta page saying they saw Ezra King here in Heather Moore and then hearing that he'd been looking at property here..." Her voice tailed off. Then she carried on. "Look, I wouldn't blame you for one second if you doubted what we're telling you, but I swear we're both genuine."

These two young women in front of me, bunched up together, reminded me a little of myself. All they wanted was to make contact with the man who could be their real father and find a part of themselves they had every right to discover. I'd been swallowed up by Declan's obsession with money and deceit and I felt like I too had lost myself along the way, but now perhaps, the air was beginning to clear.

"We'd be more than happy to supply you with our mothers' details, should you wish to speak to Toni or Jules for yourself, to be certain we're not making this up," insisted Caroline.

Laura agreed. "Although, being honest, we'd prefer it if you didn't contact our mothers. At least not yet."

"Neither of them knows you're here?"

Laura pulled a face. "No. They've made it clear they'd prefer us not to reach out to Ezra King. They're both very independent women."

Caroline sighed in frustration. "We did try to reach out to him via his agent, but no luck. The official line is that he's been inundated with publicity requests since the book came out and so he's had to take a hiatus from that side of things for a while.".

"Ah. I see." I paused before speaking again. I hated being suspicious like this, but I also wasn't prepared to betray Ezra's trust if they weren't genuine or were out to exploit their connections to him. Thoughts rattled around inside of me. I had to tell them something; but I couldn't and wouldn't put Ezra in jeopardy.

"So, he hasn't been in here, then?" probed Laura.

I found myself crossing my fingers behind my back. "No… But look, why don't you both give me your contact details and if Ezra King does ever come in here, I'll be sure to pass them onto him?"

Caroline and Laura forced out disappointed smiles.

"Ok. We'd appreciate that so much. Thank you."

"No problem."

I smiled at them in what I hoped was a sympathetic way. There was no harm in me secretly forwarding their details to Ezra, who could take it from there.

Caroline delved with one hand into her Radley bag and handed over a thick, white business card, containing her contact details.

Laura did the same and gave me hers.

"Thank you so much, Bailey. We were fired up about hunting down his address and just turning up on his doorstep, but you're right. Better to take things one step at a time." She shrugged. "He hasn't been our father for almost thirty years, so what's another few days or so?"

"I understand," I said. "Sometimes, it's best to take things slowly."

Caroline adjusted the collar of her blouse under her thick coat and gave me a long look. "You sound as if you're talking from experience."

I half-laughed and walked with them back towards the shop door. "Something like that." I instantly regretted letting that slip, because Laura pushed her hands into the pockets of her thick beige coat and studied me for a few moments longer than was necessary.

I cleared my throat, almost making her jump.

"Sorry! You must think I'm being rude. It's just that you seem familiar, somehow. I can't think where I know you from though."

My heart juddered. Not again. Was my life going to be like this forever? Living on my wits? Always looking over my shoulder?

Shit! No, stay calm, Bailey.

I flapped my hands about, my growing panic threatening to spill over.

"Oh, I've been told that a few times before. As long as it's someone glamorous, I don't mind!"

Relief flooded through me when Laura laughed, and let the subject drop.

Determined not to look too suspicious and usher them out quickly, I went for small talk and asked them what they each did for a living.

Caroline worked in public relations for her local council and lived in Cheshire, while Laura was an architect in London. They'd decided to stay in a hotel together about an hour away, they said, until they saw how things progressed with Ezra.

"We're going to stay around for a few days," Laura said. "The way we see it, if Ezra isn't interested, then we haven't lost anything."

Once Caroline and Laura had departed, I debated what I should do.

In the end, I tidied myself up, and then rang Rowan and asked her if she could come in and cover the shop for a couple of hours. She said that was fine with her and that she'd be there in ten minutes.

Once she'd arrived, I snatched up the girls' business cards containing their contact information and set off for Ezra's home in my car. The sooner I got this information to Ezra, the better. I drummed my fingers on the top of my steering wheel at the traffic lights as I headed for his place—

This must be the scandal that Zach had alluded to; Ezra fathering two daughters to two different, high-profile women.

The prospect of Zach Stern discovering my car-crash

past faded into insignificance at the thought of speaking to Ezra about Caroline and Laura. I mulled over the situation, as I eased my car down the frost-tipped country lanes towards Duxbury Hall. Talk about a bolt out of the blue!

I pushed my foot a little harder down on the accelerator, not taking any notice of the meandering, toffee-coloured Highland cattle in the fields.

I pulled up outside the security gates. My stomach was flipping all over the place. How the hell was I going to tell him? I couldn't just burst out with it.

Could you imagine? *Hi Ezra. How're things? Oh, there were two young women who turned up to speak to me today and they say they're your long-lost daughters by two former girlfriends of yours. They're happy to take DNA tests. Oh, have you started your Christmas shopping yet?!*

I hovered for a few moments, before pressing the security intercom.

Jackson answered and we exchanged a couple of pleasantries. "I don't suppose I could have a word with Ezra, if he's available please?"

"Sure. Come on in."

I got back inside my car and watched the gates swish inwards. My heart hammered a little louder in my chest, as I eased down the driveway and parked up.

Ezra was waiting for me. He was sporting a pastel-pink jumper and beige trousers.

I managed to force out a strained smile.

"Everything all right?" he asked, encouraging me inside.

I waited until Jackson vanished.

Ezra beckoned me into his sitting room and took up a seat on the opposite sofa. "You look very serious."

I opened and closed my mouth a couple of times.

Oh God. How the hell do I get myself into these situations?

I took a breath.

Right. Get on with it.

And so out it came; about Caroline and Laura visiting me; them believing they were Ezra's daughters and how they came to track him down to Heather Moore.

Ezra's expression twisted from surprise to shock and then disbelief.

Then he made a noise that sounded like a gasp. "I don't believe it." His eyes were troubled. "I mean, I had gorgeous women flirting with me everywhere I went and I couldn't resist a pretty face, but daughters I've never heard of?" He shook his head and looked thoughtful. "Technically, it is possible, I suppose, but..." He looked me directly in the eyes. "No. I'm certain it's a ruse."

I shot him a careful look. "Well, they seemed genuine to me."

Ezra's brows knitted together. "I know you mean well, my dear. But I'll bet good money that they'll have dreamt this up between the two of them... in all likelihood to get money out of me." He narrowed his eyes, then. "You really shouldn't have got involved? You're my friend, or so I thought."

Now it was my turn to make a wounded sound. His words stung.

"Of course, I'm your friend and you know you can

count on me, but these two women asked me for help in trying to contact you." Frustration gnawed at me. "And I can assure you I never once let on that I had ever met you or seen you in Heather Moore." I paused. "And what if Zach Stern had got to them first, what if he'd found out who they're claiming to be? I can only imagine what he'd do with the story." I rubbed at my forehead. "I didn't know what to do for the best, Ezra. You trust me and so you should, but there's an investigative journalist lurking around and two young women who are desperate to reach out to you…" I let my hands rise and fall as I sat there. "I wouldn't betray your trust." It was important to me that Ezra knew he could trust me. "All I said was if you ever wandered into Flower Power, I'd be sure to pass on their details to you."

Ezra looked away; his hawkish profile uncompromising. Bursts of a delicate, popping red poinsettia were exploding behind him from a gold pot on an occasional table. "It's very convenient that they've materialised, just as my much-anticipated autobiography was released."

He threw me another irritated glance.

They didn't come across as money-grubbing.

"Well, they both said they'd be happy to undertake DNA tests." I folded my arms across my chest. "I'm sorry if you think I shouldn't have got involved, but I was trying to do what I thought was best and it's not like I've told them anything. I promised you I wouldn't tell people you're here and I didn't." I rubbed at my face. "I denied I'd seen you and that you came into the shop." I hesitated. "But Zach Stern's presence is worrying me." I let out a weary sigh. "Both these girls came to my shop looking for you. They were desperate."

"Yes, desperate for fame and money, no doubt. I bet it's all some con."

I dragged a hand through my hair. "They both said they approached their mothers about you, but they refused to help. They didn't want to know."

Ezra's mouth contorted. He shot a guarded look around his opulent sitting room. "Yes. Well, we know why that'll be. It's all a tissue of lies. Or the four of them are secretly in on it." He let his hands flap in frustration. "I don't mean for this to sound dismissive, Bailey, but there are some very mercenary people out there; convincing too." He tried to smile. "I know you only meant well, but in all likelihood, they aren't who they say they are."

I eyed him. "I appreciate that, Ezra, but for what it's worth, I think Toni Rushmore and Jules Maddox could've capitalised on this years ago if they'd wanted to. I've told them nothing."

Ezra's tanned face froze. He gawped over at me for a few seconds. "What?! What did you just say?"

I blinked at him. "What part?"

"The names," he faltered. His expression carried an odd look. "The names of the girls' mothers. Tell me them again."

I repeated the names Toni Rushmore and Jules Maddox.

Ezra's expression was stricken. He looked lost in his own world for a time.

I gave Ezra a meaningful look. "Both these young

women said you'd named their mothers in your autobiography and that you said you'd had affairs with both of them?"

There was a charged silence. He struggled to look me in the eyes. "My God." Then he gave the briefest nod of his head. "Yes. I did name Jules and Toni." He paused. "And I was involved with both of them." He shot me a look. "They were intelligent, gorgeous women."

A dark cloud settled over his features. His hands tumbled over each other in his lap. "And that's definitely who they said their mothers were? You're sure?"

"I'm certain. They showed me birth certificates."

I moved to speak again, but Ezra cut me off. "That doesn't mean I'm their father though." He shook his head, hurt and confusion rearing in his eyes. "I don't know what to think right now and that includes about you too, I'm afraid to say."

I blinked at him. "Sorry?"

"I thought you were different, young lady. Everyone has always wanted a piece of me in some way or another, but I thought you were open and honest."

"Ezra," I began, "what are you talking about? You know you can trust me. You always can. I haven't told anyone anything and you know that."

The light from Ezra's huge windows cast shadows across the pale carpet. "What do you get out of this?"

I frowned at him, hurt. "What do *I* get? What do you mean?"

"Well," he said, glowering. "I imagine that trying to get a fledgling business off the ground nowadays isn't cheap."

His implication twisted in my chest like a knife. Did Ezra believe I offered to help Caroline and Laura for my own ends? That I would then go to the press and sell the story of the acclaimed elder statesman of the British acting world discovering he had two grown-up daughters?

Ezra didn't say anything else, but he didn't have to. The furious glint in his eyes answered my question.

It was ironic. He wouldn't be contemplating the idea of me bleating to the press for money if he knew who I really was.

Hurt lodged in my throat. My mouth opened and closed a few times, resentment alight inside me. After what I'd been through with Declan. Now, I was being accused of betraying Ezra's trust? "How dare you!" I ground out finally. The insult burned in my chest. "How could you even think that I'd even contemplate doing something like that. I told those two women I'd never seen you. I protected your privacy, just as I promised." I swallowed. "And I even tried to find a solution by suggesting a doppelgänger... You know nothing about me, Ezra. If you did, you'd see how alike we are in many ways."

My voice was on the brink of cracking. "I've been let down by a lot of people in my life and I understand what that feels like; how you feel like you can't trust anyone again; how you have to build this barrier around yourself, as that's the only way you won't get hurt..."

I drew up. I'd said enough. I knew how important it

was, to find out who you were, what you wanted to be and how you were going to get there, but I halted my tongue. I couldn't tell Ezra that.

Ezra raked a hand over his grey hair. His tone was dismissive. "Yes. Well." He let out a self-conscious cough. "How old are they? Twenty-eight? Thirty? They must be about your age. They should have a sodding good idea who they are by now."

"Oh, come on," I snapped back. "That's not fair and you know it." The next sentence shot out of my mouth before I could stop myself. Indignation and hurt were swirling around inside of me like a typhoon. "And anyway, that's rich coming from you."

"Meaning?"

I dropped my voice lower, in case Jackson or Mrs Watson were in the vicinity. "You're a famous actor with a very successful career and yet you leave London and move to a little Scottish town whose major claim to fame is a historical tree?"

Ezra looked awkward. "What's your point, Bailey?"

"What are you running away from?"

His jaw hardened and he looked away, an odd expression charging across his craggy features. "I'm not running away from anything."

He wasn't telling me the whole story. Zach's reference to some sort of scandal that Ezra was supposedly caught up in, nudged at the corners of my mind again. "I think you're running away to escape having to take responsibility for whatever it is that you've done."

Ezra's Adam Apple bobbed up and down. He blinked back at me, his features thunderous. He jutted out his chin. "You don't know what you're talking about."

"Oh, believe me, I do."

There was an icy silence for a few moments.

Ezra closed off. He stood up. "On reflection, I don't know if I should go ahead with having you supply your floristry services."

I stared up at him, wounded.

He thrust his hands into the pockets of his trousers. "Under the circumstances, I feel it wouldn't be appropriate."

Bubbles of hurt exploded inside me. I'd expected Ezra to be stunned about what I'd just told him but to be so cruel. So dismissive. I struggled to maintain a level of dignified calm in my voice. I got to my feet.

"Well, that's your prerogative, of course."

I made a noise that was a cross between a grunt and a sigh. It was all I could manage.

"I apologise if you think I've overstepped the mark, but those women asked me for my help and I did what I thought was best at the time." I tried to keep the emotion out of my voice. "I wanted to tell you straight away. That's why I came here." I buried a ball of upset rising up in my throat. I steadied myself and carried on. "The funny thing is that Caroline and Laura reminded me a bit of myself."

Ezra cast his light gaze downwards for a few seconds towards his cream carpet. Then he scanned my face.

"If I hadn't been trustworthy or if I'd been a fraud, I

wouldn't be standing talking to you like this right now. I'd be blabbing everything to the media."

I began to march out of his panelled sitting room, but then stopped, swung round and strode back towards him. "If you stopped for just one moment to think about this, you might just realise that you can trust me, but I do understand how difficult it is to take that step, when you've been let down so often."

I pushed out my chin, trying to stop the swell of hurt. "Must be such a shock for you, that the world doesn't solely revolve around Ezra King after all."

Ezra's eyes widened in surprise. Then he set his jaw. "Please cancel my booking with you. I won't be requiring your floristry services for the house or my party. I'll make alternative arrangements. Oh, and I can deal with Zach Stern myself. No need for dramatics with Joshua. It was doomed to failure anyway."

"Fine." I gritted my teeth. "You do what you think is best."

Ezra drew himself up.

He looked as if he were debating whether to speak again, but then a shadow passed over his face.

I marched out across the tiled hall. Jackson was glancing at his mobile as he reached the bottom of the stairs. He darted forward and opened the front door for me.

My hurt and anger burned white hot as I drove back to my shop.

Chapter Eight

That evening, I closed my curtains and fired on my table lamps.

I wanted to call Marcus back. It was only just after 10pm and I felt guilty I hadn't taken his call earlier but I had been preoccupied making dinner. I'd also still been stewing over what had happened with Ezra. At least Zach hadn't appeared today, but that in itself was troubling me. I wondered what on earth he might be up to.

Marcus answered after a few rings.

I sank down onto my sofa and stretched out my legs. My toes uncurled themselves and I sighed under my breath.

"So, what's your latest news?" I let out a snort. "Tell me something funny. Mum hasn't roped you into baking again for the Women's Institute, has she?"

He didn't reply. There was an odd gulping noise down the line. "When did you last speak to Mum and Dad?"

"A few days ago. Mum was trying to talk me into

coming down for a visit. She said I've got to move on from what happened with Declan and I think I'm slowly beginning to now—"

"Well, I think it's sodding ridiculous!" he erupted. "Ok, he was a tosser and he hurt you, but you can't live like a bloody nun for the rest of your life."

My eyes widened at my brother's harsh words.

"You loved him and we can't help who we fall in love with, but you can't hide in Heather Moore forever."

"I'm not hiding," I snapped back. "I've been taking stock and trying to move on. And I miss all that vacuous, constant partying like a hole in the head." I let out a laugh. "It's all right for you though, all loved up with the gorgeous Jacob. I'd rather get a puppy than get involved with someone else again."

I gave a theatrical shudder.

Marcus wasn't saying anything.

"Marcus? Are you ok?"

I shot forward at the sound of my older brother's voice suddenly cracking.

"What is it? What's wrong?" My imagination took off like a rocket from a launch pad.

Marcus was struggling to compose himself. "It's Jacob," he managed after a few moments.

"What about Jacob? Oh God, what's happened?"

There was a splinter in his voice as he spoke. "It's over."

"What?"

"The engagement's off. Jacob's finished with me."

I couldn't believe it.

It didn't make any sense.

Marcus and Jacob were the epitome of a serious, loved-up couple. They were often on the verge of finishing each other's sentences. They would take off on their bikes together for hours, with cute picnics and matching outfits. Dad would often joke that if you weren't constantly seeing them together in the same room, you'd start to wonder if they were the same person.

They met three years ago, when Marcus was allocated Jacob's environmental enterprise account at the marketing firm where he works.

From the moment he met him, I'd never seen my brother so happy.

I jumped up from the sofa, struggling to take in Marcus's news. "But why? What happened?"

There were a few heartbroken gulps down the line.

"I never saw it coming," he managed in a small voice. "Everything's been great, or at least I thought it was. Then, out of nowhere, he came home earlier this afternoon and told me we need to talk."

Marcus sniffed. "Jacob told me to sit down while I was in the middle of preparing dinner. Then he just came out with it," he gulped. "He said he'd been thinking about things for a while now and had changed his mind about getting married."

I paced up and down my sitting room. If Jacob Geddes were in front of me right now, he would be bent double and nursing two very red and swollen testicles. "I just don't understand, though. Where's this come from? Have you two had an argument?"

"No. That's the thing. I can't comprehend any of it."

Random questions loomed in my head. "Look, I hate to ask this, but do you think there might be someone else involved?"

Marcus admitted that thought had occurred to him too. "I did ask him that, but he denied it. He said his business is really taking off and it wouldn't be fair on me if we went ahead with the wedding."

Fury festered inside my chest. "How very magnanimous of him."

I wanted to bundle my brother up in my arms right now and tell him everything would be all right. "Do Mum and Dad know?"

"Yes," answered Marcus, clearing his throat. "I called them as soon as Jacob had packed an overnight bag and left the flat. He said he was going to crash at a friends for a few days."

"How did they take it?"

Marcus sniffed into my ear again. "They came over straight away. Mum was quite pragmatic about the whole thing, though. Plenty more handsome fish in the sea, she said. Dad wouldn't stop hugging me and said he wanted to go and punch him."

Marcus let out a wounded sigh.

"Mum and Dad said they'd stay over tonight, but I assured them I'd be all right. I want some space and couldn't face the thought of endless questions and conducting a post-mortem over it."

It was as if I could hear my brother's addled brain struggling to make sense of it from here. "We were looking to get married next spring, sis. We'd even started looking at wedding venues."

My teeth ground together as his voice collapsed again.

"Right, Marcus. I'm not debating the matter with you, ok? I want you to pack some things and come and stay here with me for a few days."

"But my job, Anastasia!"

"I thought you said to me the other week that you had some leave due."

He went quiet. "Well … yes, technically I do. I haven't taken any holiday for a good couple of months, as things have been so hectic."

"Well then. Ring the agency first thing tomorrow and explain to that boss of yours, Paul, what's happened. Didn't you say he and Jenna broke up recently?"

"Yes. They split a couple of months back."

"There you are then. Paul will understand how you're feeling."

I ramped up my powers of persuasion. "And you can work from home here if you need to. You've said yourself often enough how much stuff you get done on your laptop when you're out of the office."

I could hear my brother's husky voice beginning to weaken.

"Come on. A change of scene will do you good. You need a break. Especially now."

My appeals were met with silence for a few moments.

"You need a breather. Stop being so stubborn."

"Ha. That's ironic coming from you, little sister."

There was an agonised sigh and a few more beats of silence. "Ok," he muttered, sniffing down the line. "You win. I'll pack a few bits and ring Paul before I set off for yours tomorrow."

The next day saw chilly, intermittent November downpours, which drove extra customers into Flower Power for refuge.

Locals let out discernible sighs of relief as the warm, twinkling interior of the shop, festooned with the sweet scent of flowers, welcomed them in. I'd also strategically placed pretty bowls of festive cranberry and fig potpourri around the place.

Flower Power was well and truly easing into Christmas, with two stout fir trees, decorated with gold lights and festooned with ribbons, standing either side of the shop door. Amber and Rowan had strung more matching fairy lights along the edges of the shelves, around the door and along the counter, together with some thick, golden tinsel.

All I had to do now was finalise my ideas for the shop window display. I'd decided to go with the white, cream, and gold ice palace theme. I had more time to work on that now that Ezra had cancelled his agreement with me, I concluded with an internal sigh.

I'd ordered some reels of crepe paper to use in the display from the local stationers, so I jumped in my van and shot down to the other end of town to collect it.

No sooner had I thanked Mrs Appleby and was negotiating the wodges of crêpe paper out of the door, than I almost collied with the tall, dark, and looming shape of Zach.

Oh, not again! Was he following me?

Zach stuffed his hands into his long coat pockets. "You look like you're struggling there."

"Not at all," I puffed, hoping I didn't trip over the pavement and land arse over head in front of him. "They aren't that heavy." I angled myself past him. "Doing some shopping, are we?"

He flexed a brow. "No, doing my job."

Of being a pain in the neck, I grunted to myself.

I willed my van to move closer, but it sat there in all its pink and white glory further up the kerb. "Ha. Allow me," he announced, before sweeping the fat rolls of crêpe paper out of my arms and into his.

I was ready to protest, but he just strode on ahead with them, like they weighed nothing.

His mouth trembled, as he approached my van, clutching the crêpe paper. "I take it this sporty little number is yours?"

"Whatever gave you that idea?"

I cranked open the back of the van and he slid the rolls inside.

I banged the doors shut again. He was towering over me, all black hair and blazing eyes. "Thank you for your help."

"You're welcome. See you again soon."

And with that, he sauntered back off along the pavement.

My laptop was set up on the counter as I scrolled through my inbox, in between dealing with customers, after I arrived back from the stationery shop.

A new email flickered up on the screen, taking me by surprise, although given what had happened, it shouldn't have been unexpected.

Hi Bailey,

Hope all is well with you.

I'm Corrie Hardwick, assistant to Ezra King's manager, Densie Gold.

This is just to confirm that after careful consideration, Mr King has decided not to proceed with your floristry services for his home, nor for his private party on 31 December.

I realise this must be a great disappointment to you, but I understand it is not unexpected due to recent circumstances.

We will, however, be more than happy to compensate you

for any time you've already spent working on the floral displays.

Look forward to hearing from you soon.

Best,

Corrie

Sublime Entertainment Management Agency

A heavy feeling lodged itself in my stomach.

Well, that was his prerogative.

My head was jammed with memories of what I'd been through with the press. Ezra wanted what I wanted; a peaceful existence; a chance to breathe and re-set. And yes, I didn't want Zach finding out about who I was. Was that so much to ask?

My mobile buzzed under the counter. It was a text from Marcus, saying he was on his way, the traffic on the motorway was slow but steady and he estimated he would arrive within the hour.

I dashed a reply back, promising to have the kettle on for his arrival and told him to take it easy. I was looking forward to having him come and stay. It would be nice to have his tall, rangy, brotherly presence around the place for a few days.

Thoughts about Ezra and the niggling worry over Zach lurking around made me feel off-kilter. Boy, I needed my big brother right now, every bit as much as he needed me.

Forty-five minutes later, Marcus arrived.

He carried a leather holdall in one gloved hand and his laptop case in the other.

His skin was pale and his light brown hair was damp from the weather.

I hurried towards him and scooped him into my open arms. Marcus didn't say a word. He just clung to me in a cloud of citrus-scented bodywash. I took a step back and held him at arm's length. Lack of sleep was evident in his puffy, powder-blue eyes.

"I parked round the back," he said in a faltering voice. "I hope that's ok."

I nodded and squeezed his arm. "That's fine."

I studied him. "What would you like to do first? Do you want me to give you the spare key to the flat and you can go upstairs and have a lie down? You look like you could do with some sleep."

"You know how to boost my morale."

"You're still handsome, even during a personal crisis." I paused. "I've made up the bed in the spare room."

Marcus gave a weak smile. "I know I look like crap, but I don't feel tired. Can't I just stay down here in Flower Power with you for a little bit?"

I patted his gloved hand. He was dressed in his heavy navy coat. "You do whatever you want."

I lowered my voice. "Just remember when we have company around, that my name's Bailey, ok?"

Marcus rolled his eyes. "Your life is like some bloody soap opera."

"Please."

"Ok. Ok."

Marcus deposited his holdall and laptop behind the

counter for now, while Amber returned from my office with a spare chair. I'd explained to her that my brother was coming to stay following a painful breakup and I'd say the same to Rowan when she arrived for the afternoon shift. I didn't want them interrogating him and opening up fresh wounds while he was trying to heal.

Amber offered Marcus a kind smile before insisting he have a cup of tea.

"She seems really sweet," Marcus commented, as Amber wobbled off in her platform fur-lined boots to make a fresh pot.

"She's a gem. A bit of a chatterbox, but I wouldn't have her any other way."

"And the other girl? How's she working out?"

"You mean Rowan? She's fantastic too. A real asset."

Marcus tried to push out a smile. Perched on that chair, his shoulders hunched, he was like a shadow of his usual self.

Marcus fluttered his right hand. "You don't have to stand over me and watch me. You do what you have to do. I'm fine here."

I noticed that his scalloped gold engagement band was missing from his left hand.

Amber returned with a tray of steaming mugs of tea and we all sipped in silence.

"I can take a bit of time off while you're here," I said to Marcus. "I do have a bridal bouquet and two birthday orders I'm working on, and I need to order the ornaments for the Christmas wreaths, but that's not a problem."

Marcus shook his weary head again. "Stop mollycoddling me! I'm fine."

I started to insist again that I wanted to spend some time with him, when the shop door flew open, bringing with it Zach Stern.

Bugger. I knew he'd reappear at some point, but not just after I saw him earlier when I was struggling with the crêpe paper and he'd been taking the mickey out of my van.

Standing there with the shards of heavy Heather Moore rain pelting down behind him, he reminded me of some wild, historical hero who'd just made his way across windswept moors to declare passionate love for a willowy heroine.

His black hair was flopping forward, looking damp but inviting.

What I was about to say to Marcus dried up in my throat as my gaze collided with Zach's.

An odd feeling zipped through me. He looked delectable.

Oh no. No. Absolutely not.

He was the enemy. He was the Kryptonite to my Superman. And what had I promised myself? That I wouldn't get involved with anyone again. I could only trust myself. It was the safest way.

I raised my chin, annoyed that my ears were morphing into a bright shade of pink. "Good afternoon, Mr Stern. How can I help you?"

My attention strayed to Marcus. I noticed one of his brows had arched up towards his hairline. He was watching the two of us as though he'd stumbled across an intriguing thriller on Netflix.

Amber was trying not to make it obvious she was observing everything too, even though she was supposed to have gone to tidy up the stock room for me.

Zach flashed me a long look. "Oh, I'm sure you *can* help me, Ms McArthur. Whether or not you *will* is another matter." He took a few slow, deliberate steps towards me. "I'd appreciate a quick chat."

I tried to look nonchalant. "About what?"

He shoved his hands into the pockets of his long, stylish coat. "I'd prefer to talk in private, if that's all right."

I looked at Marcus, mentally willing Zach Stern and his beautiful dark eyes to bugger off back to Glasgow. "But my brother has just arrived for a visit and I'm afraid we're busy catching up."

Zach meandered casually away, as though he was browsing the Christmas wreath selection.

Marcus pulled an irritated expression and whispered, "I'm not five, Anastasia!" He jerked his head at Zach and continued to speak in hushed tones. "You go and do what you have to do with Mr Hottie over there."

I glanced over my shoulder at Zach. Heat rose up my neck. "I don't have to do anything with him. He's a right pain in the arse."

"I'll keep an eye on your brother," insisted Amber. "He'll be fine."

Marcus pulled a sarcastic face. "Hello? I'm sitting right here, you know."

He appraised Zach approvingly. "I know I'm off men," he hissed out of the corner of his mouth, "and they're all utter bastards and selfish arses, but…"

"But what?"

Zach was now perusing a couple of my yucca plants, unaware he was the sole topic of conversation.

"But that one's delicious!"

"Marcus!" I insisted. "It's not like that. I mean, there's nothing… He's an arrogant tit! I can't stand the man."

Amber giggled. "Then why have you gone red, boss?"

"No, I haven't."

My brother peered at me. "Yes, you have. I could fry an egg on your cheeks."

I faffed and flustered at the counter. "I haven't a clue what you two are on about."

I turned and bathed Zach in what I hoped was a cool smile. He abandoned his browsing of the nearby Christmas plants and strode back over. "Come with me, Mr Stern," I said grudgingly.

He pinned me to the spot for a moment, his expression indecipherable. "Please, call me Zach."

I blinked back at him. "Oh. Right." I cleared my throat. I didn't want to appear rude or give him any glimmer of suspicion about me. "Well, in that case, call me Bailey." Was this some sort of awkward truce? Or was he trying to lull me into a false sense of security? Make me think we'd hit some sort of understanding, when in fact, he wanted to bleed me dry of any information I might have?

I led the way towards my office and made a point of

saying to Amber and Marcus that I wouldn't be long. I had to stay on alert. It was mentally exhausting, but it had to be done.

I eased open my office door and encouraged him to go first. "I don't know how you think I can help you, Mr Stern. Er, I mean, Zach."

He gave me a withering look. "I can't help it if I'm an eternal optimist."

I scowled at him and shut my office door. Smart arse!

"So that was your brother?" he asked, all long legs and broad shoulders as he sat down opposite my desk.

"Yes."

Zach seemed to be waiting for me to give him a little more information, but there was no way I was doing that. The less information he had about me and my family, the better.

Zach folded his arms, his gaze travelling over my face. I found myself shuffling in my seat. I instructed myself to sit still.

The man is an arrogant cretin!

Yes, oozed an inner voice. *But a very handsome one with come-to-bed eyes.*

For something to do, I snatched up a pen from my desk and twiddled it around and around in my hands, trying not to think about bed and Zach.

"It's nice that he's visiting you."

"It would be, were it under different circumstances."

A questioning look lit up in his eyes. *Ah. Ever the journalist.*

"Is everything all right? Can I help?"

"What, by writing about it?"

Zach cocked a brow. "Ouch. That hurt."

"Sorry," I mumbled. He kept staring at me with an expectant look on his face.

God, he was good. Quite easy to talk to, if you ignored the self-satisfied smile. I let out a resigned sigh. I knew I shouldn't be confiding in him, but those dark, inviting eyes were hypnotic.

Jesus!

Zach tilted his head to the side.

I tried to refocus. "Relationship heartache."

Zach looked solemn. "Sorry to hear that. How's he doing?"

"Not great. He's doing what he always does when he has a problem; putting on a brave face."

Zach's gaze misted over for a few seconds before it hardened.

"He'll get over it. If you ask me, folks would be better off concentrating on the things that really matter, not relationships. They never work out."

Ouch. His blunt tone made me blink. "Well, speak your mind, why don't you?"

Zach gave a dismissive shrug. "I'm just being honest. You're far better off relying on yourself. No risk of getting hurt." He hesitated. "Or hurting someone else."

Blimey. He didn't believe in sugar-coating, did he? "What other things should people focus on?" I asked. He sounded just like me. "Their career?"

Zach's jaw clenched. "Absolutely. Far more rewarding. Relationships are overrated."

He paused for a moment before speaking again. "I've dropped by about a couple of new tip-offs I've received."

Zach's voice made me refocus. "About what? Ezra King again?"

He raked a hand through his thick, dark hair. "No. Well, at least one of them is."

"Oh?"

He pulled a brief smile.

Confusion burrowed in my chest. What the hell was going on?

I stared over my desk at him. "So, what's this all about?"

Zach lasered me with his black-lashed eyes. "Firstly, I've been told by a very reliable contact that Ezra King has two daughters by two different high-profile women. But he doesn't know they exist."

My stomach exploded in a swarm of worried butterflies. This is exactly what I was afraid of. Surely Caroline and Laura hadn't been going around telling everyone?! Oh God. Did that mean they were scammers after all? Had I been about to be duped by them as well? Anger and disappointment began to flare up inside me.

"Really?" I croaked. "Sounds like something you'd see on daytime TV." I paused, trying to couch my words. "How did you come by that information? Did you bump into these two 'high-profile' women in the street or something?" I was mentally willing it not to be the girls themselves who'd told him. I was weary of being sceptical of people and wanted to be proved wrong.

Zach arched one brow. "A friend of a friend in the showbiz management world."

"Right." I heaved an inward sigh of relief. Ok, it wasn't definitive evidence that Caroline and Laura were genuine, but at least it didn't seem they'd been the ones blabbing to journalists about their possible connection to Ezra.

Zach leant forward in his chair. I could make out his shadow of dark stubble. "My editor, Adam, was tipped off yesterday." Light flashed in his dark eyes. "If I can get exclusives on both of these stories, it'll give a huge boost to my journalistic career."

"Bully for you," I ground out.

Zach gave me a look.

"And then there's the other thing." He paused. "Adam was at an editors' lunch yesterday in Glasgow and he said there was some drunk guy hanging about outside the hotel. He got Adam's attention by fawning all over him and saying how wonderful *Stargazer* magazine is. He'd obviously done his homework. Then he told Adam he was once in a relationship with a Scottish aristo party girl."

I sat up straighter, as though someone had just fired an electrified current through my whole body.

No. It couldn't be. It was too much of a coincidence.

The breath felt trapped in my throat.

"Adam said he was a right scruffy individual and didn't look the type to be marrying someone like that." Zach carried on talking, while the panicked buzzing in my ears got louder. "But he said this guy sounded genuine."

I licked my lips. "And?"

Zach steepled his hands in his lap. "The guy told Adam he'd sell his story. Adam said he was wittering and slurring, and he could smell the booze off his breath, but this guy insisted he almost married her but got cold feet at the last minute."

Cold feet? The lying, cheating bastard! He's a crook!

My heart charged against my ribs so hard, I thought it was going to burst. Was Declan going to risk telling a lot of lies to the press? He was the one who left me at the altar, so to speak. Ok, I dodged a bullet, but that lying toad ran off with the money I gave him. It should be me who was talking to the press about him if anything. Not that I would ever do that.

Aware that Zach was studying me, I forced my expression into a neutral, calm one.

"So, a drunk guy accosts your editor in the street, claiming he was engaged to some aristocrat. So what?" I said.

Zach shrugged. "I know what you mean, but Adam said there might be a good story in it and the guy did seem the real deal. Claims that his ex is living somewhere in this area, but she's trying to keep under the radar." Zach's eyes shone. "If I'm lucky, I might be able to get a double exclusive: Ezra King and the Bollinger Babe."

My insides shuddered at the name the press labelled me with. "Sounds scintillating," I said dryly.

Zach's mouth twitched. "You'd be surprised at the appetite for this kind of thing,' he said.

"Really?" I said, as though it wasn't the entire reason I'd changed my name and my appearance, to get away from the gossipmongers and the pack of press dogs.

"Must be something in the water around these parts," Zach went on. "Adam and I did think it odd that Heather Moore cropped up again, but there's been a few instances recently, of celebrities buying boltholes in more remote parts of the country." He gave an easy shrug. "But hey … as long as there's a good story, I'm not going to quibble."

My stomach clenched. How the hell had Declan found out about me being here? Who'd told him?

I bit back a ball of bile in my throat. Morbid fascination was tightening its grip on me and I couldn't shake it off. More than one life looked like it was verging on implosion. Who would be first? Ezra or me?

"Do you have a name for this drunken character?" My office walls were suffocating me, crushing my chest and pressing down. The Christmas fairy lights and tinsel I'd strung up on the walls were burning my eyes.

Oblivious to the panic ripping through me, Zach pushed his hands into his coat pockets. "The guy was about to give Adam more details, but a couple of cops moved him on. He thinks the man might've said his name was Sean but like I said, he was very pissed, in a state and not all that coherent."

My mouth dried up. It must be Declan. Sean was his middle name. It was all about the money. It always was with him. He was obsessed by it. He must be desperate when he was crawling out from wherever he'd been hiding. Obviously, he was prepared to take a risk to get his hands on more cash. That was his aim in life.

Zach gave a sarcastic smile. "It happens more than you think, this sort of thing; desperate folks approaching us, trying to cash in on non-existent stories for their fifteen minutes of fame."

Zach's hypnotic, dark brown eyes shone with determination. "But Adam said the guy insisted his ex was that Bollinger Babe party girl who the tabloids nicknamed a few years back."

My mouth opened and closed. I gripped the edge of my desk. My knuckles morphed into blobs of anxious white.

I was fighting to speak. Thoughts were tumbling through my mind. The first being what the hell was Declan's game here?

This was quickly followed by messy, painful memories of our relationship and how it ended.

Though my brain was working overtime, nothing was coming out of my mouth, except for random bursts of panicked air.

Zach began to fiddle with his phone while he was talking to me from the other side of my desk.

Oh God, please don't let him find a picture of me!

My cheeks were flaming. Any minute now he was going to notice.

Right. Take a breath. Try to stay calm.

I let out a strangled cough. All my fears were coming true. Would I never escape the past?

My fingers knotted and tumbled over each other as I sat there. "So, you don't have a lead on her then?"

Zach jabbed at his phone screen and flashed me a glance as he scrolled up and down the screen. "Our Lady Anastasia seems to have vanished into thin air. Talk about lying low. We've run some checks and investigated social media but she doesn't use that any more. She hasn't posted on any of them for a good couple of years." Zach sat up straighter. "She might think she's able to hide, but not for much longer. I'm asking around."

Zach eyed me. "I'm telling you all this, in the hope you might know someone who can help us locate her or who might have some information. It would be worth their while." My spine stiffened. My office walls were squeezing the breath from my chest harder and faster, like that famous scene in *Indiana Jones*. To my own burning ears, my voice was a hoarse, harried mess. Hearing Zach say my real name, was like hearing a ringing in my ears. "About her being here in Heather Moore?"

Zach pushed his phone back into his coat pocket. "Yes. Gotta start somewhere and Adam said that guy was insistent she might be basing herself around here now."

"He was hammered," I insisted, trying not to sound panicked. "Not sure he'd know what day of the week it was, let alone be a reliable source of information. And anyway, I'm sure someone like her would stick out a mile in a town this size."

Zach frowned across at me. "You sound very sure about all this, Bailey."

I flapped my hands. "Well… You know, knowing Heather Moore like I do."

Zach glanced around at my flower photographs on the office walls and my newly erected Christmas decorations.

My heart iced in my chest. It had been coming, I suppose. It was inevitable. I'd been deluding myself if I thought I could carve out a fresh life for myself here. I'd been lucky to have six months hassle-free.

Zach's voice dragged me back. "Well, people slip up at some point. They make a silly mistake and leave a trail. It's human nature."

My whirring thoughts were freewheeling around my head and refusing to stop. Declan Rooney's evil shadow was still following me around. What was he trying to do? What did he hope to achieve? Duh! Silly question. Money.

It sounded like his music "career" was a no-go, if he was stumbling around the city streets, drunk. Not content with what he stole from me for the imaginary music foundation, now he was back for more.

And how the hell had someone found out about me being here? I'd tried to be as careful as I could, but that couldn't have been enough. I'd been a tabloid it-girl; the partying aristo. I'd been in so many newspapers and magazines. Had someone local recognised me and blabbed? I'd been deluding myself, if I thought I could start again.

I made a show of noting something else imaginary down. My fingers trembled as they gripped the pen. "The poor woman probably just wants to live quietly and start over. Isn't she entitled to that?"

"Of course she is, but when there's a potential human-interest story like this, it deserves to be told."

"Does it? Whose interest?" I bit back. "Hers or yours?"

Zach's eyes shone back at me. He angled his head to one side. "You seem very interested."

I whirled my pen around and around. I tried to make my voice sound airy. Every word I was saying sounded brittle. "Heather Moore isn't exactly a throbbing metropolis."

"Precisely. So, it could well appeal. Somewhere inconspicuous to live her life. It makes sense."

My heart revved up so hard against my ribs, I thought they would splinter.

A steely edge gripped Zach's handsome features. "When it comes to a story, I'm never deterred."

I dropped my gaze and rattled my pen on my desk for something to do. It spun this way and that on the polished wood. If I continued to fiddle with the pen any longer, it was in danger of exploding ink everywhere. This was agony.

Zach eyed me from across my desk. "In my line of work, dogged determination is everything, as is telling the truth."

I set my pen down. "And does that go for blowing apart people's lives too?"

"It depends what they've done. If you're talking about exposing the rich and powerful for being manipulative and behaving like they're above the law, you mean? Yes."

I unscrambled what was going on inside my head. My cheeks stung.

"So, this guy told you he was going to dish some dark secrets, did he?" I asked. "Has it occurred to you he might be lying? That he just wants to make some money?"

Zach smiled. "Sure, he could be lying. I mean no one really knows why the marriage didn't go ahead. Her family's PR made sure of that."

"Hmm." I gave him a fake smile back. "And you're just assuming that she's the villain?"

He let out a cynical bark of laughter. "I'd put money on it," he said. "A lot of folks who live very privileged lives lie and deceive with impunity. They don't consider anyone but themselves, and they're not the ones who suffer."

He pushed his chair back and stood up. "Believe me, I should know."

This was morphing into a nightmare. Zach couldn't have got it more wrong, but there was absolutely nothing I could do about it without revealing my true identity. I could see my new life evaporating in front of my eyes – and Ezra's too.

I rose to my feet, my head pummelled by thoughts.

Zach towered over me. "Stories are like buses. Nothing good for ages and then two come along at once."

"Oh well," I bit back. "Good to see you're changing the world one celebrity gossip scandal at a time."

His eyes never left my face. "You have a very dim view of me."

I straightened my back.

"I'm a good journalist with an ethical code."

My eyebrows shot upwards.

"You're judging me without knowing me. I want to reveal the crooks, the liars, and the cheats. I want to give people a voice who don't have one. They deserve to be heard loud and clear."

"By writing about people's private lives and dragging their names through the mud?"

Zach looked like he wanted to say something else. He opened his mouth and closed it again. "It's nothing personal. It's my career."

I struggled not to be captivated by his eyes, even though he was at risk of upending my entire life. I didn't want to become an exhibit here. I was happy with how I was moving things on. I didn't want to be the centre of a pity party or have the locals think I'd deceived them in any way. I didn't want to be back in the papers, splashed across the pages, having my past dissected and my previous life choices examined. I'd done enough of that myself. I didn't know what Declan was planning to spill, but it would be a pack of lies.

"I'd appreciate it if you could ask around; keep your eyes and ears open for any snippets of information about our party princess and these two daughters of Ezra King."

I jerked my attention away from Zach's scrutiny and shuffled around a few invoices. "Why on earth would I help you?"

Zach jerked open my office door and lingered there. His ink-black hair flopped onto his brow. "Because I helped you this morning with all the crêpe you were carrying."

"Oh, very funny."

Zach gave me a shadow of a smile. "You'd receive payment of course, for any valuable tip-offs. Would come in handy, I'm sure, some extra money, seeing as you've only been open a few months."

He hesitated.

"It's not going to be easy," he admitted, surprising me with his unusual candour. "Especially if this aristo's parents have sections of the press in their pockets." He ground his jaw. "I've known for that to happen before. But I don't give up and I don't give in, Bailey. On anything."

I blushed, feeling heat shoot up my neck. Cue more paper flapping.

"See you again soon," he murmured, his attention lingering on my face.

I watched him stride out of Flower Power in his flapping, long coat. Amber's admiring eyes trailed after him, while worry took great bites out of me.

I couldn't concentrate for the rest of the morning.

I faffed around with a couple of birthday bouquets and attempted to come up with something interesting for my suggested "Plants of the Week" for the shop's social media accounts, but failed. Zach kept drifting into my mind and it unsettled me.

In the end, I used Marcus as my excuse to take an early lunch and disappear back up to my flat.

"Why are you so quiet, A? What's going on?" asked my brother.

A battle was raging inside of me as to whether I should confide in him.

He had enough to contend with at the moment, nursing his broken heart, without being told that his baby sister might find herself splashed across the newspapers – again – taking with her the rest of the family. Snapshots of their horrified faces loomed in front of my eyes.

Oh God.

Mum would need to lie down in a darkened room for the next three months.

But the other half of me was desperate to offload. *Tell him!* screamed my inner voice. *He has a right to know. He's your brother.*

What if I didn't confide in Marcus and Zach did unearth everything? My brother wouldn't forgive me. I knew if the situation were reversed and Marcus found himself caught up in something like this, I'd want to know. If I found out he hadn't told me, I would be livid.

I eyed his holdall which was currently regurgitating clothes onto the chair in the spare room.

We never kept secrets from one another. When we were younger, we always took the blame for each other's misdemeanours.

"Anastasia."

I snapped my attention back to my brother and sighed.

I pushed back any lingering doubts and steeled myself. "I've got something to tell you. It's about Declan."

Marcus contorted his mouth. "The prick!" His expression grew serious. "Hold on. He's not here, is he? Has he reappeared? He's not threatening you?"

"No, well, he's not here in Heather Moore, or at least I don't think he is."

Marcus frowned across the bed at me. "What are you talking about?"

I picked at the bedspread. "It turns out that a drunk, dishevelled Declan accosted the editor of *Stargazer* magazine the other day in Glasgow. Said his name was Sean. He blabbed that he'd been in a relationship with the Bollinger Babe and almost married her – until he got cold feet."

With his bright blue eyes growing in his face, Marcus let out a stream of horrified gasps. "Are you joking? Oh shit!"

"And not only that, he also told the editor that he'd heard I was living in this neck of the woods."

Marcus shot out his hand and seized mine in his. "Jesus, A! What the hell's been going on here? How did he find out? Did you let slip to anyone by accident?"

I blew out a cloud of worried air. "I haven't said a word. I've tried to be careful."

"So how much information did that rat Declan give this editor?"

"Not as much as he wanted to, by the sounds of it. He was moved on by the police for making a nuisance of himself."

Marcus scratched at his chin. "Thank Christ for that." He hesitated. "But this is still awful!"

I squeezed Marcus's hand. "I didn't want to involve you when you've got so much going on at the moment, but it's a total nightmare."

He shuffled closer. "So, what happens now?" His eyes grew bigger. "Is it that hottie who was in today who's investigating you?"

My ears prickled with heat. Marcus noticed me squirming.

"Why have you gone so red again?"

"I haven't gone red. It's the light in here and the reflection from the duvet cover."

Marcus looked at me like I was crazy.

"Zach's editor has told him to investigate Declan's ramblings and see if there's any truth in his story. But there's always the risk that Declan could call the magazine when he's sober and then I really would be up to my neck in it."

Fretful tears found their way to the corners of my eyes. "I like my new life here, Marcus. I've got Flower Power, my cosy little flat and I feel like I'm finally beginning to move on from Declan and everything that happened."

We both fell quiet. Then Marcus spoke again. "You're going to have to tell Mum and Dad."

"What? No! I don't want to worry them. It might not come to anything anyway."

Marcus let out an incredulous laugh and waggled my

hand. "Anastasia, Declan is a toerag and he can't be trusted. Mum and Dad need to know."

His voice vanished when he picked up on my shame-faced expression. I avoided his gaze and concentrated on the bare trees I could see through the window.

"It's not fair to keep it from them. Imagine if they opened up a magazine and you're all over it like you used to be."

I blew out a cloud of embarrassed air. "I'm not stupid. I know that."

"Well stop sodding well acting like you are!" His blue eyes blazed out of his handsome, open face. "Zach Stern's a journalist and a bloody good one, by all accounts."

"How do you know that?"

"Because I was curious and looked him up online. And even if that snitch Declan doesn't remember much after his drunken stupor, there's still a good chance Zach will find out about you anyway."

"Zach might be accomplished, but he's still working for a gossip mag."

Marcus pulled in his lips. "What's that got to do with anything?"

"He has prestigious journalistic awards as long as Loch Lomond and yet he's working for a publication like that." I squinted at my brother. "Don't you think it's a bit weird?"

Marcus gave a frustrated shrug. "That's up to him. Maybe they offered him a telephone number salary? Right now, I'm far more concerned about you."

I tried to dismiss his worries. "I'll just have to try and stay one step ahead of Zach."

Marcus shook his damp hair. "How on earth do you think you can do that?" He toyed with the belt of his dressing gown. "And when exactly do you intend to tell Mum and Dad about all this?"

"I don't."

Marcus looked exasperated. "Oh, for pity's sake! Why not?"

He opened his mouth to protest, but I stopped him. "I will tell them, if the situation demands it, but not right now. It's safer all round that the fewer people who know what's going on, the better. I haven't told Amber or Rowan about who I used to be for the same reason."

He shot me a disapproving frown.

"Marcus, please. I'm asking you not to say anything to Mum and Dad. Not yet." I dragged a weary hand down the side of my face. "Please. Just let me handle things for the time being."

He flicked back a strand of hair. "Ok! Ok! I still think you should tell them, but you know you can trust me."

"Thank you." I offered him a small smile. "After all this, I wouldn't blame you for wanting to head straight back home to Edinburgh."

Marcus was incandescent. "Are you kidding me? I'm not leaving you to deal with this mess on your own!" He stroked the candy-striped bedspread. "I was planning to stay a few days, if that's ok?"

"You know you can stay with me for as long as you want."

"Thank you. And anyway, let's face it, I've got nothing to rush back for."

I didn't want to push Marcus into talking more about Jacob before he was ready, but I didn't like the thought of my brother bottling up his emotions either. "You don't have to go into details yet if you don't feel like it, but I'm just wondering if Jacob has said any more about why he called the engagement off? It's just so sudden."

My brother's mouth folded downwards. "I haven't heard from him. I still can't fathom it either and believe me, I've been giving it a lot of thought." He clicked his fingers and flinched. "Our future. Up in smoke. Just like that."

My eyebrows gathered. It didn't make sense. "And there were no indications from him that there were problems brewing?"

"Nope."

He stared past my shoulder, his bright blue eyes dimming again. "Even Mum and Dad were shocked. Mum especially. She said he must've realised he wasn't good enough for me, which is a load of old bollocks of course." He shook his head. "I mean, it was so thoughtful of Mum and Dad to ask Jacob round the other week for dinner, when I was away at that training course in London. They've been so good to him."

A kernel of suspicion began to grow. That was odd. Mum hadn't mentioned anything to me. I frowned at him. "You never told me that."

Marcus dismissed it. "It was no big deal."

I turned this over in my head. "What day was that? Can you remember?"

Marcus snatched up his mobile beside him and checked his electronic calendar. "It was a week past, Thursday."

A warning bell clanged in my head. "Are you sure?" I pressed. "Definitely the Thursday?"

Marcus waggled his phone at me. "One hundred per cent. Why?"

I forced my face into a casual expression. "Nothing. Just having random thoughts, that's all."

Marcus gave me an odd look, before tossing his phone back onto the bedspread.

Our dad hadn't been at home at Bannock House that evening. He'd been away overnight with his golfing buddies in St Andrews for their annual soirée. I remembered because I'd called Mum, she hadn't picked up and so I'd rung Dad instead to say hi and had been serenaded by half a dozen pissed, middle-aged men.

Confusion welled up inside of me. Why would Mum have chosen that night to have invited Jacob round? She would have known Dad wouldn't be there.

A discomfiting sensation took hold. I felt ashamed for even thinking it, but did Mum know something about Jacob that we didn't?

Lunchtime swung around and my preoccupied thoughts kept morphing to Declan lurking around in Glasgow.

I couldn't settle or concentrate on anything.

I felt useless, standing here, while the spectre of my sleazy ex-fiancé kept insisting on haunting me.

I actually thought I was beginning to push him out of my past and now he emerges again, trying to cause havoc.

My hands fiddled with the giant amber- and claret-coloured gerbera bouquet I was creating for Mrs Sweeney's mother's ninetieth birthday.

A thought bounced about my head, gathering traction. What if I tried to find Declan? What if I could speak to him? The prospect made my stomach churn, but what else could I do?

I was flinching every time the shop door opened and my bell let out its merry tinkle. Would he try to show up? That was very likely, knowing him. But if I tried to cut him off at the pass? Let him know I was onto him? Would that be a deterrent?

Something told me it might take more than me speaking to him, to have an effect, but surely me doing something was better than doing nothing? There was every chance he'd try to extort money out of me, to keep quiet but I realised I was prepared to take that risk. Too much was riding on this.

Declan might only keep his mouth shut if he did indeed get something in return. He must have been hoping to sell "our story" for a tidy sum, after all.

I eyed my half-eaten cheese and salad sandwich on my plate further up the shop counter. I couldn't carry on like this, knowing Declan was only a couple of hours' drive away from my new life here.

I picked up my mug of tea and drained the remainder of it.

Yuck.

It was cold.

I pulled a face and thumped it back down again.

Then I reached for my coat and bag which were hanging on one of the hooks behind me.

I thrust on my coat, refusing to dissect what I was doing in case I changed my mind. "Girls, I've got to pop out for a few hours. Could one of you tie up this bouquet for Mrs Sweeney please, with a piece of tangerine satin bow? I've just finished it."

Rowan came striding over. "No problem. I can do that."

Amber paused as she swept the floor. "Off anywhere nice?"

"Er ... just checking out a flower market on the outskirts of Glasgow," I lied, wrapping my long scarf around my neck and hoisting my bag onto my shoulder. "Now both of you just call me if you have any questions or worries, ok?"

"Sure, but don't worry," beamed Rowan. "We'll be fine."

"And make sure you both get your lunch—"

I froze as I heard the shop door clatter open behind me.

"Off out, sis? I was going to suggest we take a walk for half an hour, if you can drag yourself away from your blooms."

Bugger!

Marcus was standing there, buried in a grey woollen scarf and his coat.

"Yes ... erm ... flower market near Glasgow. I'll be back as soon as I can."

Marcus's expression brightened a little, which made me feel even worse. "Oh, I'll tag along then, if you don't mind. I could do with a break from the laptop—"

"No!" I snapped before I could stop myself, then tried to disguise it with a small laugh. "I mean, no, don't worry. You stay here and relax. It won't be exciting for you and it's a bit of a schlep."

Marcus narrowed his eyes at me. "Bailey..."

But I was already grinning like a maniac. "See you soon. Bye!"

I banged Flower Power's door closed and raced round to the rear car park, to jump into the van.

Chapter Nine

I reached the outskirts of Glasgow a couple of hours later and pulled into a parking space at the back of The Old Barrell pub.

This was where Declan had told me the landlord, a Bernie McKew, had given him and the rest of his band, their first series of gigs. It was situated up a cobbled lane, next to a betting shop and a small café, the kind that has Formica tables and laminated menus.

I sat there, frozen in the driver's seat, for what seemed like ten minutes before I reached across to the passenger side and double-checked in my bag that I had my big, Jackie Onassis style sunglasses and pink, pearly bobble hat with me. With my new hair colour, the little weight I'd gained and my change of style, I was unrecognisable to people who didn't know me well, but I'd met Bernie McKew before and I wasn't taking any chances.

So, taking a leaf out of Ezra's disguise handbook, I

thrust on my Jackie O sunglasses and my hat, pulling it low down over my ears. I also wrapped a scarf around my neck so that it almost covered my chin and fluffed out my loose hair at the ends. If I kept all this on in there, hopefully, Bernie McKew wouldn't recognise me.

I'd only met Bernie once, at our engagement party a couple of years ago, at Bannock House. Declan had invited him to our wedding that never was and he'd accepted.

I jumped out of the van, locked it and examined the exterior of the pub. It was one of those old-fashioned, glass-bottled windowed affairs, with a brown and gold sign swinging above the heavy, double doors of a pirate with one leg raised and his foot resting on a barrel.

Inside, the atmosphere was laidback, with Sir Tom Jones belting out one of his classics from a nearby jukebox.

The bar was set in front of what looked like a collage of bright, stained-glass shapes of more pirates and barrels. A couple of older gents were stationed at one end of the bar, cradling pints and grumbling to one another about football results, and I was sure that was Bernie McKew stood behind the bar, with his stout frame and polished, balding head.

I approached and tried to make my voice sound a little hoarser. "Mr McKew?"

Bernie snapped his head up. "Aye. Can I help you?" He eyed me in my sunglasses and bobble hat.

"I'm looking for someone I think you might know. Declan Rooney?"

Bernie set down the tea towel he'd been fiddling with. "And you are?"

"Bailey McArthur."

"Police?"

"Oh no," I rushed, before realising that my voice was reverting back to a higher timbre. "No," I went on, in the deeper lilt. "He owes a friend of mine money and we need to track him down."

Bernie squinted over at the two customers perched at the end of the bar, then swivelled his attention back to me. "You and me both, lass," he growled. "All the help I gave that lad and he goes and throws it back in my face."

A sliver of relief shot through me. I felt empathy for Bernie, but was also a little relieved that I didn't seem to be the only one who'd fallen for Declan's lies. "How did he swindle you?"

"Told me he wanted to go into the pub trade and that he'd spotted these great little premises on the West Coast. Showed me photos, spec, took me to see the place, the whole kit and kaboodle." Bernie shook his head. "Declan said he knew his music career, such as it was, wouldn't last forever and going into the pub trade with me would be a cushion to fall back on."

"But it was a scam?"

Bernie's face stung at the memory. "Aye. It was. I agreed to go into partnership with him and was looking forward to the challenge of taking on another boozer."

"What happened?" I asked, studying him through the lenses of my smoky sunglasses. "He did a runner with my investment. Just upped and vanished. We'd organised a wee party to celebrate going into business together at the new pub, but he never showed." Bernie scratched at his clean-shaven chin. "I was left standing there in my best suit, clutching a pair of gold scissors to cut the ribbon across the door, surrounded by my family, friends, and folks I've known in the pub trade for over thirty years." Bernie looked like he wanted the sticky wooden floor to swallow him up. "Talk about feeling a dick. Oh, excuse the language."

"Don't worry."

Bernie eyed me across the bar. "So, are you saying he's come back here? To Glasgow?"

I tried not to fidget on the spot. I was supposed to be a cool, calm, and collected shady character. "So I've heard. You haven't seen him?"

"No, I haven't," he grunted. "He'd be eating hospital food through a straw if I had." Then a wounded look shone out of his bull-like, pale eyes. "I lent him money when he was short, gave him and his band gigs in here; I even acted as his manager for a while. Then he got himself that poor Lady Whatsit. Look what he did to her. Heartless toerag!"

I swallowed. "Yes, it was awful what he put her through."

Bernie wiped his hands on the tea towel. "Just goes to show how some of us can be such a poor judge of character."

His beefy shoulders straightened and he turned round to give one of the glasses a polish with another tea towel. "I'll get onto the cops and tell them he's been spotted. He just disappeared with my cash and that Lady Whatsit's money too." He breathed hard through his nose. "Bet there's been more folks conned by that little shit than we know about." Bernie continued to give the wine glass a good buff. "In a way, I can't believe he's got the cheek to rock back up to this neck of the woods after what he did. Then again, he always was a confident bugger." Bernie started to turn around. "Now, I'm going to call the cops, so if you could give me your details… Hey, miss! miss!"

But I'd left the pub, shot round the corner and phoned the police, before streaking off back to Heather Moore.

The following morning, November was bringing its usual concoction of weather so changeable, it made the heads of the Heather Moore locals spin. Sharp, sleeting showers were replaced by gunmetal-grey skies that delivered bursts of snow. It was only about five weeks now till Christmas, so it was to be expected.

The surrounding hills were sugar spun and the country lanes glistened with bursts of holly berries.

People were gearing up for the festive season, darting from shop to shop to buy gifts and purchasing poinsettias, as well as my artificial flower and candle table arrangements.

Rowan, Amber, and I were going through each day in a hectic blur, ensuring Christmas wreath orders and bouquets were in hand.

The Heather Moore Christmas lights were now in situ, glowing down onto the slick roofs and pavements and the local shops were decked out with multicoloured tinsel, trees, and festive ornaments.

Everywhere smelled of cinnamon and the likes of Mariah Carey and Sir Elton John were already belting out their Christmas classics. Mrs Anderson, who could be relied upon for the intimate details of Mr Barr's gallbladder operation and Mrs Daly's penchant for t'ai chi in her front garden – "She wears skin-tight leggings, you know, and at her age! Jings!" – came bustling into Flower Power, to reveal that the "famous footballer" who had bought Duxbury Hall had apparently transformed it into a playboy mansion, with three rose-gold chandeliers, mirrored ceilings, a pole-dancing suite, and leopard-print furnishings. She was so excited; I didn't have the heart to tell her none of it was true.

There were moments when I still felt awful about getting involved with Ezra's family affairs. I hadn't seen or heard from him since then and surmised I wouldn't. He'd taken issue with me, that was clear. As soon as Zach had told me that he'd been made aware that Ezra had two daughters, I'd called them both to warn them.

Caroline and Laura confided in me that despite a couple of further attempts to contact Ezra through his agent, they'd still had no success. They'd even reached out to a few of his celebrity friends, but they'd politely dismissed their appeals for help; probably concerned about it being a potential scam. Every avenue they'd tried seemed to have resulted in a dead end.

Pessimistic about making any possible headway with

the man who they believed to be their biological father, they'd both returned to their jobs and lives in England.

I realised they must be genuine. If they hadn't been, they would've gone straight to the papers. Instead, they seemed to have all but accepted defeat and returned home, picking up their own lives again. I suppose there was no point in them hanging around if Ezra wasn't interested in making contact and especially now, with the media on their tail.

My thoughts were a mash-up over my brother and Declan resurfacing. Then I thought about my own parents next and Marcus's insistence that I tell Mum and Dad about my ex's tentacles reaching out to me again.

Whether it was my pride hissing at me not to be cajoled by my brother, the stubborn side of me was kicking in. And even though I knew what Declan was capable of, I was inclined to handle this situation myself. Though if things did progress, if Zach found out who I was, then it would open up old wounds, and I couldn't allow that or be responsible for it. But did I feel strong enough to gird my loins and return to Bannock House for a visit?

Marcus's pain-seared blue eyes and his confusion about Jacob kept coming back to me. Something didn't add up about any of this and I couldn't stand seeing my brother heartbroken. I knew I had to find out if Mum knew more about Marcus and Jacob's split than she'd led everyone to believe. I hoped my suspicions were wrong.

Marcus had told me Mum was away with a few of her charity fundraising cronies on a pre-Christmas shopping trip to New York. She wasn't due back for a few more days.

I gritted my teeth. I wouldn't voice my concerns about Jacob to Marcus, not until I'd spoken to Mum first, but his breakup with my brother smacked of my ending with one, Finn Coulter, who I'd met about eight years before at a local Farmers' Market close to Bannock House, just after I'd graduated from uni with my English degree,

Finn had been charming the market browsers with his ready smile as he assisted his father and younger brother at their cheese stall. Finn was tall, good-looking, outdoorsy and possessed a shock of naturally sun-streaked hair that women everywhere regularly paid their hairdressers a fortune to recreate.

The Coulters were well-known in the area for being a hardworking farming family and I was flattered that day, when Finn had turned his spotlight on me and we'd begun a long, flirtatious conversation. We'd been so engrossed in each other that before we knew it the market was closing down for the day. Around us, the other stallholders were packing up after a successful Friday of trading, dismantling the steel rods, wooden benches, and flapping canvas of their stalls.

When Finn asked me out, I didn't have to think twice about it.

We spent a happy summer together, wandering hand in hand through the bright fields, indulging in picnics and getting up close and personal in the riots of woodland that ran around Bannock House.

My father liked him and admired his work ethic and Marcus thought we made a cute couple, but as soon as my mother found out about me dating a young farmer, she became stiflingly overprotective. "You two aren't serious, are you? It's just a summer romance?" she once asked, making it sound more like a statement than a question. She gave me a forced smile. "I understand, darling. I really do. He's a good-looking young man and you wanted to experiment. Try a bit of rough, as it were."

I had stared, horrified, at her across the breakfast table. "Finn is anything but that. He has more style and substance in his little finger than most of the stuck-up sons of your friends!"

My mother had flapped her hands, exasperated. "Oh, I'm not disputing he's a very pleasant young man, but nothing's going to come of it, Anastasia."

I still remember upending my cereal bowl and storming out of the dining room, with her desperate calls echoing behind me. "Darling. I didn't mean to upset you. I'm just looking out for you!"

I carried on dating Finn until the night of Halloween when we were supposed to be going to a fancy-dress party that one of my friends was throwing. I stood on the steps of Bannock House waiting for him to pick me up. I was dressed as Alice in Wonderland. Finn said he was going as The Mad Hatter. But he never turned up.

Refusing to accept that he wasn't coming, I stood there

and waited – the fresh October air, tinged with the scent of burnt leaves and pumpkins – until Marcus eventually managed to coax me back inside.

I finally received a curt call from Finn later than evening, to say he'd been mulling things over and he'd decided we were "on different paths" and that it'd be best to remain friends.

But we didn't even remain that.

Weeks later, I heard Finn had decided to move to the Lake District to head up a new organic foods business venture of his dad's and I never saw him or heard from him again.

Despite my mother's insistence she'd had nothing to do with Finn's decision, I always suspected otherwise. She had comforted me and murmured words of support, but hadn't seemed surprised when I'd sobbed into Marcus's shoulder in front of her.

The way Finn had spoken to me on the phone that evening…

The well-rehearsed platitudes and the infuriating *It's not you, it's me…*

If I hadn't known better, I'd have thought it was my mum I was talking to and not Finn.

I was ashamed to say I'd even wondered for a dark moment whether my mum had offered him money to vanish.

I aired my suspicions to Marcus at the time, but he said he could never imagine even our mother sinking to such depths.

As I'd sat there that night in my bedraggled Alice outfit with panda eyes and a runny nose, my big brother suggested that even if Finn had been on the receiving end of Countess Tweed Muir's machinations, he could have said no. "He could have stood up to her and refused. That's if he really lov—"

He had drawn himself up as he clasped my hand in his. My eyes were blurry with self-pity and tears. "You were going to say if he really loved me."

Marcus had pulled me into a big hug and I remained there for what seemed like forever, burying my heartbroken face into the crook of his neck.

Back in Flower Power, the afternoon limped along – the terrible weather had put off locals from venturing out, even for Christmas gifts. Having despatched Rowan and Amber home, I was just putting the finishing touches to a winter bridal bouquet, while preparing my "snow" (layers of cotton wool) in the window in preparation for my ice palace and winter wonderland display.

I stood back to admire my bouquet handiwork of frosted pine cones and berries, laced around spray roses and seeded eucalyptus.

Marcus was upstairs in the flat, finishing off a Zoom call with one of his clients and had insisted he would rustle us up some dinner.

Satisfied with my work, I sighed, scooped up my coat

and bag from beneath the counter, clicked off the shop spotlights and turned the sign round to CLOSED. Trudging upstairs to the flat, I knew I had to find a way to join the dots between Jacob's volte-face on Marcus and Declan's exit from his relationship with me…

Chapter Ten

Through the shop ceiling the next morning, I could hear the faint creak of the floorboards, signalling that Marcus was out of bed.

Mornings seemed to be the toughest part of the day for my big brother at the moment. I guessed it was waking up and realising that he and Jacob were no more. I sympathised. The first few mornings after Declan had deserted me were tough for me, too. I'd got through it by sleeping in and remaining in my dream world for as long as possible – until I'd decided to end the pity party and made plans for a new life, that is.

I'd caught Marcus a few times reaching for his left hand and blinking down at his empty ring finger, as though he couldn't quite believe it.

I hadn't told him the truth yet about my sudden visit to Glasgow, or that I planned to confront Mum. But if Declan did try and disgrace or implicate my family in some way, then at least they'd be prepared.

I waited about an hour or so before slipping upstairs to the flat to see how Marcus was. I was relieved to see that he was hard at work on a Zoom call with a client. Reassured that he wasn't moping, I glanced at my phone. It was Thursday. If I was going to go to Bannock House, it had to be this weekend. Mum was returning from her pre-Christmas trip to New York on Saturday and would either be full of good cheer, or be jet-lagged, shopped out, and grumpy.

I could feel an incubation of butterflies exploding in my stomach at the prospect of re-entering Bannock House. It carried such dark memories of the weeks after Declan had left me. As doubt started to sneak in about what I was planning to do, I made myself think of Marcus. He'd stood by me ever since we were kids, when we were teased by some of the jealous school kids about being Lady Anastasia and Lord Marcus. He'd supported my decision to marry Declan (even though he'd later confessed he'd harboured some reservations about him at the time). It was the least I could do to try and help him, to try and get to the root of why Jacob had called time on their engagement so that Marcus might be able to move on.

To quash my increasing trepidation over returning to Tweed Muir after more than a year, I concentrated on the customers flooding through the door, asking to place more orders for Christmas wreaths and table arrangements or purchasing the new russet, amber, and white carnation festive bouquets I'd started selling. I'd also made a note to chat to the girls about putting a couple of finishing touches to our Ice Kingdom festive window display.

When there was a lull mid-morning, I snatched the opportunity to leave Amber and Rowan at the helm and dart up to the flat.

Marcus had showered and dressed and was setting up his laptop on the kitchen table. There was a half-empty cup of tea and toast crumbs on a plate at his elbow. At least he'd eaten some breakfast. The lilac smudges of disturbed sleep under his eyes were still very much in evidence though.

I adopted a cheery demeanour. "The forecast isn't as bad today. Fancy a walk a bit later?"

"Sounds good."

He hesitated, staring at his laptop screen as it fired up. "I just took a call from Jacob."

"What did he want?"

"Nothing. It was just to say that he's moving the rest of his things out of our flat this morning."

"Where's he staying?"

"Well, he was crashing at Gareth's, but he's secured a rented place now." Marcus dragged a frazzled hand down his face. "Look, Anastasia, you've been amazing, but I can't keep imposing on you like this."

"You're not imposing."

He glanced back at his laptop screen as it shimmered into life. "I can't hide away. I'm going to have to return to Edinburgh and get on with things. Paul has been fantastic, but I can't stay away from the office forever."

Right. Come on. Tell him about your trip to Glasgow and the reason for it.

Marcus began to talk about when he should head back, but I cut him off. "I didn't go to Glasgow yesterday to a flower market. I went to try and find Declan."

Marcus's fingers hovered over the keyboard. They stilled. "You did what?!"

"I went to the pub that he played some of his gigs in with his band when I first met him. You heard him talk about Bernie McKew, right?"

Marcus shook his head in consternation. "Yes. Vaguely." His eyes widened. "I thought your story about suddenly taking off to some flower market sounded suspicious."

I gave him a sheepish look.

"I knew you were hiding something. Jesus, A!" He rolled his eyes.

I let my hands flail. "You've no idea what it's like, jumping every time that shop door opens. I keep wondering if he's going to show up."

"And what were you planning to do if you did come across him?"

I felt my cheeks redden. "Try to reason with him; alert the police." I let out a sudden, deep sigh. "Which I did as soon as I got back in the van. Ring the police, I mean." I rubbed at my forehead with feeling of desperation. "I need closure on this, Marcus. I'm trying to move on. How can I, when I think he's still capable of ruining my new life?"

My brother considered what I'd just revealed to him. "What did the police say?"

"Not a great deal. They took a note of it, but as I haven't actually seen him and nobody else has reported sighting him, they don't have much else to go on at the moment."

I was about to speak again, but was interrupted by a knock on the front door. I stepped out into the hall. I could see Amber's distorted features through the frosted glass.

She was apologetic as I opened the door. "Sorry to interrupt but you have a visitor in the shop." She offered me a knowing look. "It's that Zach Stern."

My stomach fluttered like a cage of wild birds. Why was I reacting like that? The man was a total knob and he was threatening my future. "Did he say what it's about?"

"Just that he needed to speak to you."

"Ok, thanks, I'll be down in a minute." Shutting the door, I strode back into the kitchen. Marcus must have overheard our conversation, because his mouth had formed into a flat line. "Do you want me to come with you? What if Declan has been shouting his mouth off again?"

I folded my arms. "Do you think you could say that a bit louder, please? They won't have heard you in Shetland."

Marcus pulled a sarcastic face.

"No, I'll be fine, thanks. I promise I'll shout for reinforcements if I need to." I raised one hand and made a flicking motion, as though to dismiss everything. Inside though, my stomach was performing cartwheels of an Olympic standard. Had Declan really rung Zach or his editor? What if he'd given them a lot more – false – information about me?

Fighting to control my worry, I gave Marcus a quick hug

and went downstairs to Flower Power, where aside from Amber in her red tartan skirt and Doc Marten boots, I saw Zach standing with his broad back to me.

When he turned around, my heart raced up to my throat.

He was wearing a three-piece suit in navy pinstripe which made him look like he'd just stepped from the pages of a glossy advert in one of those high-end men's fashion magazines.

The man was an arrogant sod who could upend my life. So why was I admiring him? God, he was gorgeous, though. I managed a cool smile. "You're looking very dapper for a Thursday morning."

His eyes crinkled up at the corners. "I've just finished interviewing the new director of that renovated theatre in town."

"The Albany?"

"That's the one."

"I hear it's beautiful inside now and they've managed to restore a lot of the Victorian architecture."

Zach studied me for a few moments. "Yes, they have. It's spectacular."

Amber sidled back up to the counter, awarding me loaded looks which I ignored.

"Anyway," announced Zach. "I've got some news."

Before I knew what was happening, he was in front of me and his hand was steering me by the elbow towards the rear of the shop. His long, tapered fingers against my skin triggered exploding bubbles of excitement inside me. I had to get a grip. *It's just because he scrubs up well,* I assured myself. I ordered myself to concentrate. "What is it? What are you doing?"

Rowan came past, then, armed with boxes of white snowflake decorations for our window display from the store room. I saw her share a conspiratorial grin with Amber.

"Please, come in to the office," I told Zach, smiling as normally as I could at my colleagues. Closing the door behind us, I struggled not to register how irresistible Zach looked in that suit. "What's going on?"

I stopped myself from asking if Declan had been in touch with him, that would just look weird.

Zach smiled, while I retained a fake smile as my heart pumped furiously.

"I was thinking," he said, seriously.

"Oh, dangerous." I laughed a little too loudly.

Zach gave me a withering look. "Moira tells me that back in the day there was an aristocratic family who used to holiday here in Heather Moore. At least, that was the rumour."

A horrified shiver raced down my back, as though someone had just rammed several ice cubes down there. Bloody Moira Telford and her big mouth. Perhaps this was karma, because I'd sent Zach in her man-eating direction. I feigned casual interest. "Really? Did she tell you who they were? The aristo family, I mean?"

Zach glanced around my office. "No. She doesn't know. They kept themselves to themselves, apparently."

My past zipped in front of my eyes. Marcus and me as kids, tumbling down Heather Moore's grassy hills and splashing about in our wellington boots. Dad channelling his inner cave man with a barbecue and Mum floating around, her dark hair streaming down her back.

I prayed that Zach couldn't sense the tidal waves of discomfort swallowing me up. This situation was becoming too precarious. "Right."

His melting brown eyes became more animated. "But I was thinking… If Moira remembers this family, then there must be other locals who might be persuaded to tell me more."

"They're a loyal bunch around here," I countered, through sharp prickles of worry.

Zach barked a laugh and brandished his phone. "Bailey, I think you'll find that money talks."

Any glimmers of optimism that Zach might be wasting his time evaporated. The world I had lived in meant I knew very well how some people, especially if they were struggling for cash, dispensed with their principles if a wodge of money was dangled in front of them.

"I believe in following a hunch," he went on. "After all, my instincts rarely let me down. It's what's got me this far in my career."

I made myself refocus on Zach across the desk from me. "Really?" I blurted sarcastically. "Didn't you used to work for some of the well-regarded newspapers?"

Zach jerked his handsome face away from his phone screen. His shutters clanged down. "Your point is?"

Through the closed office door, I could hear Amber and Rowan deliberating over a string of bright white versus electric-blue fairy lights.

"Well," I said. "It just seems a bit strange that a journalist of your calibre, who's known for investigating hard-news stories, should end up chasing tabloid rubbish like this for a gossip magazine."

Zach's shoulders tensed before I saw a hint of a smile in those hot eyes as they locked with mine. "You know, you'd make a good reporter yourself, Bailey. I think you've the nose for it." He eyed me. "And something tells me you might have one or two secrets of your own."

"Is that so?" I stalled for time. He was using diversion tactics, not answering my questions but instead turning them round on me. I pushed out my chin. I hoped I could retain a poker face. "I could say the same about you, Zach."

"Meaning?"

"You're good at asking the questions, but not so keen on answering any."

"Huh." The light disappeared from his eyes and his face hardened as he stashed his phone back in his coat pocket, his gaze hardening. "My job is to investigate and ask questions, not talk about myself." He stepped closer. "And I know there's something you're not telling me."

I rolled my eyes as though he was ridiculous. "Sure, Zach," I said dryly, then decided to change the subject. "Any luck on Ezra's daughters or this rumoured scandal circling him?"

Zach's lips twitched. "You enjoy seeing me squirm, don't you?"

"Not at all. I'm merely making small talk."

He narrowed his eyes. "Not much progress yet, but I'll get there. Anyway, I do have other stories to investigate."

"So, why keep dropping in to speak to me?"

He rose to his feet. His eyes blazed down at me. "Just thought I'd keep you in the loop. I know you're interested in the goings-on in Heather Moore as a concerned member of the community."

A lame answer, that emboldened me.

"And no other reason?" I asked, way more calmly than I felt.

There was a charged silence, in which I realised I didn't want to pursue this line of conversation after all. I now wanted to put as much space as I could between us. I shot out my hand and fumbled with the door handle. It was stuck.

I jerked the handle up and down, aware that Zach was watching me.

"Here. Let me."

"It's ok, thanks. I can do it."

Our hands brushed against one another. I let out a short, sharp gasp as my heart performed a somersault.

It was as if my office was holding its breath.

Zach's dark-rimmed pupils grew. He studied me for what seemed like forever before he reached for the handle and gently manoeuvred it open. "There we are." His voice was softer.

I cleared my throat. "Thank you."

"You're welcome." He gestured to the handle. "A squirt of WD40 should help."

My mind was scattering thoughts like confetti right now.

"Oh. Yes. Thanks."

I watched him stride towards the shop doorway, turn around and offer me a pensive glance.

Then he was gone.

Chapter Eleven

It was a welcome relief to kick back and relax in the flat with Marcus that evening after dealing with Zach and another flurry of pre-Christmas orders for table decorations and purchases of our new mini-potted Christmas trees,

Weary from the week, I decided we should have a quick and comforting dinner. I unearthed a frozen lasagne and crusty garlic bread, topped it with a dusting of Parmesan cheese, and put both in the oven. Worry was nibbling at me about Moira Telford shooting her mouth off, but I tried to stem my rising panic. I was still clinging to the hope, like a raft in a stormy sea, that Zach didn't know who I was – and used to be – yet, so I just had to pray that the situation would stay that way. He hadn't said anything. It was just rather disconcerting, the way he kept reappearing. Just as disconcerting, though, was the unmistakeable charge between us. I hadn't imagined it. During the embarrassing door-handle debacle, my skin had zinged at his touch.

It was nuts! No way could I allow myself to fall for Zach. It was a disaster waiting to happen.

Marcus noticed something was on my mind and had been offering me long, thoughtful looks and asked me a couple of times if I was feeling ok. I fobbed him off, saying I was tired after a busy day. If I told him the truth, he'd think I'd lost the plot. Mooning after a journalist who worked for a gossip magazine!

After we finished eating, I rinsed off the dirty plates and slid them into the dishwasher. Marcus materialised at my shoulder. He leant against the edge of the kitchen worktop. "I've made a decision, sis. I'm going to return to Edinburgh on Saturday."

I turned off the kitchen tap. "But that's the day after tomorrow. Why so soon? You're welcome to stay as long as you like."

He studied his stripey socks. "I know that and I appreciate it. But like I said, I can't put my life on pause, just because Jacob turned out to be an utter dickhead." He fiddled with the hem of his cream cable knit jumper. "Paul has been terrific about me taking time off but I don't want him to think I'm taking liberties." He gave an eyeroll. "Losing my job would top things off nicely this close to Christmas."

I gestured to him to give me a hug. "As long as you're sure, but you know there's always a home for you here whenever you want it."

His smile quivered. "Thanks. Anyway, I want to get cracking with my application for a digital online marketing course. It'll look good on my CV and give me something else to focus on."

I stepped back to study him. "Good for you. I'm so proud of you."

His chin wobbled.

"So, if you're leaving on Saturday, we'd better make the most of tonight and tomorrow then." I gestured to one of the cupboards above the sink and asked Marcus to fetch down some of the extortionate ninety per cent dark chocolate that he liked and which I'd bought especially for him.

"Whoa! You really know how to live, sis!" He reached up to locate the chocolate. "Just promise me one thing."

"What?"

"You'll stop this Miss Marple act over Declan."

I pulled a face.

"I mean it. It could be dangerous. Just sit tight. Promise me. Please." Marcus set the bar of chocolate down on my kitchen table. "I think he wouldn't be as stupid as to turn up here. Too risky. Whereas if you go looking for him…"

"Ok. Ok. I promise."

Marcus awarded me a small smile. "Good. Glad to hear it."

"I wonder how Mum enjoyed her New York jaunt," I said, keen to move the subject onto something else, and hoping my tightening features weren't betraying me. I'd decided not to tell him of my intention to travel back home on Sunday afternoon to talk to Mum about his broken engagement. He'd enough to contend with at the moment, without fretting about anything else, and there would be plenty of time to talk to Marcus about it later, if and when I found out anything more.

"Riotous, no doubt," he said wryly as he sloshed white wine into two glasses, just as my mobile let out its familiar tinkly ringtone from the hall table.

I stared at it, wrinkling my nose and Marcus laughed. "Want me to get it?" he asked.

"Yes, please."

He set the wine bottle down and padded out of the kitchen, his socked feet slapping on the kitchen floor. A few seconds later, I heard him murmuring something, then his footsteps came back into the kitchen. He proffered the phone, arching a brow. "It's Zach."

Oh God. A zinging sensation rose up in my stomach, as though I was about to set off on a wild rollercoaster ride. I struggled to meet my brother's eye as I accepted the phone.

"Thanks." I watched Marcus vanish into the sitting room as I put the phone to my ear. "Hi Zach. How are you?"

"Good, thanks. Just chilling in my hotel room with a glass of full-bodied red."

The way he said the words "full-bodied" made my heart speed up. I needed to get out more. I was going to end up a frustrated middle-aged florist. I gave myself a mental shake.

"I'm also hiding from a certain lady hotel receptionist," he continued.

The image of Zach, approximately six foot one, trembling in his hotel room at the thought of diminutive, redheaded, sixty-something Moira Telford, made a smile break out across my face, despite my niggling worries. "Might you be talking about Moira, by any chance?"

"Congratulations. You guessed correctly."

There was another frisson of something, which I couldn't quite put my finger on: casual chatter; a smooth easiness between us; smiles down the line.

"I just wanted to hear a friendly voice, Bailey."

I blinked at his words. His deep, educated voice was like honey. "Oh?" I managed, wishing I could think of something more insightful to say. I eased myself down into one of my kitchen chairs. "So, what would you like me to talk about?"

"Anything," he replied in a teasing tone, which caused my stomach to ripple. "Although I hope you don't mind me saying that you're not exactly Miss Chatty when it comes to revealing much about yourself."

Hold on. Did he think I was stupid? Did he think that by flirting with me, I'd do some of his dirty work for him? That I'd try to help him and do some digging amongst the locals on his behalf? Get him some info on the Bollinger Babe and Ezra King? Was the attraction on his part all just an act? After Declan and his deceit, I wasn't sure about my judgement.

Then again, what if I was just too cynical and he was genuinely interested in me?

Bollocks! My head was beginning to spin. Whatever this was that was happening between us, it could become dangerous. It wasn't worth the hassle. There was too much at risk. I wouldn't allow myself to trust anyone again. I would be the one in control from now on. And yet, Zach's eyes, his smoking hot body—

"Bailey, about what happened this morning in your office." Zach cut across my conflicting thoughts.

I was about to answer, about to admit the undeniable chemistry between us, when the unmistakeable sound of a female voice in the background pulled me back, sending a brutal and sudden punch to my solar plexus, just as Zach said, "The posh coffee is over there, Astrid..."

There was giggling from Astrid and then a throaty laugh from Zach. Crashing disappointment gripped me. Anger at myself for allowing slivers of hope to creep in contorted into shame-faced embarrassment. Served me right for allowing my ridiculous imagination to spiral out of control. He really had been playing with me; teasing me; letting me think there might be something developing between us. All to secure a good story. To keep me onside?

Zach came back on the phone, apologetic, but breezy, as he cut through my pain. "Sorry about that."

It's for the best, I reminded myself. *The guy's a journalist for pity's sake!* It would be like a diver going into a shark tank with a lump of fresh meat tied around their neck.

"No problem," I struggled, feigning indifference.

Zach switched the subject, oblivious. "Anyway, as I know it's piqued your interest, I just rang to say that I've another idea in order to try and locate our missing aristo."

"Oh?" I managed nonchalantly, as though my interest in the subject was minimal. "And what might that be?"

"Ex-boyfriends, hangers-on... I'm sure the lure of a few

quid will make them talk," said Zach. "I'll mention it to Adam. We can put an appeal in the magazine for information leading to the discovery of the Bollinger Babe. As for Ezra's daughters, I've got a couple of solid contacts looking into that."

I was fighting to calm the swirling worry in my chest. "Good for you… Look, I'd better go. You sound rather busy."

I didn't give him a chance to answer before I ended the call.

I'd got it wrong about Zach being attracted to me, but what did it matter anyway. If anything were to happen between us, it wouldn't be long before he knew who I was. I sighed. Would I ever be able to move on and create new and fulfilling memories like I'd imagined when I'd planned my new life here in Heather Moore?

As it was, my attempt at a reboot seemed like it was beginning to take me down a different path. Where that path was headed, I had no idea…

Chapter Twelve

Marcus set off for home the following morning, after prolonged, fierce hugs from me and requests from him that I take care and not do anything risky.

It was as if he thought I was going to parade up and down Heather Moore with a placard around my neck, proclaiming, "I'm the Bollinger Babe".

"I promise I'll be careful," I told him, with an eyeroll. "Now, go, and I'm always here if you need me."

Saturday was my favourite day of the week in Flower Power because of the more relaxed atmosphere it brought with it. There were no trains to catch, no buses to flag down, and no congested roads to negotiate, so customers were free to spend quality time in my shop, savouring the delights of the flowers, browsing our arrangements, and losing themselves in the warm scents.

Amber and Rowan were both in a buoyant mood.

Rowan was gushing about my brother's ideas for publicising her little side-hustle – a dog-walking business – which she'd discussed with him during his stay. "Marcus suggested giving new clients a ten per cent discount on their first two walks and offering a small range – at least to begin with – of A Walk in The Bark merchandise," she explained, buzzing. "He thinks I should start off small with some mugs and keyrings featuring the image of my clients' dogs. If it goes well, I could expand on it." She clapped her hands together. "He's so brilliant!"

I smiled at her, thinking it was typical of Marcus to deal with heartache by throwing himself into work – his and other people's. He'd never been one to mope or sit around waiting for things to happen. Hell, he was even planning to enrol in an evening class, for heaven's sake!

A flash of my own aggravating predicament appeared in my head, with Zach sneaking his way back into my thoughts. I'd been out of my mind to harbour attraction for some sleazy tabloid hack, though admittedly a very hot one, who could be on the verge of destroying the new life I was building for myself.

I felt a chill in my veins at the sensationalist news stories that would no doubt be splashed across the tabloids if my location was revealed. And I hoped that Caroline and Laura could continue to avoid Zach for a little longer, before he tracked them down.

I picked up my phone and navigated to my mother's number. I was returning to Bannock House tomorrow to talk to her about Marcus and Jacob and wondered if I should let her know I was coming. Then again, turning up unannounced meant she would be thrown by my sudden arrival, and off-guard, with no prepared answers to my questions. She'd be more likely to be honest. I hoped.

As much as I wasn't relishing the prospect of stepping back inside Bannock House again, it had to be done. I couldn't hide from the ghost of Declan forever. I refused to let him win.

"Hi, Bailey."

I jumped at the sound of Zach's voice as he walked through the door and up to the counter. Of course, he looked amazing, in his thick navy polo neck, winter jacket, and dark jeans. My insides pirouetted, not just because he was undeniably gorgeous, but because every time I saw him, I expected those immortal words – *Aha! I knew Declan's former It-girl aristo was you all along!*

I drank in his burning brown eyes, before recovering myself.

"Hi there. How are things?"

"Oh, ok thanks. On a late lunch break at the moment. Been busy asking around doing some important research."

"Uh-huh," I said. I was damned if I was going to ask what about. Like I didn't know. Instead, I plumped for something polite but vague. "Any luck?"

"Things are moving in the right direction. The good

news is that I was called today by a guy who claims he does actually know who the Bollinger Babe is."

My stomach lurched. It was happening. My past was catching up with me. It felt like Flower Power was beginning to spin.

Not appearing to notice my stricken expression, Zach's bright, dark eyes shone out of his chiselled face as he went on. "He's going to ring me back later this afternoon with more information. Sounds like our party princess is enjoying life tending the land."

It took a few moments for me to process what Zach had just said. What? My throbbing heartbeat was pounding in my ears. "Sorry? What did you say?"

Zach glanced around him at my clusters of red and green plants and the twinkling Christmas lights. He lowered his deep rumble. "According to this caller – and he seemed very sure of himself – there's a woman who owns some farmland just outside of Heather Moore. She's blonde, well-educated and has a penchant for flashing her cash." Zach looked like the more he considered this notion, the more the jigsaw pieces were slotting together. "I think she could well be our missing Lady Anastasia McLaren-Kerr. The description fits."

I opened and closed my mouth, before ramming it shut. What was he talking about? Who was he talking about? Farmland? It took a few moments for me to join the mental dots. Oh God. No. It couldn't be. Realisation dawned.

He was talking about Joan Webber, who lived up in McShand Lodge. I conjured up an image of Joan, with her long, hippie-style, dirty-blonde hair, sea shell necklaces, and penchant for chasing anyone from her property with a cocked shot gun.

I didn't know whether to laugh, cry, be pleased, or offended! Who the hell thought she could be me? That she was the so-called Bollinger Babe? Who was this guy who'd called him, convinced Joan Webber was the Bollinger Babe? Joan hadn't been near a bar of soap for years. Why would someone think that?

My mouth formed a series of odd shapes. Talk about barking up the wrong tree. More like the whole forest. "That's a good call," I stuttered, fighting a sudden, relieved urge bubbling up inside me not to laugh. "I know you reporters don't usually name your sources, but I wonder who called you about Joan?"

One of Zach's black brows arched. "He told me he wouldn't give me his real name. Scared of repercussions, he said. He told me to call him Mark Darcy."

Mark Darcy? I didn't know anybody of that name, apart from a character in *Bridget Jones*. My mouth did that weird, popping open thing again. Mark Darcy.

My eyes widened. *No!*

I almost laughed out loud, but managed to turn it into a cough when Zach slid me a curious look. Bloody hell! It couldn't be. Could it? Marcus had rung Zach and deliberately set him on the path to Joan Webber?! The more I thought about it, the more it seemed like too much of a coincidence. Marcus's favourite movies were the *Bridget*

Jones ones and he'd always harboured a crush on Colin Firth.

Joan Webber was a bit of a mysterious, reclusive figure around these parts. I concealed an emotional smile as memories of the two of us being greeted by Joan, Hettie, her late father Sandy, and their two-family sheepdogs, Lachlan and Lauder, wavered in front of me.

As children, Marcus and I managed to endear ourselves to Hettie whenever we came to Heather Moore, even though they were a family who didn't tend to mix with the rest of the locals and she would even let us assist Joan in pouring in the double cream when she was making her delicious golden butter.

A glow of emotion lit up inside me. Even though he had his own troubles at the moment, my big brother had made time to look out for me and throw Zach on a wild goose chase. It must be him. It all fitted together.

It wouldn't deter Zach long-term – as soon as he found out that Joan had lived here all her life with her family, he'd know she wasn't me – but maybe it would buy me a little more time, and take some of Zach's attention away from Ezra and his long-lost daughters, and whatever scandal surrounded him.

"Can you excuse me for just a second please, Zach? I have to make a quick call to one of the suppliers. Then I'll be with you."

"Sure."

Grabbing my phone, I darted up to my office and clattered the door shut behind me. I pulled up Marcus's number. He barely had time to say hi. "Are you Mark Darcy?" I gushed.

There was a rumble of laughter down the line. "What do you think?"

I let out a gasp. "I knew it!"

"Has it worked?"

My head popped with thoughts. "Yes. Well, for now."

Marcus dropped his voice. "Glad to help. But be careful, ok? Love you."

Back on the shop floor, Zach's voice broke through my thoughts. He looked a little awkward, which wasn't like him at all. "I actually came by because I could do with your help."

"Oh, yes?"

"I'm looking for a present for someone. A plant or bouquet."

"Sure," I replied. "Who's it for?"

"A friend. She's a special lady."

She?

Astrid. Jealousy pierced me in the chest. I moved out from behind the counter towards him. I was fighting to look unphased. "Any preferences?"

Not that it was any of my business and I didn't care either way.

"No. I was hoping you might have one or two suggestions." Zach pushed his hands into his trouser pockets. "I read a while back that the Victorians were really keen on giving flowers that had a specific meaning."

I strode over to a corner of one of my new winter displays,

which housed a spray of cream and white tea roses, mingled with berries and twigs. I wished I could pass Zach over to one of the girls to deal with. This was excruciating. "That's right. They were. All flowers have a specific meaning." I straightened my back. "What flower you choose really depends on what she means to you and what message you're trying to convey."

Zach drew up beside me, his intent brown eyes scanning the blooms I was pointing at.

"I want to get her something a bit different. I'm not bothered about the cost."

Ram it down my throat, why don't you?!

I tossed a frosty glance at him. I felt childish, but couldn't help myself. "I do everything I can to keep the prices of my stock at a reasonable level. I'm not in the habit of trying to rip off my customers."

Zach blinked at me. "I'm sure you don't."

God, this is horrible.

A part of me was tempted to recommend something like yellow carnations, which signify rejection, but I reminded myself that I was a professional. Or at least, I was supposed to be.

In the end, my conscience took over. "If I were you, I'd go for something like this." I picked out one of our frilly sugar-pink camellias and tried to conceal the pain in my voice. "They represent love and missing someone." I cast a long look at Zach and buried a sudden ball of emotion. "I love the scalloped petals. They remind me of a rose but have a bit more attitude about them."

I touched the petals, losing myself for a moment in their deep, riven shape.

I looked up and noticed Zach was staring down at me, an indecipherable expression on his face.

I was certain Astrid would love the camellia. It never failed to lift my spirits.

Zach gestured to the flower. "Thanks. It's lovely. I'll get this one then."

He offered me an odd smile, but I struggled to return it. In the end, the smile I did finally manage to conjure up must have made me look like my bra was too tight.

I made my way back behind the counter, cradling the camellia in my arms and proceeded to put Zach's purchase through the till.

He pointed over at a couple of our Christmas wreaths for sale, decorated with satin tartan ribbons. "I'd better not bring Astrid in here. I'd never get her out again!"

I snatched some pretty cerise ribbon from under the counter and tied it around the pot of the plant to dress it up a bit. "Oh, please do," I said through bared teeth, not meaning a word of it. "The more custom, the better."

"I guess that's true," he said, his eyes lingering on me. "Bailey, is everything ok?"

I pushed the credit card machine towards him. "Absolutely." I gave a rictus grin. "Why wouldn't it be?"

Zach finished paying and returned his credit card to his leather wallet. I imagined Astrid to be some willowy Scandinavian goddess.

"Buying something for a seventy-year-old church elder is a bit of a minefield!"

My envious thoughts juddered to a halt. I gawped up at him. "Sorry?"

"Astrid," he said, as though I should've known all along. "Astrid Connor. She's a lovely woman. She's staying in my hotel at the moment while her house is being redecorated. She's lonely, poor thing, so she's been popping to my suite to talk to me, mostly about her late husband, who was a Fleet Street reporter back in the day."

I clutched at the edge of the counter, my horrified cheeks zinging with colour at Zach as he continued to explain. "She happened to pass by my hotel room when I was letting myself in," Zach continued to explain. "I get occasional migraines and last nights was a real doozy. Astrid made sure I got into my room ok and proceeded to administer water and fetched me painkillers. Even when I started to feel a bit better and wanted to make a few calls, she insisted she stay a little longer to make sure I was all right. I suggested she stay and have a coffee with me."

I listened, trying not to show my complete embarrassment at getting it so wrong.

"She said I remind her of her son, who lives in Texas," Zach went on. He indicated the plant, now cradled in his muscular arms. "I just wanted to get her something to show my appreciation."

I winced. What a lovely thing to do. I'd been marching around like a hormonal schoolgirl who'd just learnt her pop star crush had a girlfriend. I wanted the ground to swallow me whole. I'd been having murderous thoughts over a kind church elder?

I was fighting to bring myself to look Zach in the face. "That's very thoughtful of you," I croaked. "I'm sure she'll love it."

"Oh, I'm sure she will. Thanks again, Bailey, for your help."

I gestured to the camellia, its scalloped petals waggling around in Zach's arms. "Tell Astrid that camellias like acidic soil and partial shade. An area that gets morning shade is the best, as direct sunlight tends to dry out their petals."

"Right. I will. Thanks."

"They're woodland plants," I added, faffing around at the counter, red-faced.

I realised I was wittering on and stopped talking. Zach was studying me over the top of the frothy, bright pink plant.

"Ok. I'll tell her. Thank you."

He loitered for a few moments, as though he was debating something before giving a self-conscious wave that was at odds with his usual cool, controlled exterior.

My gaze followed him out of the shop. Then I dropped my head in shame onto the counter and pretended to thump it against the pink-painted wood.

Chapter Thirteen

That evening, upstairs in my flat, I finally unzipped my boots and threw my old jeans and cable knit jumper on top of the bed. The flat was so quiet without Marcus. I missed the scent of his Dior perfume in the bathroom, and the sight of his charcoal tartan scarf hanging up in the hall.

It had been a busy but productive Saturday, what with Heather Moore's dazzling Christmas light display going into overdrive, because of Santa's appearance with his reindeer (aka Tony Mullen, a local farmer) and the additional visitors they brought in.

Amber, Rowan, and I had finished the ice palace window display, which had transformed the two windows of Flower Power into a sparkling, white and silver cornucopia of snow, white and blue snowflake lights, and clusters of cream and white winter roses. They surrounded a Disney-style sparkling palace I'd located for sale online.

The whole effect was stunning and was attracting customers, particularly families with children, who would press their little red noses against the glass for a closer look.

Slipping into a pair of PJ bottoms and one of my favourite strappy tops, I struggled not to think about earlier, when I made myself look like an utter muppet in front of Zach.

I closed my eyes, again seeing his bemused expression. No bloody wonder. He must've thought I was having some sort of episode.

I hoped he hadn't realised the real reason for my behaviour. I let out a painful groan, hoping I could dislodge the excruciating memory of it and decided to put up my Christmas tree to distract me. The earlier festivities had put me in more of a Christmas mood, despite what was swirling in the background with Zach, Ezra, Marcus, and me.

I slid my new tree out of its box, which was an artificial silver and white affair. I didn't believe in using the real thing because it always filled me with anger after the festive season, when I would see real pine trees unceremoniously slung out onto the pavement. I erected it in the corner of the sitting room, right by the window, and began trying to drape it with rose-gold lights and matching thick tinsel.

The tinsel wasn't so much of an issue, but I found myself struggling to wrap the long lights around it. Any moment now and I was going to be trussed up like Harry Houdini! I paused and fetched the new silver star I'd bought to pop on top.

Ah. I hadn't realised it was as big as it was! I'd bought it in rather a hurry online and had been so captivated by its realism, not to mention the fab reviews, that I hadn't taken notice of its measurements.

I then made a number of valiant efforts to install the star on top of the tree, but failed.

Growing increasingly frustrated, I set the star down and wandered through to the kitchen, leaving the lights drooping from a few of the lower branches. I knew I had a set of steps stashed somewhere. I'd have to find them.

I glanced down at my watch. It was approaching six-thirty in the evening and I knew I should really make some dinner first.

I opened the fridge and sighed. What did I feel like eating?

I'd just reached for some diced chicken and a box of Chinese vegetables when there was a knock on the door.

I closed the fridge door and paused.

I edged up the hall. It was almost dark and so whoever it was appeared like a long, looming shadow through the glass. "Who is it?"

"It's your friendly, neighbourhood journalist."

I could almost hear him roll his eyes on the other side of the door, as I hesitated.

"It's me, Bailey. It's Zach."

Zach?

What was he doing here? Wild-eyed, I flew to the hall mirror. I didn't feel at my best. Some of my make-up from earlier in the day had vanished and I was slouching around in PJ bottoms that'd seen better days.

"Hang on a second," I called. "Just getting out of the bath."

I whirled around in panic, remembering I'd dumped my shoulder bag on top of my bed when I arrived home.

I scooted down the hall and pinched my cheeks, before adding a flick of lipstick. Then I fluffed up my ponytail. That would have to do. I couldn't keep him standing out there all evening. His eyelids would freeze shut. But then something made me draw up. What was I doing? Sprinting around my flat in a panic? I was like little Red Riding Hood inviting in the wolf.

I stared at his tall, willowy silhouette again through the pane of glass at my front door. I knew what I wanted to do, but whether it was wise or not, I wasn't sure. No. Scrub that. I knew it wasn't wise. I could just imagine Marcus's horror at me even contemplating allowing Zach in.

But my heart was overruling my common sense.

Bracing myself, I unlocked the door.

Zach had changed his clothes from earlier and was now rocking a casual V-neck and black jeans under his long coat. Not only did he look devastating, but there was the delicious, warm aroma of food drifting in.

Zach lifted up his right hand. Dangling from his fingers was a Chinese takeaway. "Egg fried rice, lemon chicken, crispy shredded beef, and a couple of vegetable spring rolls. I tried to play it safe in case you had any food allergies."

I must've looked perplexed.

Zach buried a smile. "It's food," he explained. "I thought we might eat it."

I recovered myself. "Sorry, but…"

What on earth is he doing here?

Zach smiled, almost shyly. "Sorry, I should have checked with you, but I wanted to make up for bothering you with all my questions, lately," he said. "So, I thought I'd treat you to a takeout after a busy day at work." He stepped into the hall. "I took a chance on you having no plans."

"Er … thanks," I said. "That's kind of you."

I hadn't expected my Saturday night to take such an unexpected and annoyingly perfect direction. I walked into the kitchen to get some plates.

"Did Astrid like the camellia?" I called out, batting away cringeworthy memories from earlier.

Zach materialised behind me. "She loved it. Thanks so much. It was a real winner."

"No problem."

"Where do you keep your cutlery?"

I directed him to the second drawer down near my microwave and he set the kitchen table while I fetched glasses and peeled open the cartons.

My stomach let out a desperate grumble at the sight of the rich, scented delicacies.

We dived in with several large serving spoons and delivered the tasty food onto our plates.

As I snatched a look across my kitchen table at Zach, I experienced a confused, excited rush. *Why is Zach here on a Saturday night? Isn't there some glamazon he should be seducing somewhere?*

Zach took another spoonful of glistening, crispy

shredded beef. He regarded me across the table. "I decided to drop by Joan Webber's place this afternoon."

Ah. A swell of disappointment washed over me. So, despite him saying he'd come round with a compensatory takeaway, tonight was clearly all about finding the Bollinger Babe. I should have known.

My fork, piled with fried rice, halted as it reached my mouth. "And how did that go?"

Zach arched a cynical brow. "Put it this way. Joan's like Clint Eastwood in a blonde wig and so is that eccentric mother of hers."

I could feel a bubble of laughter rising up in my throat. I jammed my lips together for fear of breaking into a grin. "So, not good, then?"

He folded his arms. "You could say that. Joan Webber threatened to set her two dogs on me. She was marching about with a shotgun."

I swallowed back a laugh. That sounded like Joan. And well done to Marcus for thinking of sending Zach up to her farmhouse in the first place. I was struggling to keep my face straight. "Do you think she could be who you're looking for then? This elusive so-called aristo?"

Zach's lips twitched. "If she is, I'm Tom Cruise."

I picked up my water glass and buried another grin in it. Then I rearranged my expression. "Oh dear. Well, no harm done then, eh?"

"No harm done," he echoed. "I do have other stories I'm trying to work on. That was a waste of my time."

I prodded at the lemon chicken with my fork. "Well,

whoever tipped you off must've believed Joan Webber could be this woman."

Zach scooped up more of the shredded beef. "Yeah, sure they did. I think it's more likely someone was throwing me a deliberate curve ball." He offered me a loaded look. "Again."

I hoped my face didn't betray me. "Why would someone do that?"

He shrugged. "Who knows? Any ideas?"

I gave a dismissive shrug. "I don't mean to sound like I'm saying I told you so, but like I mentioned before, it's a close-knit, friendly community here in Heather Moore. The locals tend to look out for each other."

His dark, brooding eyes lasered me across the kitchen table. "Yes. You've said that before." He looked thoughtful. "It could be a friend of Lady Anastasia's who deliberately set me up with this. A relative maybe."

I pushed down a shot of alarm, as Zach laid down his fork for a moment. "But the day wasn't a complete waste of time."

"Really?" I popped some rice in my mouth.

"Yes, things took a bit of an intriguing turn with another story."

"How so?"

"There are rumours of dodgy working practices regarding a family by the name of Temple-Davenport."

I recognised the name. I didn't know the family, but I'd heard of them. They owned land not far from Bannock House, which they'd transformed into a fruit market cottage industry, producing strawberries and raspberries. "What's the issue with them?" I asked, intrigued.

Zach curled his mouth up in disgust. "A whistle-blower who was employed by them contacted me to say they've been exploiting their staff. It's all low wages, long hours, and poor working conditions."

I shook my head, appalled. "That's dreadful. Bad enough a couple of hundred years ago, but it's hard to believe it's still going on today." I hesitated. "Sounds like a really worthwhile story for you to get your teeth into."

And with any luck it would get him off my tail.

Zach retrieved his knife and fork and cut off a chunk of juicy lemon chicken. "*Stargazer* won't be interested, of course. It's a strong news story that deserves to be told. But I still have contacts at some of the old newspapers I worked for who would be." His jaw clenched. "There's no way I'm ignoring the plight of these people. I'll look into it and write up the story. I'm sure one of my editor friends will jump at the chance to expose that lot."

I blinked, heartened by his passionate reaction to the story of these poor, exploited workers.

"This sort of thing shouldn't be happening in twenty-first-century Scotland. It shouldn't be happening anywhere."

"I agree. You should expose what they've been doing."

"Oh, I will," he replied with renewed determination. He eyed me across my kitchen table. "Why are you looking at me like that?"

My cheeks blanched. "What do you mean?"

"Like I've just told you I've got the Koh-I-Noor diamond in my pocket."

I tried to look nonchalant. "It's just ... you know ... a bit of a surprise..."

"What is? Hearing that I actually have a conscience?"

"You said that, not me."

He gave his dark head a playful shake. "I don't know. Anyone would think I had no scruples." Zach's eyes stayed locked on my face. "They couldn't be more wrong."

There was a sizzling silence between us. Then Zach seemed to recover himself. "Some of these entitled families like the Temple-Davenports are only concerned with one thing – themselves – and sod the little people. They make me sick."

I landed back in reality with a fierce bump. I squirmed in my kitchen chair and made a show of tackling one of the crispy spring rolls. Zach sounded so disgusted, and rightly so, but not every titled family behaved that way. The idea he'd think that kept punching me in the chest. I realised I wanted to prove to him that there are always exceptions.

I decided to change the subject. "You haven't said much about your background," I faltered, trying to keep my voice steady. As soon as I said it, I realised with a huge bolt of hypocrisy that I hadn't either.

I'd read up about Zach online, of course, but hoped I could keep that to myself. I didn't want him thinking I was checking him out.

Zach's fork hovered in mid-air. "There isn't much to tell.

I'm from St John's Wood in London." He took a sip of his iced water. "My late father was a journalist and my mother writes historical romances, so I suppose writings in my blood."

I wondered if he was intending on saying more, but he snatched up his glass of water, took a thoughtful gulp, and returned to safer ground. "So, what about you? What's your life story?"

I stiffened in my seat. "There isn't much to tell. My parents and brother live in Edinburgh."

Zach's expression urged me to reveal more.

I stifled a pang of worry. "My mother undertakes a bit of charity work, my father retired after years being involved in land management, and I've just the one brother, who you met." Again, I didn't mention Marcus by name. The less personal information I furnished Zach with, the better.

"What does your brother do?" he asked, taking another spoonful of rice.

Oh God. All these questions. "He works in marketing."

"Oh, whereabouts?"

"Edinburgh," I answered vaguely, desperate to reroute the line of questioning. I daren't give Zach any more details, otherwise he could look up my brother online and soon the trail would lead to the Bollinger Babe – and me.

"Does he enjoy it?"

"Oh, he loves it."

All I wanted to do was divert any more questions away from my background. This was getting too close for comfort. I felt like I was skirting around the edges; prodding at a wound that at any time could burst open again. I moved the chat on. "Heather Moore is pretty, isn't it? The scenery's so spectacular and dramatic. It seems to change all the time and you always see something new."

"So, you and your brother are both creative types then?"

Oh shit. We're back to talking about me. I forced a smile. "Yes, I like to think so."

Zach appraised me over the Chinese takeaway and I held my breath, hoping he wouldn't probe any further, but he changed the subject.

"Oh, I forgot to say, I've had another interesting tip-off about Ezra King, and this time it seems legit."

Inwardly, my stomach plummeted. I'd thought, or at least hoped, the Ezra saga might be dead in the water.

I forced a pleasant, curious tone. "Oh, yes?"

"Yes." He flexed his brows. "As it turns out, my visit to Joan Webber's house wasn't a complete waste of time."

A sliver of worry jabbed at me. "What do you mean?"

"She's given me a pretty good steer on where exactly Ezra King lives."

"Joan told you this?"

With Joan, if it didn't have udders, she usually wasn't interested.

Zach nodded. "Some local lad has been doing some work on her land. He previously worked on Ezra King's house as a labourer, and Joan overheard him bragging about it to one of her farm hands."

Shit. I could feel the colour draining from my face.

Zach examined me from under his brows. "Are you ok, Bailey? You've gone a bit pale…"

I felt my shoulders go rigid. "No, I haven't."

"Yes, you have." Zach appraised me over the takeaway.

"I'm fine," I croaked. I snatched my water up and took a big mouthful.

Zach looked unconvinced, but took a very slow sip of his water and moved the subject on. "Anyway. If it's true about Ezra, it sounds like he's been hiding in plain sight." Zach's face adopted a determined expression. "I'm going to check it out."

Panic began running through my head. If Zach tracked down Ezra, it'd only be a matter of time before Caroline and Laura were unearthed too. The three of them would be thrust into the media spotlight then. Recollections of my own life splashed across the tabloids and magazines were all too fresh. At first, I'd embraced the attention, maybe even relished it. But after a while, the intrusion became like this living, breathing creature I couldn't control. I became a caricature of who I was and my family began to get caught up in my stupid press games too. And when everything had imploded with Declan it had become a living nightmare. I hadn't deserved the constant scrutiny, the violation of my privacy and neither did Ezra and the women who thought they were his daughters. Anxiety was replaced with anger, and I lifted my chin at Zach.

"Why do you do it?" I said. "Why spend so much of

your time on grubby stories like this, when you could be exposing more slave labour situations and social issues that affect so many people?"

Zach looked like he'd been attacked with a cattle prod, then arched an eyebrow at me. "Because it's what the public want. Stories like this. It makes them feel … I don't know, *satisfied* that the privileged and rich of this world pay a price for it."

I maintained eye contact with him. "Is that really what they want, or is that what gossip mags make them think they want, by feeding them endless tittle-tattle?" I leaned forward. "Is it just that you're trying to justify what you write?"

There was a sudden, icy atmosphere across my kitchen table.

I set my fork down with a decisive rattle on the side of my plate. Should I appeal to Zach's better nature? I jutted out my chin. I had to do something. Perhaps honesty was the way to go now.

I took a sharp intake of breath and decided to go for it. "I know Ezra King… Well… I kind of know him … a little bit… He came into the shop a couple of weeks ago."

Zach's dark-lashed eyes widened. "You do know him? But you said—"

I fidgeted and struggled to make eye contact with him as he stared at me. Then he lowered his knife and fork, frustration flashing in his dark eyes. "I don't believe this. You stood there, watching me chase my tail over this story. You've watched me make an utter tit of myself."

I threw up my hands. "But it's none of your business! What's he ever done to you? I don't owe you the truth. You're not the police on the hunt for a murderer!" I shot back.

Zach rolled his eyes, which only spurred me on.

"Like I said, this isn't storytelling. It's not journalism. It's grubby and invasive when people are just trying to live their lives. All you care about is circulation figures."

Zach didn't say anything for a minute. He examined me with an indecipherable look in his eyes. "So that's why you didn't tell me the truth about Ezra King? Because of your principles?"

I nodded. "Ezra's right to privacy is more important than your search for a story! To be honest, I still feel that way." I swallowed. "But I've got to know you a little and you seem like a decent person. That's why I'm hoping you'll do the right thing. I'm trusting that you won't splash his private life over the pages of *Stargazer*." I paused. "Don't you think trust is important?"

Zach let out a grunt. "Of course, I do. Finding out the truth and being able to trust people is my job." He flashed me a long look that ripped into my chest. "Speaking of which..."

I flinched in my kitchen chair and felt heat rising up my neck.

"Speaking of what?" I said, as calmly as I could.

Zach continued to appraise me. He seemed to be struggling to decide whether to say something else. In the end, he threw his head back, stared at my kitchen ceiling and then back at me.

"Well… You clearly know far more about what goes on around round here than you've led me to believe."

I frowned over at him. "What do I know exactly?"

Zach lowered his voice, even though it was just the two of us and debris of the takeaway. "The tip I received about Ezra having two grown-up daughters he didn't know about."

The blood leeched from my face, like a watercolour left out in the rain.

Zach hauled a frustrated hand through his dark hair. He looked momentarily wounded. "So, my instinct was right then?" His broad shoulders slumped.

"What are you so afraid of, Bailey? Why won't you let me in?"

"Let you in?" I scoffed. "Zach, you work for a gossip magazine!"

The sudden, almost vulnerable softening of his face took me by surprise.

"I thought … we were getting on," he said. "I've shared things with you, haven't I?"

Yes, about Astrid, I thought. And as endearing as that had been, he'd hardly divulged truly personal information. I battled my conflicting thoughts. On the one hand, there was nothing I wanted more than to feel I could confide in this tall, drop-dead gorgeous man. On the other, I still couldn't be sure he was playing up the chemistry, the connection between us, so that he could get the information out of me he wanted. Not to mention him finding out who I really was. I decided to turn the tables on him.

"It's a bit rich of you," I said. "Wanting me to open up to you. Because every time I ask about your background, you shut me down." I shook my head. "You're fine delving into other people's lives and exposing private things, but you won't talk about your own. Hypocritical, wouldn't you say?" I fiddled with my water glass. "There are two women here who could find themselves thrown into the spotlight and they didn't ask for it. They don't want that. Why are you so determined to expose them when they've done nothing wrong?"

Zach's chiselled expression was serious. "Listen. You have my word. Whatever you tell me right now, is strictly off the record."

I stared across at him. I wanted to believe him. More than anything. "Yeah. Right. How often have you said that?"

"Bailey, I promise you that whatever you tell me, stays between us." His warm, autumnal eyes never left my face. "I couldn't… I wouldn't betray you like that…"

The atmosphere in my flat had shifted. It was crackling. What was going on here?

I bit my lip. Could I trust him? Maybe it would be a relief to unburden myself of the secrets?

I heaved a sigh, then pinned him with my gaze. "If any of what I tell you gets published, I will hold you personally responsible."

Zach nodded. A soft, understanding smile tugged at the corners of his mouth. "Understood."

I clasped my hands together on top of the kitchen table. I felt like I had one foot over a precipice. I swore I'd never trust anyone again after what Declan did to me. And yet, here I was, about to open up to Zach.

"Bailey. I promise you. Whatever you tell me right now, stays in this room."

I closed my eyes for a few seconds and leapt. "All right. Yes. Ezra King did decide to escape from London." My fingers laced and unlaced themselves. "We became friendly and he offered me a floristry commission to create flower arrangements for his home."

Zach's brows waggled up and down. "Ok. I sense there's a but coming?"

I rubbed at my face.

"Bailey?"

I felt like I was teetering on the brink. I took a long breath. "Then two young women showed up here at Flower Power. They told me they believed they were Ezra's daughters, but that he had no idea they existed. They managed to track him down to the area." I paused and carried on talking. "I said I didn't know him but if he were to come into the shop, I would pass on their details to him. Then I went to see Ezra and told him about his two daughters. He was furious and pulled the plug on my commission. He'd been planning to hire me to arrange the flowers for a private party as well, but that's now dead in the water too. I haven't seen him since."

Zach sat and listened, his arched brows lifting higher.

I sank back in my kitchen chair. "Caroline and Laura only discovered that Ezra might be their father recently." I left out the detail about their mothers and the affairs Ezra had had with them. "It was in Ezra's autobiography."

Zach listened and gave a brief nod of understanding.

"Ezra thought I was meddling and I guess I was. Perhaps I deserved it." I shut my eyes for a few seconds. "I should've left well alone, but I only wanted to help. I didn't want word getting out about his daughters." A wry smile flashed across my mouth. "Things haven't turned out well."

Zach digested what I'd just told him. He leant forward, scanning my face. "I think you're being too hard on yourself. I don't think you interfered."

"You don't?"

He shook his luscious, dark sweep of hair. "What else were you supposed to do? Ignore them? Like you just said, you did what you felt was right at the time." He offered a small smile that made my heart zing. "If you hadn't made an effort to speak to Ezra about Caroline and Laura, you might have been denying a family the opportunity to reunite." Zach leant both arms on the edge of the table. They carried a smattering of dark, wiry hair. "Just imagine how you'd have felt if something had happened to Ezra and you hadn't done anything? You would've regretted it."

My mouth flipped into a quirky smile. "Blimey. If I didn't know you, I might start to think you're trying to make me feel better."

Zach gave me a look. "Don't get me wrong. I'm still

irritated at you for not coming clean about Ezra at the beginning. It would've saved me so much time and hassle." He hesitated. "But I understand why you did it."

I wrinkled my nose. "I was perfectly within my rights not to tell you. It's your problem if it annoyed you."

Zach laughed. "Fair enough."

I gazed across at him, dumbfounded. There was another side to this man that I had no idea existed. But in a way, I felt even more wretched. What would Zach say if he found out who I really was?

While we cleared away the debris from our meal, Zach told me he'd heard Ezra's autobiography was a juicy read. "Apparently, Ezra King started off as a successful fashion model before breaking into acting."

"Really?" A picture of Ezra, all cheese grater cheekbones and cut-glass English accent, swaggering down the runway in his youth, jumped into my mind. I could see him doing that.

"Yep. And from what I've been told through my contacts," he continued, "His revelations have got certain TV and film executives worried."

I hesitated, a dirty plate in one hand above the open dishwasher. "So, what do we do now? I mean, you want the story about him moving here and your editor is expecting you to come up with the goods." I offered Zach a glance. "But at what expense?"

Zach gazed at me. "I'm not the ogre you think I am, Bailey. Please believe me."

I fiddled with my hair. "And I'm not trying to make

your search for news difficult. I'm just trying to let you see what impact these stories can have on people."

He nodded. "I understand."

There was a sudden softening in his eyes and we continued to clear up in comparative silence.

Once we finished despatching the takeaway debris, Zach sauntered into my sitting room and spotted my Christmas tree. His attention fell on the star I'd set down on my coffee table. "Your tree looks great – or at least it would do if the lights were on it as well."

"I was struggling with wrapping the lights around it and with putting the star on top." I felt myself blush. "I hadn't realised the tree was so tall."

He flashed a grin, picked up the star, and in one long stride, was over by the glittering white and silver tree.

I watched him attach the star to the top of the tree with ease. He took a step back to admire his handiwork. Then his attention drifted to the messy lights.

His face softened. "Let's do it together."

My stomach tangled itself up in more knots than my tree lights.

Zach gathered up the delicate lights at one end, I took the other, and we eased them around the tree, lacing them this way and that. It was much easier having another pair of hands to help me.

A couple of times, we inadvertently bumped into each other. The brush of Zach's body against mine sent my breath into a spin.

We finished decorating the tree in silence, with

electrified glances exchanged between us. I noticed how the rose-gold lights emphasised the cut of his jaw and the sweep of his nose as they flashed against his face.

A few times, he looked like he wanted to say something, but then he switched his attention back to decorating the tree so fast that I wondered if it was my imagination playing tricks on me.

Zach lingered by my front door at the end of the evening.

"Thank you for the takeaway. I really enjoyed it."

"Me too."

There was a pregnant pause. "And thank you so much for helping me decorate the tree. I dread to think what state it would be in right now, if you hadn't been here."

Zach towered over me, his magnificent eyes trailing across my face. They came to rest on my lips. Rasps of excited breath knotted at the base of my throat.

"You're welcome, Bailey."

But just as a corner of my mind wondered whether he was going to kiss me, he seemed to collect himself. He took a step backwards, flipping into professional journalist mode again. "I'm going to contact Ezra King's management team and see if they'll talk to me."

The spell broken; I wrapped my arms around myself.

My God! Hasn't he listened to a word I'd told him?

Did the intimate looks between us while we decorated my Christmas tree mean nothing? The dinner we shared...! My eyes hardened.

"So, you still plan to expose him and chase after his daughters, after all I said?"

Zach hesitated. "Bailey, it's not what you think. Things have moved on. It's complicated…"

Stupidity rained down on me. Shit! When would I ever learn? I'd sat there, torturing myself over what to tell Zach – if anything – and now he was turning the tables again. I let out a bark of sarcastic laughter. "Why the hell did I think I could trust you? Jesus, what was I thinking? Me of all people should've realised—"

I clamped my mouth shut.

Zach studied me. "If you could just stop talking for a moment and let me explain please."

I glowered at him, as the sparkly late November stars danced across the sky behind him through the open door.

Zach shook his head in frustration. "You have my word that I'm not here to needlessly invade Ezra's privacy, or his two daughters." His voice was deep and earnest. "If someone does that, it certainly won't be me."

I blinked up at Zach. "Are you serious?"

He nodded. "You have my word."

"But then … what?" I stumbled. "Why are you approaching Ezra King's management?"

Zach jerked up the collar of his coat. "There's been a development… Something genuinely of public interest. You know I'm interested in the truth, that's all." His attention drifted from my eyes to my mouth again, making my legs turn to jelly and my stomach churn at the word "truth".

We stood there, staring at one another, unaware of the brisk cold.

I gazed at a small scar on his chin hidden amongst his shadowy stubble.

"I can't tell you what's going on yet, but I will." He hesitated. "I don't suppose there's any chance you could speak to Ezra King on my behalf and persuade him to talk to me?"

I sighed. "I highly doubt it. He was absolutely furious when I talked to him about Caroline and Laura. I'd be surprised if he ever speaks to me again."

Zach reached out one hand and squeezed my shoulder. The sensation of his fingertips skimming against my skin made me bite back a gasp.

He stood over me, a kaleidoscope of emotions travelling across his face. "Bailey..." Then he blinked and snatched his hand away. It was like touching me had scorched him. "You were trying to help. It's a shame he couldn't see that."

I was silent for a moment. Zach was right. I had only been trying to help. But Ezra hadn't seemed too interested in finding out the truth. Like his denial was more important than connecting with his own flesh and blood.

"Why do you need to speak to him if you're not doing an article on him?" I asked then.

Zach cocked his head at me. "Trust me, Bailey. Please."

I felt like I was in free-fall whenever I looked at him. I nodded after a few more seconds. "Ok, I will."

Zach gave a brief smile. "If Adam finds out about me dicking around and hesitating over writing up about Ezra's daughters, my P45 will be in the post." He started to move away and then turned around again. "I'll let you know how I get on."

I began to close the door.

"Bailey." His eyes glinted back at me.

"What?"

"Trust me. Please."

Chapter Fourteen

Sunday morning's drive to Bannock House was actually very pleasant. There was a wintry breeze, signalling the definite arrival of December, but the coquettish sun persisted in flirting in and out of the stippled shreds of icy clouds.

Still, the secret I was keeping from Zach was very much on my mind. How long could I carry on like this? I didn't want to lie to him or deceive him. It made me feel shabby. But, despite telling him I trusted him, how could I when it was his job to expose the truth?

I was even taking a risk driving back home. What if Zach was tailing me? It didn't seem that likely, not after what had happened between us last night, but it wasn't impossible. I checked my rear-view mirror but the coast was clear. It looked like I was the only car on the road.

I relaxed a little, though I was still struggling with a combination of guilt and longing. I wanted to be the person

Zach thought I was. Despite my protestations that I'd never allow myself to fall for another man again, let alone trust one, here I was, doing it anyway.

When I stopped at some traffic lights, I studied my eyes in the little mirror on the back of the visor that I'd pulled down to protect against the bright flashes of occasional sunlight. My eyes were preoccupied and pale grey, like an unsettled loch on a winter's day. Squirming nerves, like a basket of eels, slithered in my stomach.

As I left behind the main roads, the familiar scenery of the countryside emerged. In the distance, there was the faint, craggy hillside. the thrusting peaks of the roofs and the higgledy-piggledy shops. Everything looked festive, as though it had been sprinkled with glitter.

I passed the familiar spread of farmers' fields on the left, with their shaggy, amber-haired Highland cattle and then turned right into the private road that led up to my family home. The trees on either side thrust their branches in dramatic, twisted curves, casting spidery shadows over the roof of my car. The Georgian wrought-iron gate with its fussy leaf carvings stared back at me as if to say, "Oh, long time, no see!"

I got out of the car and jabbed the security code into the panel that was wired into one of the gate posts. It still worked. It hadn't been changed since I was last here over a year ago. My parents were rather lackadaisical about that sort of thing.

The gates glided open.

My tyres crunched over the driveway gravel, with its

candy-pink chips, grumbling in consternation as I passed banks of rustling undergrowth.

It felt like I'd never left.

Bannock House glinted under the intermittent rays of the watery sun, its grey coade stone proud and resilient against the Scottish weather.

The house had two storeys and a taller central tower with numerous other turrets rising phoenix-like from its high walls. The entrance was imposing and consisted of a large oak door which was reached via a broad set of stone steps.

An impressive walled garden was situated at the rear, which contained an arboretum dating back to the late nineteenth century and nurtured many glorious North American conifers. Surrounding that was an abundance of various trees, ranging from elm and sycamore to beech and Scots pine. The gardens still captivated me every bit as much as they did when I was a child.

I parked my car at the rear of the house and collected my handbag from the passenger seat. The throb of birdsong felt like a welcome serenade.

My favourite go-to place here, apart from the sprawling gardens, was the library. It was an alcove affair in beech wood, with a single high window and a gothic-style fireplace. There was a Cairngorm tartan rug on the floor in a palette of greys.

I used to love perching myself on a stool, surrounded by the volumes of books and drinking in the scent of paper and the delicate floral perfume of Scottish bluebells, which Mum would place in a china vase on the nest of tables.

I made my way across the gravel and round to the front entrance to be greeted by a surprised and delighted-looking Mrs Bamber, our housekeeper. She bounded out of the door. "Miss Anastasia! Oh, my goodness!"

She enveloped me in her arms and I clung to her. She was as much a fixture of the house as the arboretum was.

"How are you, Mrs Bamber?" I asked. "All well?"

Mrs Bamber's apple-cheeked face glowed. "Stanley and the boys and I are grand." She sighed, drinking in my appearance. Her hazel eyes sparkled at me with affection. "It's been too long. Far too long. And look at you! All grown up and sophisticated." She stroked my ponytail. "I almost didn't recognise you."

I laughed. "I take it you mean in a good way."

Her cheeks flushed. "Sorry, Miss Anastasia. But yes, I must admit I do. You look wonderful." She asked me if anyone was expecting me and how things were going with Flower Power.

"Everything's fine. Well, more than fine actually. The shop's doing great." I hesitated. "Business is picking up now after a bit of a slow start." I dropped my voice. "And no, I'm not expected."

Then I mentioned Marcus and Mrs Bamber's expression darkened. "Aye. The poor lad. That Jacob turned out to be a right charlatan." She drew a little closer. "I hope I'm not speaking out of turn, Miss Anastasia, but I never warmed to the man. I always thought there was something right shifty about him."

"Mrs Bamber? What's going on? Who is it?"

I looked over Mrs Bamber's shoulder at my mother emerging into the hall. Both our eyes locked on one another.

Mum's lip sticked mouth fell open. "Anastasia? Oh my God! Why didn't you tell me you were coming?!" She bounded over the polished, black-and-white chequered hall floor and bundled me into her arms. Her words came out in one long rush. "It's wonderful to see you. Your dad's out on the golf course. I'll ring him."

"No, don't do that," I laughed. "He'll never forgive us."

Mum was wearing one of her heavy trouser suits. This one was in ghost grey.

I gave Mrs Bamber's arm a supportive squeeze.

"I'll go and rustle up some tea," she insisted. "And you couldn't have timed this any better. I've just finished icing a ginger cake."

I smiled fondly after Mrs Bamber, aware that my mother was still staring at me, as though I was some kind of apparition.

I pointed at Mum's trouser suit. "A New York purchase? It's lovely."

She nodded and beamed at me, her dark coiffed hair skimming her shoulders. "I'm glad you like it, sweetheart. Oh, you do look so well!"

I glanced about the hall, as though seeing the sweeping watercolours and elaborate urns of grassy reeds for the first time. Two sage-green Christmas trees were standing to attention near the bottom of the staircase, waiting to be decorated. "I hope you don't mind me dropping in like this, Mum, but there's something I wanted to talk to you about."

She linked one arm through mine and steered me towards the lounge. "You can talk to me about anything, darling. You know that. It's not about your business, is it?"

"Oh, nothing like that. Things are going well."

"That's great. Then what is it? Oh, I'm thrilled you're here!"

We approached the panelled door of the lounge.

"I've come to talk to you about Marcus."

Mum's jewelled right hand flew to the oval pendant around her neck. She proceeded to play with it. "Yes. Awful. That bastard Jacob." She paused. "I understand Marcus came to stay with you for a few days while I was in New York. Your father told me."

I levelled my gaze at her. "He did."

Mum's dark blue eyes glistened with something. "So, what is it, sweetheart?"

The square heels of my taupe suede boots tapped on the floor, as Mum's manicured hand reached out for the handle and opened the lounge door.

"Jacob came here for dinner with you, right before he ended it with Marcus."

Mum stiffened. She opened her glossy mouth to say something, but I cut her off with a raised palm. "And before you go saying anything else, I know Dad wasn't here at the time. He was away on his annual golf jaunt with the boys."

Mum squirmed in her high-heeled boots.

"Well, am I right?"

Her complexion tightened under her make-up.

We stepped together into the sunlit lounge. "I think we need to talk, Mum."

I followed her into what Mum liked to call our "drawing room" but it was more like a second sitting room, decked out with a walnut-coloured sofa, armchairs, and a huge vanilla stone fireplace, which was now festooned with a frothy, festive garland of silver leaves and holly. A smaller Christmas tree was stationed in the far corner, dripping with gold baubles.

She had redecorated since I'd last been here and the walls were now painted pale apricot, instead of toffee.

I also noted Dad had finally got his own way and there was now a fifty-inch plasma TV stationed in the top left corner of the room.

I sank down into one of the armchairs and propped a velvet cushion at my back. Outside the window, the morning sun swept across the manicured lawn and flower beds, which were bearing odd clots of heather and some hardy winter plants of baby pink cyclamen, witch hazel and red-studded viburnum. Frost danced across the lawns. Christmas was flirting with everyone's senses.

Mum seated herself opposite me. "You have a different air about you."

"I feel different, Mum. In a good way." It was strange. I'd expected Declan's malevolent spirit to jump out at me as soon as I stepped back into Bannock House, but it hadn't happened. There were no painful memories flooding my brain. Instead, he'd just fizzled into the background, like some fancy firework that had failed to spark. I wouldn't take responsibility for Declan anymore, or for what he did to me. He was consigned to history, along with my party-girl past.

Shards of optimism glowed in me. I really was moving on with my life at last.

Could Zach be a part of my new life?

I appraised Mum's long, slender legs angled to one side. I'd always been rather in awe of her. She was always so self-assured; an inherent sense of self-worth beamed out of her like a beacon.

I decided to get straight to the point. "So, why did you invite Jacob over for dinner?"

An odd look flitted across her features. She lifted a slim wrist and brushed a hair away from her face. "He was going to be my son-in-law. What's so strange about asking him over?"

"What's so strange is that you didn't tell Marcus you were inviting his fiancé over for dinner. If it was all so innocent, why not mention it? And why did you want to see Jacob on your own?"

Mum let out an unconvincing laugh. "Darling, what's this about?"

"I take it you haven't told Dad about this?"

Mum's dark blue eyes glittered out of her face. "What is this, Anastasia? I didn't realise I had to run my social events by the rest of the family."

There was a prickly silence, except for the steady click of

a carriage clock on the writing bureau. "What happened, Mum? What's been going on?"

Mum pursed her lips. "Honestly, I sometimes wonder where you get your fanciful ideas."

"They aren't fanciful. I haven't forgotten about Finn Coulter, Mum."

My Mother's fingers clenched in her lap. "Oh please. Not that again."

I leant forward in the armchair. "I don't get any of this. Everyone knows how well-suited Marcus and Jacob are."

She slid me a look. "Yes, well, that's what you think."

"What's that supposed to mean?"

Mum raised her long neck upwards. "You haven't been here. You don't know the full story."

I angled my head to one side. "Well, I'm here now, so tell me."

She sighed. "I wish I'd protected you from that money-grabbing bastard Declan. I should've stepped in."

"I wouldn't have listened, Mum. I loved him. I thought I knew him. Still, at least I found him out in the end. At least I didn't end up marrying him. He did me a favour, dumping me at the altar."

"Yes, after fleecing you for money and causing untold embarrassment on the family."

"It was *my* embarrassment, Mum."

"You let your heart rule your head," murmured my mother. "We've all been there."

I dragged a hand over the top of my ponytail. "Yes. I did. More fool me."

I focused my attention on the wintry grounds, where the bare trees stood like iced statues. Winter berries popped like red jewels in the hedgerows. "Look, Mum, I want to know what the hell's been going on here. Marcus is in bits."

When she didn't answer, I rose from the sofa.

"Perhaps I should speak to Dad about this. I'm sure he'd be very intrigued to know what you've been up to."

Her red-slicked mouth flatlined. She let out an agonised noise. "Yes. All right. Enough of the amateur dramatics."

I sank back down again onto the other couch.

My mother wedged her tongue in her cheek for a few seconds. "He's better off without him. Marcus, I mean."

"And you hastened his departure?"

She widened her eyes melodramatically. "I don't know what you mean?"

Good grief. She may be wonderful at fundraising, but her acting skills were appalling. "Oh, just stop, Mum!" I stared her down. "I know you were instrumental in Finn leaving the area. What did you do? Remind him he wasn't posh or rich enough?"

Mum blustered. "If he'd been keener on you, he would've hung around, wouldn't he?"

I dismissed her protests. "And what about Jacob? Would he have hung around if he was keener on Marcus?" I asked pointedly.

Mum twisted her scalloped dress ring around on her right hand. "I was very fond of Jacob, but you have no idea what's been going on here. You're sitting there, making accusations and blaming me when you don't know the real situation."

I let out a disbelieving laugh. "Oh, I cannot wait to hear this. What's the story this time, Mum? Have you discovered Jacob's grandfather didn't drive a Daimler? Or perhaps his mother was born on a council estate?"

Mum swallowed.

"Doesn't it matter to you that he and Marcus love each other? Can't you see how heartbroken—"

"Jacob's been cheating on your brother with Samuel," she interrupted me, her tone brittle, and I shut my mouth. Her words hung in the air like acrid smoke.

"Samuel Lawson… from Marcus's work?"

My mother's gaze bore into me as she nodded. "It's true. I wish it wasn't, but it is."

Samuel and Marcus had worked together for a few years and become friends. I knew that Marcus and Jacob had gone on numerous double dates with Samuel and his partner, Lee.

"N-no," I stuttered, watching my mother stride backwards and forwards in front of the window in her expensive clothes. "Who told you this?"

Mum's jewellery rattled. "I didn't want to be right about this. I really didn't."

This couldn't be true. For the last few months, Marcus had been brimming with excitement and anticipation at spending the rest of his life with Jacob.

Mum laced and unlaced her fingers as she continued to stride backwards and forwards in front of me, like a traumatised zoo animal. "You might not believe me Anastasia, but I didn't want any of this. I was hoping it was just my imagination. But you must understand that I had to protect your brother." Her voice cracked. It was as if she were fighting to get the words out. "And my daughter, although I didn't do a very good job of that."

I blinked up at her.

She stopped in front of one of the two big windows. The naked trees out in the grounds weaved and swayed like exotic dancers in the wind.

"I'd had my suspicions for a few weeks. Jacob began cancelling when he was supposed to be meeting Marcus to visit wedding venues or go out, citing work pressures, and then when he visited here, I noticed he was distracted by his phone. He always seemed jumpy." A pleading look stole over her serious features. "You have to believe me. I didn't want to be right."

My head was muddled, struggling to accept what my mother was telling me. "I can't believe he and Samuel would do that to Marcus."

"Well, they did."

Poor Marcus. Oh God. To be betrayed by your fiancé, but to also be betrayed by one of your friends. My anger was stoking up. "How did you get him to admit to it? Jacob, I mean?"

Mum flicked me a hot look out of the corner of her eye as she examined the graceful mermaid water feature tinkling outside. "He couldn't deny it. Not after they were spotted together in public. It was Ruth Keegan from my

Women's Institute days who saw them – holding hands and sharing an intimate dinner in a hotel restaurant in town."

I felt sick. I could hardly believe it.

Mum turned away from the window. "Ruth asked to meet me for lunch just the other week and she told me what she'd seen," she said, folding her arms, her bracelets jangling. "That's when I decided to confront Jacob about it."

My frustration was all-consuming. "Mum, don't you think you should've spoken to Marcus instead?"

Mum sank down again opposite me in her armchair. The anger in my eyes must have registered with her. "Yes, well, on reflection, I should have. We all make mistakes, believe me."

"What, even you?" I asked dryly.

She bristled. "All I could see was that Jacob was making a fool of your brother." She shook her head, as if playing through the events again. "I let Declan do that to you and I wasn't prepared to let history repeat itself again with Marcus." Her voice took on a more brittle edge. "I've met men like that before."

An odd, faraway look clouded her eyes, before she composed herself. "Anyway, even before Jacob had the chance to sit down, I told him I knew what had been going on and that he and Samuel had been seen together in some gaudy restaurant."

"And how did he react to being found out?"

Mum snorted. "Would you believe Jacob denied everything at first? He said he was having regular catch-ups with Samuel because they were discussing the wedding!"

She let out a snort. "He even had the cheek to say that he and Samuel had been meeting in secret because he was planning some major surprise for your brother as part of the wedding ceremony."

"And then?"

She got up and paced again, her heels placed deliberately one in front of the other. "I wouldn't let it drop. I said I had been suspicious when he was always glued to his phone while visiting here." Her pointed chin shot forward. "Finally, he admitted that he and Samuel had been having an affair." Mum's lip curled. "He was like a cornered animal in the end," she sighed. "Despite my suspicions, I couldn't believe it when Ruth told me." Her brow furrowed. "He and Marcus made such a wonderful couple – or so I thought – and I always considered Jacob to be a principled young man, especially when you consider his environmental work." Then she snorted. "If all of us who'd been deceived by someone we trusted were lined up side by side, the bloody queue would stretch to Mars." Her features twisted into a mask of hurt and she fell quiet.

"Mum? Are you ok?"

She steadied herself. "Oh. Yes. Of course. I'm just being silly."

I reached up to massage my temple.

Shit. What a mess.

Maybe if I'd been around, I might have noticed something was happening?

"Does Marcus know any of this?"

"He does now." She fixed me with a look. "Your

brother's been tied up with work and, I think, deliberately throwing himself onto courses and away-days to keep himself occupied since the breakup. One of Samuel's colleagues texted Marcus yesterday and told him." She drew in her lips. "Last I heard, Jacob and Samuel were looking at apartments on the south side of Glasgow. They were talking about staying around the Edinburgh area, initially. Even looking at building a new home in Tweed Muir."

I groaned. "You're kidding. How insensitive."

Mum swallowed and set her shoulders as she continued to pace around. "But don't worry. Everything's been taken care of."

An odd feeling took over. "What do you mean by that?"

"Let's just say I had no option but to appeal to Samuel's avaricious streak."

I lurched up from the sofa. "You paid him off? Why?"

Oh, good grief. This situation was just getting better and better.

"I didn't want to. Please don't look at me like that, Anastasia, it wasn't my idea. It was Samuel's."

I looked at my mother standing there, with the gilded picture frames and velvet cushions behind her. "What are you saying?"

Mum allowed her manicured hands to rise and fall. "Samuel was shameless about it when I rang him." She contorted her lips in disgust. "He said Jacob didn't want to tell your brother about their affair, but he had no such qualms and had tried to push Jacob into confessing everything. I got the impression the vicious little sod was almost relishing it."

She stared past my shoulder, her mouth set. "Samuel said Marcus had a right to know. He told me Jacob wanted to move away and start over with him, but Samuel said they might stay around Tweed Muir."

I couldn't comprehend Samuel's audacity. It wasn't enough for him that he'd stolen his friend's fiancé, he was trying to live locally with him as well! Talk about rubbing my brother's nose in it!

"I think, underneath, Samuel was always rather resentful of your brother, professionally speaking," admitted my mother, her gaze wandering over to the fluttering red-studded viburnum outside the window. "He remained friends with Marcus for as long as it suited his own ends and for what he could get from him."

I sank down again onto the sofa.

Mum's mouth twisted into a grim line. "I told Samuel that he and Jacob should ensure they put as much space between themselves and your brother as possible. I said it was the least they could do and I thought I was getting through to him at one point, when he admitted they'd already viewed some new-build apartment on the south side of Glasgow."

"And then?"

"Then Samuel turned round and without a flicker of remorse said that unless I gave him money, he'd go to the press and tell all about his affair with Lord Marcus's fiancé." Mum eyed me for my reaction. "That would be the cost of them disappearing out of Marcus's life. Maybe I shouldn't have done it, but I was trying to do what was best for your brother."

Mum crossed and uncrossed her arms as she continued to stride around. "It might not seem like it, but everything I've done, and everything I do, is for my children."

She looked pensive as she studied the wintry garden scene. I was speechless.

"Samuel has resigned. He put out the story that he'd been headhunted by another agency. Your brother was on a residential training course for a few days and when he came back to work Samuel had already gone."

I looked at Mum. "And does Marcus know about the money you gave Samuel?"

She whipped her head round to me. Her voice was insistent; pleading. "No. And it should stay that way. It's in your brother's best interests – you'll see. I knew how hurt he'd be by all this and I wanted to try and protect him as much as I could." Her eyes shone. "I still feel like I failed you over Declan. Perhaps I thought I could make amends over you, by at least trying to create some sort of damage limitation for my son."

I drove back to Heather Moore, feeling twisted up inside with sadness and anger on behalf of my heartbroken brother, and when I got back to my flat, I tried to call him, but only his voicemail kicked in, so I hung up without leaving a message.

I didn't sleep well that night, and when I woke up on Monday morning, I felt as though I'd been battered and bruised in a rugby scrum.

I made myself a camomile tea as I prepared to open up Flower Power.

The first part of the morning seemed to crawl past. Amber and Rowan were their same ebullient selves, looking forward to Christmas and both sporting Santa hats, but I felt like I was wading through treacle.

It was only when Zach appeared around lunchtime that I was able to distract myself for a little while.

"You look … tired," he said with concern.

"Thanks," I said ruefully. I so wanted to unburden myself to him, but I knew I couldn't. Too much was at stake. I blinked up at him, touched by his concern. "I just didn't get much sleep last night."

Zach smiled. "Right. Well, I'm here if there's anything on your mind you want to offload." He then let out a frustrated sigh. "I feel terrible but I'm actually here to ask a favour of you."

I fiddled with some change in the till and shot him a cross look. "Is that why you're being so nice to me? Because you want a favour?"

"No, it bloody well isn't! Gee. Great to know you think so much of me."

I twisted my mouth up at one corner. "Is this you fishing for compliments?"

Zach grinned, exposing his white, even teeth with just a sliver of a sexy gap between the front two. "Is it working?"

I let out a laugh, trying not to register the sudden rippling sensation in my stomach. "No, but God loves a trier." I stopped what I was doing with the till. "Ok, Zach, out with it. What's the problem?"

He looked contrite. "It's not good news on the Ezra King front, I'm afraid. He's refusing to speak to me. I've tried his manager, his publisher, everyone I can think of. It's the usual excuse: he's had bad experiences with journalists in the past and now brackets every reporter alongside Satan."

Zach rubbed his jaw and moved closer to me. I got a delicious waft of his woodsy, English oak cologne.

I narrowed my eyes. "Can you blame him?"

"I suppose not. But what I'm looking into isn't your run-of-the-mill gossip, Bailey. This rumour that's circulating..."

"Yes, you keep mentioning that. What rumour exactly?"

Zach frowned. "I can't say, not yet. Just trust me on this one, ok? I need to speak to him to get his side... It's very important."

I studied him. "To get his side on record, you mean?"

"Something like that." Zach sighed, an adorable air of little-boy helplessness about him.

I fiddled with my necklace. "Ok, I'll try. But don't get your hopes up. I've already told you I'm not one of his favourite people right now."

Chapter Fifteen

Amber had finished for the day but Rowan was still working so I excused myself for a few moments and secreted myself in my office with my mobile.

I tried to contact Ezra first, but his phone rang out and he didn't pick up. Either he was busy or he could see it was me calling him and was avoiding me. Undeterred, I then rang his manager, but Denise Gold's voicemail was activated and despite leaving several messages, she didn't return my calls.

I then decided to ring Corrie, Denise Gold's assistant. She'd been so kind and sympathetic when Ezra had decided to cancel my floristry services.

After exchanging pleasantries, she apologised again for Ezra's decision not to use Flower Power. "I'm so sorry. I felt awful having to tell you. In fact, I was rather dreading it."

"Honestly, Corrie, please don't feel bad about it. Ezra had already said he'd changed his mind about using me." I hoped she'd be able to hear the urgency in my voice. "And I can assure you this call isn't an attempt by me to try to persuade Ezra to change his mind. But I really do need to speak with him about something else. It's urgent."

Corrie made an understanding murmur.

"I know Ezra hates journalists," I went on. "But this is something where … Ezra's involvement will benefit him." I hesitated. I didn't know that for sure, but I trusted Zach to have Ezra's best interests at heart. "Can you tell Ezra that I'll be here at the shop this evening and if he can come by around 6pm, I'll be waiting with Zach Stern?" I took a breath. "Ezra will know who Zach is. It's very important." My chest gave a little heave. "Please emphasise to Ezra that I trust Zach and he should, too."

Corrie sighed and I heard her scribbling down a note. "Ok. I'll pass on your message, but I can't promise he'll get back to you, let alone show up." There was a smile wrapped around her words. "You know what a cantankerous old bugger he can be."

Once I'd hung up, I rang Zach on his mobile and kept him in the loop.

Zach was pleased. "Good work, Bailey. I'll make sure I finish up this staff exploitation story I'm working on, so I can be with you about five forty-five. Do you think he'll come?"

I sighed. "I'm not going to get too optimistic. I just hope curiosity gets the better of him." I took a breath. "I emphasised when I called that I trusted you and that Ezra should too."

There was a poignant silence down the phone for a few seconds. "You mean that?"

"Yes," I faltered, breaking into a small smile, even though he couldn't see me. "I do."

His voice became like warm butter down the line. "That means a lot to me, Bailey. More than you know. Thank you."

I kept Flower Power open for a little longer at the end of the day, before finishing up in advance of Ezra's possible appearance.

When Zach materialised at the door, he looked somewhat dishevelled, with his shirt creased and his thick hair flopping onto his brow. He must have had a taxing day. But despite not looking his usual dapper self, he was still delectable.

I hoped I wasn't staring. It felt like I was. "Been a tough one?" I asked.

"Doors shut in my face and frightened staff thinking they can't speak to me. But I'll get there." He gestured around the shop. "No sign of our Mr King yet?"

I closed the door behind him, his long coat billowing behind him in the stiff evening wind. It was approaching 6pm and the hills opposite were invisible in the winter darkness.

I shook my head. "I don't think he's coming. To be honest, why would he?"

"You never know." Zach sat down behind the counter on

one of the stools. I hadn't yet switched off the Christmas fairy lights, which made Flower Power possess a magical quality tonight. It looked cosy and festive. Romantic. Aware that he was watching me, I darted about tidying the shelf under the counter, where we stored Post-it pads and gift wrap.

"You're a very determined person," he said.

My hands stilled. "What makes you say that?"

He indicated around himself. "It's not easy nowadays, running your own business."

"Careful," I laughed. "That almost sounded like a compliment."

I raised my bent head from the counter and our eyes met. A sharp knock on the fire door interrupted our conversation.

Zach raised his eyebrows.

I hurried to the back of the shop and unlocked the door.

Ezra was standing on the step, his dark trilby poised at a jaunty angle and a tartan scarf knotted around his neck and partially covering his face. With the tweed coat he was wearing, he looked more like a Guy Richie gangster than a respected thespian.

Jackson waved from the open window of the car.

Ezra regarded me for a moment before stepping inside and removing his hat with his familiar, theatrical flourish. His tone was measured. "Hello, Bailey."

We looked at one another, both struggling to gauge the atmosphere between us.

"Hello, Ezra."

The silence crackled, until Ezra's attention fell on Zach. His face darkened.

"Hello, sir," said Zach, striding towards him and extending one hand. "I'm Zach Stern, from *Stargazer* magazine."

Ezra didn't reciprocate the handshake. He took a step backwards and flapped his hat at Zach, as though repulsed. "I must be bloody mad. I was in two minds whether to come along, but curiosity got the better of me." He shot a fierce glare at Zach. "What the hell's going on, Bailey?"

Zach took a few steps towards Ezra. "Please, sir. You have to trust me."

Ezra broke into peels of sarcastic laughter. "I'll do no such thing."

I jumped in between them. "Please, Ezra. Just hear Zach out."

Ezra's distinguished features were all suspicious. He narrowed his laser-like eyes at Zach. "All right then, young man. What is this about? Tell me at once!"

I gestured to Ezra to take a seat. "Please, Ezra."

Ezra fingered the brim of his hat in both hands. "I want to know what's going on right now or I'm leaving." He eyed Zach again and then cast me a withering look. I was definitely still in the bad books, maybe even more so now.

I straightened the cuffs of my jumper and nodded at Zach to speak.

"I understand you have two daughters that you only recently found out existed."

I snapped my head round. What?!

"Zach!" I hissed. "What are you doing? You said you would keep the girls out of this." Dread pooled in my stomach. How could I have been so stupid! I'd trusted him. I couldn't believe this!

Ezra's expression mirrored mine – absolute horror and shock. "Did you do this?" he asked me, icily. "Did you tell him?"

"No." I blanched under his gaze. "Zach found out about them on his own." I glared at Zach.

Zach jumped in. "That's true, sir. Bailey's gone to great lengths to protect you."

Ezra drank in my concerned expression. His head whizzed from me to Zach and back again. "Then what the bloody hell do you want?"

"Yes, what the bloody hell are you doing, Zach?" I ground out, firing blazing looks at him again.

Zach was quick to answer. "Please, Bailey. Hear me out. It's not what you think." He transferred his attention back to Ezra. "You made some revelations in your book about the time you spent as a fashion model at the beginning of your career, is that right?"

Ezra let out an exasperated sigh. "What of it?"

"You've also named and shamed certain individuals in the TV and film industry. There are some big hitters from the past listed in there."

Ezra straightened his shoulders. "Well, at least you've read my memoir, if nothing else," he said, dryly. "And those bastards deserved it. Everything I've said in that book is true."

"I'm sure it is," nodded Zach. "That's the problem."

"What do you mean?"

"It appears you've upset a few people in your autobiography and they want to draw attention away from your book, and damage your reputation and credibility in order to cast doubt on your claims."

A slow burn of apprehension took over Ezra. "Meaning?"

"Meaning they've no qualms about getting to you through your daughters. I'm trying to warn you about what these people are capable of. Believe me, I've no intention of writing anything about your daughters." Zach gave me a soft smile. "I promised Bailey I wouldn't."

A wisp of breath caught in my throat. The way Zach was looking at me…

He faced Ezra again. "And as for the recent unfortunate event you were said to be embroiled in…"

Ezra's expression twisted. "Not guilty," he said. "Malicious gossip, that's all."

"Yes, sir. I'm sure of that."

Zach filled me in. "Mr King was accused of stealing the script of the next Brad Janson movie. It went missing while Ezra and several high-powered Hollywood executives were dining out in London a few months ago."

Ezra's face was like granite. "I would never do such a thing." He sighed. "I've been up for a few parts in a number of his previous movies, but I never quite hit the mark, despite my experience. I've never liked the man, but in this industry, you have to try and stay professional wherever you can, otherwise it bites you on the derrière." Ezra shrugged. "I thought it strange Janson didn't want to involve the police when the script went missing."

Zach nodded. "That fits. One of the executives tipped us off about what happened. Everybody in attendance that night was keen to portray Mr King as the guilty party, including Brad Janson." Zach paused. "But I've since discovered that Mr Janson isn't who he says he is."

Ezra's brow furrowed. "Interesting."

Outside Flower Power, the winter night was wrapping itself around everything, enveloping us with a surprising sense of camaraderie.

"Mr King, in your career, have you ever come across a man by the name of Kenneth Braid?"

It only took a few seconds for Ezra to consider this. "Good grief. Yes, I have. Kenneth Braid was one of the seedy lowlifes who exploited the models at the agency I worked for when I started out."

"And you've spoken about him in your autobiography."

Ezra nodded, while I just listened.

Zach eyed Ezra. "What if I told you that Brad Janson's real name was Nicholas Braid?"

Ezra's head snapped from me to Zach and back again. "They're related?"

"Yep. He's Kenneth Braid's son. It looks like he arranged for that script to be stolen, so that you would be discredited and so would the revelations you make about him in your autobiography."

Ezra let out a furious gasp. "Good grief. I've had

entertainment industry friends begin to shun me since this nonsense happened. It's been most unpleasant. A real whispering campaign. That's when I knew I had to get away." His jaw ground. "Well, when I say friends…"

Zach shook his head. "Brad doesn't care if he ruins Mr King's career by protecting his father. In fact, that was his aim, until we leant on one of the executives from that night and he told us everything. We just have to confirm a few things, before we go to print on a story that exposes *them*, not you."

"This is insane," breathed Ezra. He rubbed his craggy face and stared around himself at Flower Power's interior. He let out a desperate groan. "Dear God! What do we do now?"

Zach turned to me. "It's not only Brad Janson who has a vested interest in having Mr King's book discredited. There are others. And according to my sources, they're prepared to do just about anything to make that happen."

I rose up from my seat and leant on the counter, mad thoughts hurtling through my head.

"Well, whatever these cretins have up their sleeve, I'm not prepared to curtail my life just to suit them. I have a small, private party taking place on New Year's Eve at my home," said Ezra, haughtily.

"Do you think that's wise?" asked Zach.

Ezra shrugged. "What else can I do? Cave into their demands? It's not like I'm inviting all of the acting fraternity; just a few of my closest friends and entertainment and publishing associates."

I tried not to smile. It didn't sound too small a soirée from where I was standing.

While Ezra and Zach's voices melted around me, I desperately wanted to help Ezra, and an idea was nudging its way to the forefront of my mind.

It could well be risky, Ezra holding his Hogmanay get-together at his home here in Heather Moore. Bannock House, however, would be a perfect alternative. Holding it there meant we could control the security, the guest list, everything. Ezra would still be throwing his party, but just at a different location. There was only one giant snag in that plan.

I'd lose my anonymity. I'd have to come clean about who I was.

I swallowed, trying to muster as much courage as I could. I knew I couldn't keep my past life a secret anymore. I had to accept that my past was part of me, but that it didn't have to define me. Running away wasn't a solution. I'd been deluding myself for too long. And anyway, I didn't want to keep deceiving Zach. It had begun to feel wrong now – deceitful, in some way.

I'd been very lucky to hide my past for as long as I had. Wouldn't it be better if Zach heard it from me, rather than some stranger?

All the stress of hiding was squeezing the breath from me. I couldn't continue living like this. It had taken this precarious situation with Ezra to make me realise what I had to do. He'd looked so cornered when he learnt that Zach had first arrived here in Heather Moore, and I didn't want to feel like that. I wanted to be strong and capable. I wanted to be free.

I took a breath and pushed out the words before I could change my mind.

"Ezra, your party is supposed to be taking place at your home."

"Yes, that's right," faltered Ezra.

I shook my head. "I suggest you invite your friends over to my family home. I don't think holding it at your place is a good idea. Not when you consider what your book contains and these people could well have discovered your address by now anyway."

I carried on, aware that both Ezra and Zach were studying me with confused expressions. "If these people realise you're not going to surrender to their threats and redact the stories about them in your book, things could turn nasty. At least this way, you just invite your small gathering to my family home and there's no need to draw attention to where you live here."

Zach jerked his head to look at me as though I'd lost all sense of reality. "Your family home?" he repeated. "I'm confused. You mean your flat upstairs?"

I shook my head. "No." Then I fetched my laptop from its leather case under the counter. I set it up and twisted it round for both of them to see the screen and typed *Bannock House* into the search engine. My heart was jumping. I felt sick.

I clicked on one photograph and enlarged it. The solid grey stone of my family home filled the screen.

"Whoa!" Zach said, laughing. "That's some place. Where's that?"

I looked down, my cheeks hot. "That's my family home."

Ezra studied the screen. "Good grief. Are you serious?"

Zach gawped at me. "That's where you live?"

"It's where I grew up, with my parents and Marcus. My mum and dad still live there."

If I was going to do this, I had to do it properly. No more secrets. No more hiding. In a way, it would be a release. No half measures.

I took a big gulp of air and typed in the words *Lady Anastasia McLaren-Kerr*.

The screen shimmered before dozens of images of me in slinky gowns at various events popped up. There was me posing with Declan, me tear-stained and jilted on my wedding day, me with various celebrity friends at parties.

I didn't dare look at Zach.

Headlines raced across the screen.

IRISH CHARM ON THE LADY'S ARM; LADY ANASTASIA GETS ENGAGED; BOLLINGER BABE IN LOVE; WEDDING DAY WOES FOR JILTED LADY A– BOLLINGER BABE ARISTO DUMPED AT THE ALTAR; CONNED BY HER IRISH ROVER – LADY ANASTASIA DUPED AND DUMPED…

It was odd to see these pictures again now. I didn't recognise myself as the woman in the photos. It didn't seem like me. It didn't feel like me. Not anymore. And I was so glad.

Ezra appraised the images on screen as he perched on the edge of the stool. He angled round to look at me, a stunned expression in his eyes. He looked at the pouting blonde and then back at me again. "Oh, my goodness! It's you. You're Lady Anastasia." He stared at the photographs of me looking thinner and with swishy, long blonde hair.

My fingers hovered over the keyboard. This was like a therapy session. I hadn't known what to expect, but I hadn't expected this. It was like shrugging off chains, feeling the hard, cold sensation sliding away. An element of relief flooded through my system.

"It *was* me," I clarified, the heat rising in my cheeks. "But not anymore."

I don't know what I expected Zach to say.

I knew he would be surprised. Shocked, even.

What I hadn't expected was the depth of the wounded look in his dark eyes, like he didn't know who I was. White-hot needles of pain seared through my heart.

He pointed at the array of images of me filling the screen. His voice was flat. "Is this a joke? That's you? That party girl? The runaway aristocrat?"

"I didn't run away," I blurted. "I started over." I fiddled with the laptop trackpad for something to do. "But yes. I'm Lady Anastasia McLaren-Kerr."

Zach drank in the shots of Bannock House again on my laptop screen. "And that stately home is yours?"

"It's my parents'," I answered, struggling to look at him.

Zach's confused gaze ran over me, before returning to the screen. His puzzled expression focused on one of the photos of me on my wedding day, waiting for Declan to show up at the church.

I switched onto one of the pictures of Bannock House again.

Zach rubbed at his jaw, trying to unscramble what I'd just told him. He looked like he'd been punched in the stomach. "So, your parents…?"

I flashed a sideways glance at Ezra. "My parents are Earl and Countess Tweed Muir…"

I clenched my hands into fists by my side and then released them. "I never felt like an Anastasia. Bailey was the middle name of my grandmother and I always liked it." I couldn't look at Zach. I steadied my voice and carried on. "I opted for the surname McArthur, after one of my favourite floristry instructors at college, Katie McArthur."

I took a breath. "And yes, I was supposed to marry Declan, who I suspect was the person who waylaid your editor that day." I hoped my voice didn't betray the hammering in my chest. The trouble with opening a box of secrets was that they were all tumbling out at the same time. "His name is Declan Rooney. You probably remember the story. He conned me out of a lot of money and then jilted me at the altar. He vanished into thin air until he spoke to your editor in town."

Ezra offered me a fleeting smile of sympathy.

I felt sick. I so wanted Zach to believe me and hear what I was saying. I tried to compose the words jumping around in my mind. "I obviously thought Declan felt the same way about me as I did about him, but he didn't. He used me as a walking cashpoint, a stupid idiot who could be manipulated and squeezed for absolutely everything I had." I wrapped my arms around myself. "He told me all about this wonderful charity that he was setting up to support kids from underprivileged backgrounds. He said his aim was to help them break into the music industry. I invested in it – or at least, I thought I did."

"But he pocketed the money and then scarpered," concluded Ezra.

"Yes. On what was supposed to be our wedding day."

I bawled up one fist. "I wish I hadn't been so blind, so naïvely trusting."

Zach took charge of the laptop and clicked on a photograph of Declan and me sipping champagne at some charity event. Declan was grinning like a great white shark, as though he couldn't believe his luck.

I rubbed at my arms. "Because of Declan and my own stupidity, I lost everything – at least it felt that way. I lost money of course, but I lost my self-respect, my ability to be open and vulnerable with people. It took a long time to rebuild myself."

I clasped and unclasped my hands in front of me. "I recently travelled to Glasgow to see if I could find Declan and speak to him. I wondered if I could reason with him, more fool me. I spoke to someone else who he'd conned too, but they hadn't seen him."

I got a waft of Zach's delicious woody scent beside me.

Pain gripped his handsome face. "And you're only telling me all this now? I thought..."

His wounded expression tore at my insides, but I was also determined to stand up for myself.

"You don't have an automatic right to all my most intimate secrets just because you showed up on my doorstep asking questions! I worked hard to give myself a fresh start, and to become someone I'm proud of. You don't get to come here and demand a piece of me like you're entitled to it! I'm Bailey McArthur. End of." I turned and jabbed my finger at another photo of myself with my brother and parents, taken about ten years ago. "Can you really not understand why I wanted to lay low, start again without the past hanging over me? If I'd told you, a journalist I still don't know that well, I'd have been insane! It's no one's business but mine."

My voice cracked but I swallowed and fought to keep my composure.

"My mother is so good at all that. She embraces it and it embraces her. She knows her role and she excels at it. I always wanted to be like her – and for a while, I thought I was good at it too, but I'm not and never will be. And that's fine. I like who I am now. Finally."

Ezra's brows bunched together and it felt like he understood me and empathised with me. This celebrated and talented actor, standing in *my* shop, understood me! Zach, however, was another matter.

He turned away from me and stormed out into the street.

"Zach. Wait!" I shouted after him, following him to the shop door. "Zach, please, talk to me."

The street lamps were thronged like orange stars against the backdrop of inky sky out in the street and I shivered without my coat on.

"I thought we were getting closer,' he said, rounding on me. 'But now I feel humiliated.'

"That's never been my intention!" I breathed hard. "Can't you see that it's not about *you*? None of this is about *you*. I was protecting myself." I closed my eyes for a moment in frustration. "Zach, I'm sorry you feel hurt by this but I'm not sorry I lied." I looked back at my shop, at everything I had worked so hard to build, and I felt at peace. "I've had enough of looking over my shoulder, and I'm strong enough now to face the person I used to be and the mistakes I made in the past without it destroying me. But I won't let anyone break me again – including you. And I won't be judged for protecting myself against gossipy tabloid journalism!"

My words vanished into the darkness.

Zach was striding away from me. "I thought I was beginning to get to know you, Bailey. Or Anastasia, or whoever you are. I thought you were different. Open. Principled. The real deal." He swallowed. "I even thought I was falling for you." He let out a dry laugh. "The thought scared the hell out of me, but I knew I couldn't ignore it. Even securing some big exclusive didn't matter anywhere near as much as you." He shook his head ruefully. "Just goes to show. Some journalist I am."

"If that's how you feel, then maybe you're not the person I thought you were either."

He snapped his mouth shut but I could tell he was furious.

Well, let him be furious. I'm pretty mad too.

All I could do was watch him through a tearful haze as he disappeared around the corner to his car.

"Oh, Bailey, I'm so sorry," said Ezra. "When I returned inside the shop, I couldn't help overhearing that..."

"Thank you. At least I know you won't judge me," I said, giving Ezra a weak smile and propping my chin on my hand as I leant on the counter. Tears burned in my eyes but I refused to let them fall. "At the beginning, I had no intention of telling Zach anything. But then I began to get to know him and I wanted him to know the real me." I blinked back my emotions. "But then he started trying to track me down, after sodding Declan spilled his guts to Zach's editor and it just made everything so complicated and messy and there was no way for both of us to get what we wanted." I turned back to Ezra, willing him to understand. "I didn't want anything sitting between us, but to trust him ... after everything ... I just couldn't."

An echo of a smile played around Ezra's wide mouth. "You like him. A lot."

I nodded. "I do. But it's not like he's told me anything about himself either. I guess there's a lot we don't know about each other."

Ezra studied me with his questioning stare. "Does

anyone here know? Have you told the two young ladies who work for you who you are?"

I gave a fierce shake of my head.

"I thought as much."

We fell into a considered silence again.

I looked at him from under my tear-pricked eyelashes.

"It's hard to start over somewhere new when you want people to see you for who you have become and not for what you did in the past. I should know," Ezra said with a sympathetic smile. "But if I've learnt anything from hiding away up here, it's that you can never really escape your past. And nor should you wish to. After all, we are who we are *because* of it. I'm proud of you, Bailey, and I hope I have the same courage when the time comes for me to face my own past."

I felt the tears start to trickle down my face.

As Ezra turned to depart through the fire door at the back of the shop, he squeezed my hand. "Have an early night, dear, and we can talk again in the morning and get arrangements moving with regard my Hogmanay party. That's if your parents are all right with it being held at their home."

"Are you joking?" I tried to laugh through the tumult of emotions. "My mother will be beside herself with joy."

"Well, as long as you're sure."

I nodded.

Ezra flicked me a look. "I'm sorry about what happened between us." He pulled a face. "I was terrified by the threat of the scandal hanging over me. I thought no one would believe me. I thought it would overshadow everything else I've done in my career."

"I know what you mean. And I'm sorry too."

Ezra hesitated at the fire door and smiled. "I know it isn't much notice, Bailey, but if you have the time and the resources, I would very much like to reinstate you as my florist. The regular service for my home?"

I blinked at him through damp lashes. "Seriously?"

"Of course. If it's not too much to ask?" He smiled. "And if we can make it work, I'd like you to do the flowers for New Year's Eve, too. If your parents won't mind that?"

"I… I'm sure they'll be delighted," I said. "Ezra, I don't know what to say. Thank you. We can handle it. I'll have to get Rowan and Amber to help me. It'll mean all hands on deck."

"Well, I shall leave it in your capable hands." Ezra patted me on the shoulder in an avuncular fashion. "If that young man has a problem with who you are – or who you were – then it's up to him to address it and deal with it." He indulged me with one of his famous, lopsided smiles. "And if he's unable or unwilling to do that, then it's his loss." He plonked his hat back on his head. "I'm grateful to you for contacting me, Bailey. I wouldn't blame you for not having anything more to do with this grouchy old sod."

I laughed, despite how wretched I was feeling.

I knew Ezra had been married three times, but he told me again anyway. "I've always been a selfish old bugger, used to getting my own way." A glimpse of regret crossed his face. "I've never been father material. I guess as you get older, you become better able to accept your limitations."

He was trying to justify to himself, and to me, why he'd decided not to get involved with Caroline and Laura.

"Well, for what it's worth, I think you'd make a wonderful dad."

"You have a very kind heart, young lady."

He turned his dashing face up to the night sky and savoured the tossed array of stars. "I took out my frustration and fear about those girls being my daughters on you and I'm sorry. I hope you can accept this old goat's apology."

"Of course," I croaked. Now, it was my turn to apologise. "I shouldn't have interfered. I thought I was doing the best for you, and for them."

"Sometimes, you just have to do what you think is right at the time."

I took his hand and gave it a squeeze, and then watched him vanish into the night with a gallant tip of his trilby.

Once he'd gone, I pressed my back against the door.

What an evening!

I was so glad to have sorted things out with Ezra, but the ball of injustice regarding Zach rolled around inside of me. Why was he acting like I'd purposely tried to humiliate him, hurt him? What would he have done if I'd told him who I was right away? He'd have gone immediately to print with some salacious story about me in *Stargazer*.

Sure, I'd had opportunity to tell him more recently. But the time had never felt quite right. And besides, I still didn't know Zach that well … it was him who was putting a barrier up, not me. I didn't know much about him at all. At least nothing that really mattered.

Except his smouldering eyes, his tall, muscular body, and the kindness that had been showing itself lately.

But Zach still hadn't explained why he was working for *Stargazer* magazine, when he had a CV bursting with previous employment at some of the biggest and most auspicious newspapers.

Being born into my family wasn't a criminal offence! It wasn't like I'd asked for it to be bestowed upon me. It was an accident of birth.

Whereas Marcus was older and would inherit pretty much everything, I'd always known I would have to go a different route. Heather Moore and Flower Power had allowed me to do that. As a teenager, I'd rebelled and become a party girl, but I was older now, and it was a relief to stop socialising with people who I knew weren't real friends. They'd clung to me like needy children, simply because of my connections. They didn't have the first idea about why I loved plants so much, or know that I was driven by an entrepreneurial spirit. They didn't care that I was afraid of moths or that I loved true crime podcasts. All they saw was a ticket into the best parties and a chance of getting their photograph in the papers.

I'd said this to Declan on more than one occasion, but he'd just shrugged and said, "Everybody uses everybody else, honey."

Well, not me.

I hooked a stray hunk of hair behind my ear as I allowed my new perspectives free rein to dance in my head. I looked so different. I *felt* so different.

And I was glad.

I drained my cup of tea and leant towards my laptop, which was perched on the coffee table in front of me.

I realised that I liked myself. What I'd said in the heat of the moment to Zach was true. I was proud of all I had achieved, and I didn't regret it. I had learnt how to stand up for myself. I wouldn't let anyone take advantage of me again – I wouldn't let them use me. I just wished Zach could see the real me too.

My fingers loitered for a few seconds above the keyboard. Zach's bitter words kept turning over and over in my head.

What's he hiding? Why's he working for Stargazer? *It's possible that the magazine might have headhunted him and dangled a huge pay cheque in front of his eyes, but Zach didn't seem the type to compromise his beliefs for the sake of cash.*

I recalled his genuine anger at the exploitation of staff at the fruit farm he'd been investigating. No. Something wasn't right.

I typed Zach's name into the search engine and sat back in my PJs. I'd looked him up before, but decided to do a more thorough examination this time.

Whatever his problem was with me, I hoped he would still continue to help Ezra. I didn't want him to have to be afraid of his past catching up with him, like I was.

I rubbed my gritty eyes. I was wrung out emotionally.

I shuffled my bottom further forward. Several pictures of Zach emerged, showing him at a couple of newspaper award ceremonies in London and New York, dressed in black tie. He looked so confident and dashing.

Another sharp pain jabbed me in the chest, but I dismissed it.

I tried to bury the festering hurt and moved onto the next page, working my way through the various articles he'd written. They included high-profile court reports and interviews with shady figures in the crime world. I noticed the words *Exclusive by Zach Stern* appear again and again. It was obvious he was a first-class journalist and thrived on what he did – and that what he did was not celebrity gossip. It was important work. It mattered.

I clicked onto the following page, making my way down reams of articles he'd written. There were more striking photos of him and impressive bylines from a variety of prestigious newspapers. My laptop screen flickered as headline after headline shimmered in front of my eyes.

Then I sat up straighter.

I noticed that Zach's name was mentioned several times in an email chain on a free speech website. The message exchanges were from a couple of years ago.

I scanned the email chain:

Hi there. I have a potential lead on a land acquisition scam involving local councillors. I'm sure Zach Stern on the London Inquirer would be the go-to journalist for a story like this, but I haven't seen his byline in the paper recently?

Thanks

Adam S

Hi Adam.

No, you wouldn't have done. Apparently, Zach Stern no longer works for them.

Betty H

Hi Betty,

Really?! Do you know why? Funny, as I don't remember seeing anything about his departure in the paper.

Adam S

Good morning, all,

Sorry to jump in, but what Betty said is unfortunately true. Zach Stern is no longer a reporter on that paper.

My sister's best friend works in another department there and she heard he was let go – some sort of misconduct breach.

Sorry to be the bearer of bad news,

Harry D

I shot forward and read over the messages again. Misconduct breach?

But why? What was he supposed to have done?

I sank back against my sofa, letting this sink in.

I leant forward again and scrawled through the next few pages on my laptop screen, but there was no more mention of Zach or why the newspaper had let him go.

If this was true, what on earth had he done that had led to the newspaper dismissing him?

I chewed the inside of my mouth.

If Zach had committed a sackable offence, then that would explain a lot. It would explain why he was so evasive about his personal life and career move to *Stargazer*, and it would explain why he was so closed off when I asked him anything.

The more I thought about it all, the more it was starting to make sense. That must have been why Zach quit his life in London and came up to Scotland. Whatever had happened at the *London Inquirer* he wanted to leave behind. I wasn't the only one trying to escape a previous life. Ezra King, and now Zach, too...

Was becoming a gossip columnist Zach's way of trying to move on after his dismissal from that newspaper? It still seemed an odd choice for him, and it still left me wondering why he was let go.

I picked up my mobile from the coffee table and stared down at the dark screen for a moment. I'd no idea what I was planning to say, but the desire to speak to Zach was too irresistible a force to ignore.

My breathing galloped harder as I pulled up his number and dialled. I waited for him to answer, but he didn't pick up. I frowned as it went straight to voicemail.

I moved to say something and stopped. *What to say?* I would have to admit that I had been stalking him online because only a deep dive had revealed this. When I had googled him previously, none of this had come up on the first few pages of results.

He probably didn't want to speak to me anyway.

I opened and closed my mouth a few times, desperate to say something coherent. In the end, I hung up.

I peered at the clock on my laptop screen. It was coming up for 8pm.

Still clutching my mobile, I returned to my contacts page and sought out Mum's number. Her regal-looking image loomed at me on the screen while I waited for her to pick up.

I couldn't control whatever was happening with my feelings for Zach, but I could do something about helping Ezra. It would also keep me busy and my mind occupied.

I still felt conflicted about Jacob and Samuel now that she'd told me she'd essentially paid them to do a disappearing act. The least Mum could do in return was help me with this.

The beginning of the call was stilted. We both danced around one another. But once I assured her that I hadn't revealed anything to Marcus about Samuel accepting the money, things seemed to thaw between us. No sooner had I mentioned the words *Ezra King*, *party*, and *Bannock House* in the same sentence, Mum was salivating down the line. There was one point where I thought she was about to spontaneously combust.

"But of course, sweetie!" she gasped. "You assure Mr King he's more than welcome to hold his gathering here."

"Right. Good. Thanks, Mum. I'll ring Ezra now and

confirm that with him." I paused. "He's asked me to do the floral arrangements for his house and for the party."

There were a few beats of silence. "Seriously? You?"

I rolled my eyes heavenwards. "Yes, Mum. Me. Your florist daughter. Flower Power. As shocking as that might sound."

"Then everything's good to go," Ezra said when I rang him moments later and told him about my Mum almost biting my hand off about staging his do at our family home. "At least that will give me something to look forward to, after all this debacle with my autobiography. And no one should need an excuse for a little party!" He hesitated. "Now, you're sure you feel up to supplying me with flowers for my house and for my do on Hogmanay?"

I reassured him. "I want to keep busy, so I don't dwell on what a mess I've made of everything." I sighed as thoughts of Zach took hold again.

"That's the spirit," agreed Ezra down the line. "Before all this carry-on, I'd been planning a big Hogmanay party, partly to celebrate the success of my book, but on reflection, this is a much more sensible idea."

"I think so too. I'll fire off an email to Corrie with a link to Bannock House so they can see the venue for themselves. And at least that'll keep your team in the loop."

Ezra's voice was caring, which made me feel even

worse. "That's a great idea. Thank you. And how are you feeling?"

"If you want the truth, I feel like I've been put on a spin cycle."

I could sense Ezra giving me one of his charming smiles. "I recall the time I danced on top of a table bar in Mexico with Farrah Fawcett. Now that was some evening!"

I wasn't sure what that had to do with Zach and me, but it put a smile on my face and for that, I was grateful.

Once I finished speaking to Ezra, I emailed Corrie at Ezra's management agency, with a link to the Bannock House website, as I'd promised.

I didn't expect Corrie to reply but she did almost straight away. Exclaiming in her email, *Wow! Talk about grand. It's perfect.*

I replied back: *There's no need to worry as my mother makes lists about lists and is one of the most fiercely organised people I know. Ezra's also asked me to arrange the flowers for this and for his home. It's a bit of a long story.*

Corrie's further email response made me smile. *Well, I'm glad to hear that. But honestly, if I have to work with any more temperamental showbiz types, I think I'll end up losing my mind!*

I then texted Mum, who replied back seconds later, assuring me I wouldn't have to concern myself with anything except the floral displays and that she would see to the catering arrangements.

Zach continued to hover at the corners of my mind again. He hadn't made any attempt to text or call since I'd told him who I was. He was off licking his wounds, I supposed. We'd both been hiding things, but that didn't mean we couldn't at least be friends.

Steeling myself, I rang his number. I would tell him about Ezra's gathering definitely taking place at my home. Maybe this would be a good excuse for us to talk, now that things had calmed down a little.

My heart travelled up to my throat and wedged itself there. He wasn't picking up again.

I was on the verge of hanging up, when there was a click and a hesitant, "Hi."

I squirmed on the sofa. "Er. Hi. It's Bailey."

I decided to stick to safe ground – this conversation would be about Ezra. "I wanted to let you know that everything has been confirmed about Ezra's party. It's going to be held at Bannock House on Hogmanay. My mum's thrilled." I paused and then decided to go for it. "Do you think you might come along?"

He hesitated. "I'm not sure." There was an edgy silence. "I'm not sure what I'll be doing then. I'll be leaving Heather Moore soon, anyway."

My breathing stilled. "You're leaving? When?"

"Don't know exactly. Once this staff exploitation story is wrapped up, so maybe in a few days." There was a charged pause. "My head's all over the place right now."

Mine too, I thought.

When I went to bed that evening, my heart felt like a lead weight.

It hurt to think I might never see him again.

Chapter Sixteen

The next morning, I repeatedly wound my fingers around the silver ribbon embossed with white reindeer. I couldn't shake off thoughts of Zach. I refused to let my assumptions come between us. But there *was* no "us".

I wanted to call him again, but what would I even say? How would I get him to talk to me?

The temptation lodged itself in my mind and refused to budge. It was as though my heart was galloping off into the distance and my common sense was struggling to keep up. He was going to be leaving Heather Moore in a few days and that would be that.

I continued to play with the ribbon on the Christmas wreath as the lights sprinkled liberally around the shop danced and glittered at the edges of my vision.

Luckily, I hadn't deleted my initial notes or thrown away my sketches from when Ezra first asked me to provide the floral arrangements for his home. As soon as he asked me again, I dug them out and spent the weekend going over colour schemes and adapting them for the new venue.

I looked up suddenly when I caught a flicker of movement outside the shop window.

The breath lodged in my throat when I realised it was Zach. He was hovering there, looking in at me with an injured expression on his face.

I darted out from behind the counter, but he realised I'd spotted him and began striding away. I couldn't catch up, and the dusting of snow we'd had made everything slippery.

"Zach! Please! Wait!"

He glanced over his shoulder, hesitated, and then drew up.

I reached out to touch his coat sleeve. He stared down at my hand resting there.

"Please, Zach. Just give me five minutes."

He flashed me an indecipherable look and the briefest of nods.

I encouraged him back to Flower Power and we stood together awkwardly in the shop doorway. From inside the shop, I could hear Christmas music but it didn't ease the tension between us.

I slid Zach a charged glance.

God, he's gorgeous.

I struggled to unscramble what I wanted to say. I hadn't thought this through. A barrage of questions tumbled around in my head. In for a penny, in for a pound, as my dad would often remark. I gathered myself and took a step off the precipice. What did I have to lose?

"I know about the *London Inquirer*. I mean, I know something happened and you left."

Zach's face froze. "Excuse me?"

I felt my cheeks blanch. "I saw some stuff about it online." I hesitated, trying to read the expression in his dark eyes. "Talk to me, Zach. Please."

Zach's face thundered. "You've been busy."

"Why is it ok for you to poke around in other people's lives but it's not ok for me to do the same?"

He focused on the Christmas shoppers bustling by, their gift bags dangling and jostling. "What can I say? They let me go a couple of years back." His broad shoulders shifted under his heavy coat. Zach rubbed at his face. "You don't get it," he ground out.

"Get what? Zach, talk to me. Please."

He let out a weary sigh and hesitated. His dark eyes glittered. "I…." He gave his head a shake. "Forget it. I can't."

"Zach? What aren't you telling me?"

But he pushed his gloved hands deeper into the pockets of his long coat.

"Look, if you'll excuse me, I should get back to the hotel. I have to file a story by 5pm and then think about when I'm heading back to Glasgow."

"So that's it, is it?" I blurted, my breathing ragged in my chest. "You're not even prepared to talk about it."

Zach didn't reply.

"You're not prepared to let me in, are you?"

Zach shook his head. "What do you want me to say, Bailey? You didn't tell me the truth about who you were."

I sighed. "If you still can't understand why I didn't tell you, then I don't know what else I can say. I didn't do it out of malice or to make you look an idiot, Zach. I would never do that." I gave him a pleading look. "I did it because I thought you were going to blow my life apart. You and Declan, between the two of you. Can't you see that?"

Zach dropped his eyes to the snow-slicked pavement. "As if I would ever do anything to hurt you."

"Well, how was I supposed to know that? You were a complete stranger." *He still is, really*, I thought. I wanted to trust him, but how could I? "Why were you chasing down the story if you weren't going to publish anything?"

This was excruciating.

He raised his eyes to mine. My breathing quickened as he took a couple of steps towards me. I could make out the sexy planes of his full mouth, the long sweep of his nose and the high angles of his cheekbones.

Zach towered over me, his eyes drifting to my mouth. My heart pummelled my ribs. Then he drew back. A defeated expression took him over. "Look, I'm sorry, Bailey. I can't do this."

I felt like I'd been knifed in the chest.

There was nothing more to be said. If he couldn't get past this, if he couldn't open up, then there was no point.

It took me a few moments to compose myself.

"I'm sorry too." I stumbled over the words, blinking back the pain. "I'm sorry that you feel you can't talk to me. Still, no worries. Take yourself off to Glasgow and I'll help Ezra. You don't need to bother yourself with that." I couldn't help the bitterness that crept into my tone.

Zach reacted as though I'd just thrown off my clothes and danced around Heather Moore to the sound of "I'm Too Sexy".

"But you can't," he protested. "Not on your own."

"Who says I can't?"

Zach's dark brows knitted together.

"Bailey, this isn't a good idea. It could be dangerous."

My emotions felt like they'd been stomped over and shattered into pieces. "Yes, it could be, but I'm not going to abandon my friend. Don't you worry about me. I'll be careful."

Zach moved to say something else, but I turned on my heel, biting back tears, and marched back inside my shop.

When I glanced over my shoulder, Zach was gone.

Chapter Seventeen

Christmas was now just a few days away, which meant that Ezra's party was rushing towards us at an alarming speed.

Mum made a few flapping phone calls to me. "And don't forget that you're coming home with your brother to have Christmas with us."

Marcus. We'd exchanged a couple of brief calls and texts recently, but nothing more. He'd been really busy with work, as had I. And I still felt complicit in a lie because I knew why Jacob had left him and about Mum's part in it, so talking to him now was an uncomfortable and guilt-inducing experience. God, it didn't bear thinking about if Marcus discovered what Mum had done, even though Samuel asked her for the money in the first place.

"So, are you going to tell me what's going on?" asked Ezra.

I glanced across at him in the passenger seat of my car.

"I've already told you as much as I know. My mother called last night and suggested I take you over to Bannock House. It's so she can meet you – she's very excited."

Ezra cocked a cynical brow. "I understand that, and it's a very good idea. But what I'm referring to is the sudden disappearance of your journalist friend."

I focused on the road ahead and the banks of hedgerows sprigged with frost. My fingers dug into the steering wheel. "We're not friends. And anyway, Zach had to return to Glasgow. He's been tipped off about another big story."

Ezra switched his attention to his passenger side window. "All very sudden, isn't it?" He slid me a sideways glance. "You reveal your true identity and he announces he's leaving?"

My cheeks zinged. "Well, I suppose that's how the media world works. Fast moving."

Ezra's expression was pensive. After a pause he said, "It's very kind of your mother to invite me over, especially with it being so close to Christmas."

I was relieved Ezra had changed the subject. I tried to smile. "Oh, she couldn't wait to meet you. I'm sorry if this is interrupting any of your pre-Christmas plans."

Ezra grinned and assured me there was no need for an apology. "It's giving me a chance to take a look around your gorgeous family home anyway."

"What with you visiting today and the prospect of her having me and my brother back for Christmas, my mother can barely contain herself."

I nudged my car down a country lane, the Sunday

afternoon sky churning up blobs of moody clouds. The past couple of weeks had been manic in Flower Power, with more wreath orders and festive table decoration orders, not to mention Amber and Rowan and I throwing ourselves into sorting blooms for Ezra's party and planning the first arrangements for his home.

We arrived at the sweeping private road. I got out and entered in the security code, and the gates swept inwards.

I climbed back into the driver's seat and drove up the crunchy, pale pink, gravelled drive.

"Have I ever told you about the time I ended up in a sports car on Route 66 with Oliver Reed and two Playboy Bunnies?" Ezra said, out of nowhere.

"No, you haven't! What was it like?" I asked with a grin.

He gave me a cheeky wink. "One of the best nights of my life!"

I laughed as I pulled up beside the house and climbed out of the car.

Ezra's gaze swept appreciatively across my family home. "Well, well. It's even more spectacular in real life."

"I suppose it is." Growing up, I think I viewed it more like a museum than a home. There were always assorted antiques Marcus and I were never allowed to touch, rooms we weren't allowed to go in, ways we had to behave.

Ezra and I had barely made it up the first couple of steps before my mother came flying out to greet both of us, like an avenging angel wrapped up in pastel cashmere.

She clasped Ezra's hand in hers and pumped it up and down. "It's such an honour to meet you, Mr King. I'm a huge admirer of your work." She flushed prettily. "I loved your role in that mafia drama and I never missed an episode of your detective series."

Ezra bathed in a thousand-watt smile. "The pleasure is all mine, Countess Tweed Muir. And please do call me Ezra."

As I witnessed their exchanges, I thought she was going to dissolve in a puddle in front of him. "Oh please! It's Vanessa. No need for formalities, isn't that right, Bailey?"

I blinked in consternation. What on earth had this strange woman done with my mother? "News to me," I muttered to Ezra out of the corner of my mouth.

He grinned.

Mum ushered us into the hall and I drew up. Bloody hell! The two Christmas trees, which had been standing to attention on either side of the sweeping staircase the last time I was here, were now decorated and studded with crystal and white ribbons with matching lights swathed everywhere.

Mum swung round to Ezra, who was taking in the vaulted ceilings of the hall. "I hope our modest little home meets with your approval."

"Mum!" I ground out, embarrassed.

Ezra slid me a sympathetic wink. "It's perfect, Vanessa."

She bristled with pride. "Excellent! Well, I can assure you that everything is in hand, and Anastasia is doing a sterling job with the flower arrangements. I must say I'm a seasoned professional when it comes to entertaining," she preened. "I will take you on a proper tour of the house once we've had afternoon tea. Anastasia's father is just finishing up at bridge club and will join us directly."

I squinted through the windscreen as the light became almost ethereal over the fields on our journey back to Heather Moore.

It had been a very successful visit, with Mum pulling out all the stops to make Ezra feel welcome. She had organised for Mrs Bamber to serve us a sumptuous array of sandwiches, scones and cakes. Mrs B was known for her coconut and cherry cake, and I'd never had a better scone in my life than her homemade creations.

Ezra made a show of patting his stomach as he slumped beside me in the car on the way home. "Good grief! I think I'll have to hibernate like a bear for the rest of the winter!"

I smiled. "Between them, Mum and Mrs B always bring out the big guns when we have visitors. Mrs Bamber doesn't know the meaning of the phrase 'less is more', bless her."

'Well, it was met with much appreciation by me,' said Ezra, who turned to gaze out of the window at a couple of red deer skittering around on top of the hills. The whole landscape looked like something from a gorgeous, rural Christmas card.

He turned back to me, a hesitant look on his face. "Bailey, please don't think I'm trying to interfere, but don't you think you ought to contact that Zach chappie?"

I kept my eyes on the road. "I've tried, Ezra, but he doesn't want to know."

He let out a tired sigh. "It's Christmas in a few days. I know I can be somewhat of a Grinch at the best of times, but you're a lovely young woman. You and Zach shouldn't let your pride get in the way of something wonderful."

"You're very sweet," I said with a smile. "I'm not too proud. I've tried to reach out, and to explain, but Zach won't hear it. Or he doesn't care. I don't know." I fought not to think about Zach's intense, dark gaze as I guided the steering wheel.

"He didn't appear to me like a man who doesn't care. Quite the opposite, in fact. Maybe he cares a little too much—"

"Zach made it clear he doesn't want anything to do with me. He said he has other important stories to focus on, and he practically left tyre tracks with how fast he drove off." I flicked Ezra a look. "And Zach has his own secrets. He obviously has no intention of sharing them with me."

Ezra folded his arms beside me. "And why do you think that might be?"

I paused as we eased up to the junction that would take us past Flower Power and towards Ezra's home. "I really don't know," I said, then glanced sideways at him. "But thank you for caring. It means a lot."

"Friendship," Ezra said. "Genuine friendship, that is. Is worth its weight in gold."

I smiled. I found this charming, eloquent man so easy to talk to. I still regretted our falling out over Caroline and

Laura, which was why I'd decided not to mention them. I didn't want to rock the boat again so soon after reconciling with him. He knew they were looking for him, and he knew how to get in touch with them. I hoped he would seek out a relationship with them on his own, but ultimately it was up to him.

Our disagreement and subsequent reunion actually seemed to have made our friendship stronger somehow; it had broken down a barrier.

I drew up outside Ezra's home, noting its manicured lawns that were tipped with frost and the swathes of gold Christmas lights draped around the nearby trees. There were glowing lights from inside too, casting amber pools of light through the mullioned windows.

"Bailey." Ezra squeezed my hand. "I know we haven't been acquainted very long, but I feel I have something of the measure of you by now. And I'm not getting out of this car until you tell me what you've *not* been telling me about your handsome journalist." He gestured to Duxbury Hall. "I'll sit here all evening if I must. I've got nothing and nobody to rush in there for, apart from Mrs Watson and Jackson."

I switched off the car engine, defeated. "They don't call you a cantankerous old bugger for nothing, do they."

His expression was mock outrage. "How dare you," he said but with an impish gleam in his eyes. "I'm serious, Bailey. Talk to me."

I fumbled about with my car keys, then sighed and settled back in my seat.

"All right, then. I found out that Zach was dismissed from a newspaper for misconduct." I examined the branches of the gnarled trees wrapped in lights for a few moments. "I tried to talk to him about it, but he just clammed up." I shook my head in dismay. "It feels so hypocritical, Ezra. *I'm* not allowed to have a past, or to keep anything from *him*, but *he's* keeping so much from *me*. I just want him to feel he can trust me, but maybe there's too much … dishonesty between us now for that." I rubbed at the knees of my dark jeans. "As soon as Zach found out I was the 'runaway aristo' he'd been chasing, he just wanted to distance himself from me. He seemed so angry … disproportionately angry. Unfairly angry. I didn't do anything wrong. *I* was the one who was deceived and conned and left at the altar. I worked so hard to heal, and to start again, and I didn't want my new life to be tainted by the stain of who I used to be. Yet he's acting like *I* was the one who was conning people and stealing their money and breaking their heart." I stared ahead through the car windscreen at the twisted branches. "I don't deserve that. At least, I don't think I do. And now it turns out he's not being upfront about his own past, yet he's holding mine against me."

My shoulders sunk. "Lady Anastasia McLaren-Kerr. I never wanted the bloody title in the first place or what goes with it. It isn't me. It's not who I want to be, yet he's acting like I've committed some crime just by being born into this family." I raised my right hand from the steering wheel and flicked it. "It's not fair."

Ezra considered my words in silence for a moment. He appraised his spectacular property out of the passenger side window. Then he looked across at me, his light eyes like shards of glass in the descending dark. "I think you're wrong. I don't think he wants to distance himself from you at all."

"What do you mean?"

Ezra twisted himself round in the passenger seat. "I think Zach's gone *because* he's got feelings for you. You've made him doubt himself and his choices." Ezra's mouth pressed itself into a sympathetic smile. "Perhaps all this has brought back some painful memories for him and he's not prepared to make himself … vulnerable … and be hurt for a second time." Ezra angled his head to one side so that his thick crop of silver hair flopped onto his face. "And if something did happen in his career that he's still struggling with, then I would say it's more to do with him than it is with you."

My heart tightened. "But what am I supposed to do with that if he won't talk to me?" I rested my head back against the driver's seat and stared out at the blueberry-black sky. "I wish I'd been able to tell him who I was when Declan began trying to stir things up again, but I just couldn't." I gestured out of the driver side window. "I love the life I've built for myself here and I just couldn't face having everything rubbed in my face again. I want the people in my life to like me for me, and for my business to thrive because I'm good at what I do. I actually felt like I was being *more* honest, because this is who I am and not the title

I was born with. But Zach doesn't see it that way. He only sees my past and my name. I thought, of all people, he would understand." Hurt rampaged through me. "It's like as soon as he discovered who I really was, he pushed me away."

Ezra considered this. "Maybe he understands better than you know, and this is what's bothering him so much. I think you should keep trying with him, Bailey. His pride is hurt. But he will come round, I'm sure of it. And, remember. He's a journalist for a gossip magazine, where a story like yours is a gold mine. If he didn't care about you, he would have thought nothing of writing that story, wouldn't he?"

"He *doesn't* care," I insisted, but deep down I knew that was a lie. Ezra's words were forcing me to acknowledge that he might be right.

He's a good person, my heart told me.

"Maybe," I said quietly.

"Right-oh, I think we have made some progress." Ezra opened his door and began to get out of the car. He adjusted his woollen scarf and stooped down with a dramatic flourish that was so much a part of his charismatic presence. "I think you'll find, young lady, that I am correct on this matter." His eyes twinkled at me. "Maybe in some sort of twisted fashion, Zach thinks that by leaving you to enjoy your new life without exposing your secrets, he's showing you exactly how much he cares. How about that?"

He winked and then closed the car door before marching away towards his front door.

Chapter Eighteen

Monday morning dawned with buttery, festive sunlight and a crisp breeze. There had been more snow and a papery layer of it clung to everything.

In the shop, I snatched up my notebook as a distraction from my thoughts of Zach and the conversation with Ezra, forcing myself to try and come up with some new promotional ideas I could introduce into the shop in January when sales would no doubt be thin on the ground.

Amber and Rowan listened, shooting each other concerned glances, as I dislodged any further dissection of Zach's behaviour and reeled off the ideas I'd come up with, like an over-enthusiastic jack-in-the-box. I hadn't mustered up the courage to tell them yet about me being Lady Anastasia, though I promised myself I would, when the time was right. I was still too wounded by Zach's reaction and I wanted to get a handle on my emotions first, before launching myself into another "scenario".

"What do you think about loyalty cards?" I said. "Every time a customer makes a purchase, we could stamp a card for them and when they've made their sixth purchase, they're entitled to a free bouquet."

I used my finger to scan down my page of frantic handwriting.

"Or how about a Little Ones Gardening Club? Parents could sign their kids up to it and they can get a packet of seeds and a pot once a quarter. Might encourage the children to get interested in botany from an early age? We could also do monthly social media posts focused on a particular species of flower or a house plant that we have in stock and—"

Amber held up one hand. I noticed her nails were slicked with Christmassy, bottle-green polish infused with glitter.

"Stop right there, boss."

"Why? Don't you like any of my ideas?"

"It's not that," said Amber, coiling one finger around the end of her plait. "It's just that you seem a bit … manic…'

"Well, this is my business and I want it to be a success."

Rowan nodded. "We get that, but you need to slow down … take a bit more time for you."

Amber chewed her bottom lip. "And I hope I'm not putting my size sevens in it, but we both noticed that the sexy journalist hasn't been around for a while…"

I shrugged and hoped I looked unfazed.

"He's gone back to Glasgow. He's working on some big story," I said breezily.

Amber eyed Rowan meaningfully.

"Honestly," I said. "It's all fine."

"Sure," said Rowan. "If you say so."

Thankfully, the shop door opened, bringing with it more customers before I could respond to that.

"Right," I said, instead. "Action stations, ladies."

The morning flashed past, bringing with it a visit from a nearby nursery.

The little ones toddled around, marvelling at our miniature Christmas trees, the tubs of ruby-red poinsettia and our fake snow-decked festive wreaths. They were delighted with the little packs of sunflower seeds we gave them to plant.

Once they departed, their stubby fingers waving goodbye, I took a few moments to slip away to my office and ring my mother, to make sure there were no other last-minute items she wanted me to bring over for Christmas.

"You can bring a guest with you for Christmas lunch, darling, if you wish. Plenty of room at the inn."

I gripped my mobile, shutting out thoughts of Zach. "Thanks, Mum, but I don't have anyone to bring."

I could hear her brain ticking over. "Well, in that case, I could invite over that handsome young nephew of Lucinda Duncan's. His name is Troy Meadows and he's a chiropractor."

"For God's sake!" I snapped. "My back's fine, and I

don't want to be set up on Christmas Day with Lucinda Duncan's bloody nephew!"

Mum tutted at my outburst.

"It's Christmas dinner, Mum, not a blind date."

My mother started to make a series of protesting sounds. "I've seen photos of him. He's very attractive. Reminds me of that young man in *Outlander*. He's split with his girlfriend recently and his parents are on a cruise, so he's at a bit of a loose end."

"Charming," I grunted under my breath. "Marcus is going to be coming on his own this year as well, don't forget. Let's not rub it in."

Before my mother could come back at me with a counter argument, I rounded off the call. "See you on Christmas Eve, Mum. Text me if I need to bring anything else with me."

Amber, Rowan and I spent the remainder of the day making sure the final flower orders were placed for Ezra's event, so that we could hit the ground running on the 28th and start working on the displays. We also ensured we had enough gold, silver, and white satin ribbon in stock. I'd already delivered the first of Ezra's flowers for his home and he'd been thrilled with the myriad scents, textures, and shades I'd come up with, especially the berry, fig, and pine cone decorations.

It was a busy time, keeping up with order collections,

local deliveries, and the increased footfall. I knew January would be much quieter, so I tried to enjoy the busy period and embrace the festive chaos.

At the end of the day, the three of us each nursed a mug of tea and demolished a flapjack from the local bakery. I was so glad I'd found Amber and Rowan to help, and I hoped they felt like they were learning something that they could put to good use in the future, whatever they decided to do.

I felt satisfied as I climbed the stairs to my flat that evening. It had been a productive yet hectic day. Being occupied helped filter out thoughts of Zach.

I was shrugging off my quilted jacket in the hall and dumping my bag, when there was a loud, insistent banging on my door.

A familiar voice made me start. "Anastasia? Answer the door. It's me, Marcus."

I yanked open the door to see my big brother standing there in his winter coat. I moved to haul him into my arms. "Wow! This is a lovely surprise! I'm seeing you in two days anyway."

But Marcus was stiff and pulled away from me, his face pinched and his deep blue eyes wet. "No, you won't be seeing me at Christmas. Are you joking?!"

"Sorry?"

"Why didn't you tell me? How could you do that?" He shook his head. "You know damn well what I'm talking about. Your visit to Mum the other week. About me. About Jacob." He ground his jaw. "The money Mum gave Samuel." His expression turned to granite. "Who is no longer with the agency, but you probably knew that as well."

Dread gripped me. *Oh God.* He knew.

My stomach churned at his charged expression. I wanted him to understand how awful I felt about it, how complicit, even though Mum had kept her suspicions about Jacob from me to begin with. "Oh Marcus, I'm so sorry. Please believe me. I only found out about it from Mum the other week when I went over to see her."

Marcus's mouth contorted.

"I suspected Mum might know more about your broken engagement than she was letting on. That's why I wanted to talk to her." My voice was pleading. I was willing him to understand. "I thought I was protecting you by not telling you about Samuel and the money. You had enough heartache to deal with and I didn't want to add to it." I stopped and took in his clothes. "Have you just come from work?"

"Well, I don't normally dress like this on a day off." His eyes glistened with emotion. There were lilac smudges of tiredness under his eyes. No wonder. From what Mum had said, Marcus had been practically living, eating, and breathing work in order to blank out his heartache, or at least try to. "I've been at a meeting in Glasgow with another advertising agency," he said. "And guess who was there?"

"Who?" I reached out a hand to comfort him, but Marcus wrenched his away.

"Samuel's sister, Siobhan, that's who. She told me Mum gave Samuel money as a bribe." His eyes hardened and he clenched his jaw. "Jacob and Samuel are living together in some riverside apartment in Glasgow now. Siobhan's horrified by what her brother did. The whole family is, apparently."

When I didn't say anything, Marcus let out an incredulous laugh. He stared down at me. "Wow. I thought I could trust you. I thought you were on my side."

My hand shot out again towards him. I wanted to comfort my brother. I wanted him to believe I wouldn't deceive him. "No. You don't understand. You've got it wrong. You don't know the whole story."

He recoiled. Pain pulled at his mouth.

A lump of worry was threatening to choke me. Marcus was looking at me as though he didn't recognise me anymore.

"I'm sorry. I should've told you when Mum told me, but I wanted to protect you. What would telling you about the money have achieved, Marcus? You would've gone straight to Mum and you would have had a confrontation."

"Don't insult my intelligence."

Desperate to put things right between us, I appealed to him again. "Marcus, come in. Please. We can talk about it. Honestly. Whatever you've been told, you don't know the whole story. There's something you should know..."

He plunged one hand into his coat pocket for his car keys. "No thanks. I know enough. There's nothing left to say." He dismissed a tear trickling down his cheek with the back of his hand. Emotion tore through me like a whirlwind.

"I hope you and Mum enjoyed your cosy little chat about me. Have a lovely Christmas, won't you?"

I stared at him. "You're not coming? Marcus, please come. Mum and Dad will be heartbroken if you don't come. We're family."

"Family? Don't make me laugh. If that's family, I don't want any part of it."

I called after him, but Marcus was already thumping down the staircase towards his snow-dusted car.

Chapter Nineteen

"Marcus. Please pick up."

Hot tears clustered in my eyes. My repeated call; my pleas for him to speak to me were going unanswered. His mobile kept going straight to voicemail.

I paced in vain up and down in my sitting room, but my brother didn't ring me back.

I made the decision to call Mum next. "Marcus was just here in a real state. He knows, Mum. He knows about the money you gave Sam." I groaned. 'I knew we should have been honest with him.'

"How on earth did he find out?"

"It doesn't matter." I screwed my eyes up as my Christmas tree lights dazzled. "Marcus is the innocent victim in all this, Mum. He's the one who's hurting and thinking his own family are keeping secrets from him. I should never have listened to you. I should have told him."

Mum fell quiet down the line.

"If you must know, Samuel's sister Siobhan moved jobs recently and now works for some advertising agency in Glasgow. She attended the same meeting as Marcus today and they got talking."

"Oh bugger!"

My teeth ground against one another. "Let's face it, Mum. You've got previous form for meddling in our relationships."

Mum ignored this, of course. "I'll speak to your brother," she said briskly. "Once he realises we had the best of intentions and that it was Samuel who asked for the money with the intention of blackmailing me, he'll see sense."

My hackles rose as I honed in on my mother's use of the word *we*.

"Oh no. Don't you dare include me in all of this." I ran a frustrated hand over the top of my ponytail. "Has Dad made any attempt to speak to Marcus to try and smooth things over?"

Mum was evasive. "Your father doesn't know everything yet."

I was incredulous. "Hold on. Are you saying that you didn't tell Dad you gave Samuel money?"

"Not yet, but I will."

"I can't believe you. Are you even capable of being straight with anyone?"

I ended the call abruptly and then hurled a sofa cushion against the far wall.

My bloody family!

All I wanted to do was speak to Marcus. I wanted to explain and to beg his forgiveness and make everything right between us again. Mum's relationship meddling had been done with what she thought was the best of intentions, but the whole thing had blown up in our faces. In trying to protect Marcus from knowing about Samuel being a money-grabbing bastard, he'd concluded I was complicit by not telling him.

It galvanised my thoughts. No more harbouring secrets and willing them to vanish.

But dear God, what a horrendous Christmas this was going to be!

When my mobile rang a few moments later, I scrambled forward, almost tumbling off the edge of the sofa in my haste to answer it. Was it Marcus? Or Zach?

But it wasn't either of them. It was my accountant, reminding me about my end of January tax return.

On Tuesday, I was still festering over what had happened with Marcus. He was stubborn, like me. Mum was convinced he'd still come for Christmas but I wasn't so sure. The gift I had bought for Marcus – a gorgeous wooden pen set carved from an old Scottish whisky barrel in Tyree – was wrapped up in glossy blue and silver paper. I wasn't sure whether to pack it, but I decided to think positively just in case. My stomach dipped. I tried to call him again but he didn't answer.

He wasn't even picking up the phone to Dad – probably assuming Dad had been in on it too. Needless to say, Dad was exasperated with Mum when she finally told him, but not entirely surprised. My parents' relationship had always been a mystery to me.

I forced myself to refocus on the shop. Amber asked to leave early as she was in a blind panic about getting a couple of last-minute gifts before tomorrow when Christmas Eve would arrive with all its fanfare. Rowan was helping me tidy up, water the plants and deadhead a few of the flowers before we closed for the day. She was telling me about some gorgeous festive flower table decorations she'd spotted earlier in the week in a department store in town when Ezra suddenly burst through the door. He was out of breath and his eyes were wild.

"I don't know what to do!" he burst out from under his baker-boy cap.

"Ezra! What's wrong? Are you ok?" I said.

He scrambled about in his coat pocket and thrust a crumpled sheet of paper at me. "That journalist friend of yours said this might happen."

I frowned at him and unfolded the sheet of A4 paper. In bold type was printed:

WE KNOW ABOUT YOUR DAUGHTERS. PUBLICLY RETRACT BOOK CONTENTS OR THEY WILL PAY IN KIND.

I blinked at Ezra, revulsion taking hold. Shit.

Ezra's expression was grim as he stuffed the note back in his pocket and hovered by the counter, his shoulders sinking under his coat.

"What on earth was I thinking? I revealed all that information in my book, to do good; to name names and show those cretins up for what they really are. And now my honesty is backfiring." He shoved a lock of stray hair away from his brow. "I'm ashamed to admit it, but I feel as though it's taken something like this to give me a short, sharp kick up the rear end."

"What do you mean?"

His expression was grim. "Whoever these villains are, they're ratcheting up by their threats. I was hoping Zach had got it wrong, but it seems he hasn't." He set his jaw. "I think I'm going to contact Caroline and Laura. I don't know how serious this threat is and it could be dangerous. They didn't ask for this."

"What are you saying?"

Ezra pinned me to the spot with desperate eyes. "I have to do what's right by those girls. Christ knows, I haven't so far." He flashed me an apologetic look and rubbed at his face in frustration. "I'm not prepared to take the risk when it comes to two innocent women who may be my daughters. Whoever is behind this has to be stopped. I've got to stop thinking about myself for once."

I nodded. "Come on. Let's step outside for a moment." We moved out onto the doorstep of Flower Power, leaving behind the festive scent of pine needles.

The afternoon sun was struggling to appear from behind

the patchy clouds and our Christmas window display of the ice palace glittered against the white tea roses.

While Ezra stared straight ahead, his recognisable profile pensive, I plunged my hands into the pockets of my grey trousers. "I understand that you've focused your mind on what's important, and I admire it. But what about how you'll feel in six months or a year from now? If you do issue a public statement, retracting your comments and essentially clearing these people of their wrong-doings over the years, they'll have got away with not only what they did back then but what they are doing now." I turned to him. "Isn't that sending the wrong message to people like them?"

Ezra's mouth turned down.

I felt so bad for him. He was torn between two different versions of trying to do the right thing. Here he was, a celebrated actor, used to being the centre of his own universe and revered by so many people, and now he was confronted with the fact that he had two adult daughters who had been put in danger by his attempts to stand up for himself.

"Caroline and Laura are about the same age as me. It's not as if they're little girls. They grew up with famous mothers and will be able to get security, if they need it." I offered him a small smile. "Why don't you speak to them? Tell them what you've been trying to do in your book and tell them about this note. And also tell the police. They should take this threat seriously."

Ezra dragged a worried hand down his face.

I took a step closer to him. "I know it's hard, Ezra, and it might not be what you wanted, or the way you wanted, but you know what you have to do."

Ezra stared up at the Christmas lights strung from the lampposts. The shimmery images of Santa and his sleigh sent a golden glow onto the planes of his face. After processing what I'd just said, he looked at me.

"I suppose you're right. Come on then, Lady Anastasia. Lead the way."

I gave him a jokey glower.

Back inside the shop, I asked Amber and Rowan to keep an eye on the counter, collected my laptop and gestured to Ezra to follow me to my office, where I closed the door behind us.

"You can Zoom call Caroline and Laura on this. I'll help you set it up."

Ezra looked appalled. "What? You mean now? Right this minute?"

"Yes, why not? No time like the present. This problem isn't going to go away."

I set up my laptop, created a Zoom meeting and then texted Caroline and Laura the details. I saw the blue ticks appear, so I knew they had both received the message. I hoped they were ready to meet the man who they strongly suspected was their father...

"I'm going to meet them on this?" he said, staring with increasing panic at the blank screen. "What the hell am I going to say to them?" His voice sounded small and he suddenly wasn't the confident man-about-town I was used to.

"Just tell them the truth," I said simply. "About you, about their mothers, about your book and the situation you've found yourself in."

I offered him an understanding smile before launching the Zoom meeting. I made a move to leave to give Ezra some privacy and eased open my office door, letting the sound of Amber's pleasant chatter and the tune of "White Christmas" drift in.

I saw Ezra's startled face as the laptop screen flashed indicating that at least one of the girls had joined the Zoom call and was in the "waiting room".

"What are you doing?" he whispered to me.

"I'm going back to work."

Ezra pointed to the empty chair next to him. "Oh no you don't! You sit right there."

"But—?"

Ezra's expression brooked no argument, however, so I rolled my eyes, closed the office door again, and took up the seat next to him.

"What do I do now?" he said.

"You let them in to the meeting," I said. "They're in a digital waiting room."

"How very bizarre," he frowned. "I must admit, I wasn't as nervous as this on opening night at the Old Vic."

He clicked to let the first participant, Caroline, into the call.

Her pretty face appeared on the screen. She was in an office, talking to someone, who I presumed was a work colleague. When she saw me first, an engaging smile broke across her features. "Hi, Bailey. Well, this is a lovely surprise. How are you?" Then her voice vanished when she caught sight of Ezra.

Her eyebrows jumped under her thick, dark fringe. She gave me a hesitant look. "What's going on?"

Before I could answer, Laura was invited in by Ezra, and her pale features morphed onto the split screen. She appeared to be at home. There was a bookcase behind her and on top of it was a holiday photograph of Laura and a smiley brunette, both gazing into each other's eyes. That must be her partner.

Ezra offered me several petrified, sideways glances. He reminded me of a deer caught in headlights. "Go on," I whispered. "Just say the first thing that comes into your head."

Ezra cleared his throat and studied both images of his daughters on the screen. "Hello. Hello there. Hi. Um … hi."

Caroline gestured to the colleague hovering beside her, and seemed to be explaining that she needed to take a personal call, though she was on mute so the only sound was Ezra awkwardly greeting his daughters for the first time.

Laura ran a hand through her messy bob and gave Ezra an unfathomable stare.

Caroline sat rigidly in her leather chair. Her lipstick coordinated with the berry shade of her satin blouse and she looked elegant and professional. Like her sister, her eyes scanned Ezra with a look of shock, as though not quite believing it.

"Go on," I encouraged Ezra.

Ezra gradually began to relax and talk. He faltered at first, struggling to find the right words, but soon the story of his young life and the numerous affairs he'd had came spilling out. I could tell that the girls were wondering where he was going with this story and how long they would have to listen to it before he got to the parts they were specifically interested in. I also noticed he hadn't asked them anything about themselves. Still, at least he was here and that was a good thing.

"I had a rampant ego that was fuelled by my modelling days in London. I would languish in bed all day then get dressed up and haunt The Marquee Club. I was obsessed with David Bowie and copied everything he wore. Everyone was, to be honest, and we were like glittering jewels amongst the gaudy, neon venues of Soho."

Ezra smiled at the memory as the three of us listened.

"I had long, shaggy hair, cheekbones you could ski-jump off, and the brash attitude to match."

He regaled the girls with tales of the strict dress code of Annabel's nightclub and the various hangers-on that would congregate outside in the hope of gaining access to its hallowed chambers. "It felt rather like you were at a party in someone's opulent drawing room!" he exclaimed.

Then something clouded in his eyes. I could sense he was gearing up to a revelation and I hoped that Caroline and Laura would bear with him until then.

"I got noticed on the modelling circuit. After RADA, it wasn't what I wanted to do, but I needed the money and it didn't take much effort to lean against a wall and look brooding and rebellious." He rubbed at his chin. "I love what I do – being able to transform into someone else; to inhabit another life – but there's also a dark side to the industry. I didn't realise… There were things… Back then I was so naïve, and what I witnessed along the way…"

He trailed off, and I could see that he'd got their attention now.

"Like what?" Caroline asked. I realised these were the first words either of the girls had spoken to their father.

I watched Ezra carefully consider what he was about to say, so as not to cause the girls undue alarm. "You might have heard that my autobiography was released very recently. In it I've laid bare many of the traumatic and distasteful memories I carry with me from that time as a young model and actor."

Laura's light, whispering voice echoed out. "Yes, we're reading it now, but we haven't got to those parts yet… It's been all over the press, though. Sounds like it's rather explosive."

Ezra snorted. "That's rather an understatement." He sat back in his chair. "I've kept quiet for years because … well, for lots of reasons. Fear, shame, a misguided sense of duty… For a long time, I just wanted to forget it ever happened, but I'm not prepared to do that anymore." He shifted in his chair. "But now I'm beginning to wonder if I've done the right thing."

"What do you mean?" asked Caroline.

Ezra rooted in his coat pocket, located the note, and held it up to the screen so Caroline and Laura could read it.

"But… My God! Who is it from? And how do they know about us?"

Ezra sat forward, his cleft chin growing hard. "I don't know for sure. I have my suspicions, but it could be a few people. There are a number of names I've shamed in the book, and some of them aren't thrilled about that, to say the least. But there's nothing in the book about either of you. I didn't know about you when I wrote it, so I don't know how they found out." He shrugged his shoulders and looked down at his hands. "I… I had to leave London for a while. I had to get away because…" He took a deep breath and met his daughters' eyes. "It turns out that an eminent film director has spread rumours throughout the industry that I stole a confidential movie script, because his father is named and shamed in my book. He tried to blacklist me and I lost roles over it, but please believe me when I say that I didn't do it."

Caroline chewed the inside of her mouth. "That's awful! But Ezra, you haven't said what it was you saw during your career that's stirring up trouble. What are they afraid that you'll reveal?"

I could see how hard it was for Ezra to talk about this, especially with Caroline and Laura when their relationship was only minutes old. "The exploitation of young actors and models, blackmail, sexual assault, as well as the awful and, frankly, illegal working conditions imposed on staff at a well-known London fashion house. You name it, I saw it."

Caroline's insistent words made me start. "You have to name and shame the people responsible. It's important, Ezra. It matters."

Ezra's reluctance was clear. "But Caroline, they're *threatening* you and Laura." Realisation gripped his features. "I'm not worried about myself. I've been in this game for a long time now, but I couldn't bear it if they hurt either of you in order to get to me."

Laura appraised her father with a cool stare. "A tad late to enter the Father of The Year competition, isn't it?"

"Touché," I muttered under my breath at Ezra.

"I'm sorry but I agree with Caroline," Laura went on, "you have to carry on and not waver. You have to clear your name and you're right to expose what they did. How will anything change if you had stayed quiet??"

Ezra shifted in his chair. "But it could be dangerous. I'd never forgive myself—"

Caroline was imploring. "And we'd never forgive you if you try to redact what you've said and let them off scot-free. It's important, Ezra. This kind of thing really matters."

Ezra pushed himself upright in his chair. He studied the images of the pretty, forthright young women in front of him. "I admire your courage, I really do. I think we ought to go to the police, but that will mean that the story will leak about us ... about us possibly being family. Are you sure you're ready for that?" He sighed. "Obviously I'm not going to win any medals, but when I said I didn't know either of you existed, I was telling the truth."

There was a considered silence.

"If you want to do something for us now, you'll push on with publicity for your autobiography and make sure it continues to receive the fanfare it deserves," announced Caroline, the emotion in her voice practically bouncing off the cream walls of her office. There was also an odd expression on her face.

"Are you all right?" I asked her.

She didn't reply.

Ezra grew more frustrated. "You don't know what it feels like to have carried around something like this."

"Oh yes, I do," bit back Caroline, her distraught image on the laptop screen giving me cause for concern.

"Caroline? What is it?"

Her eyes, daubed in beige shadow, glittered with tears. "I was sexually harassed at work eight years ago."

Ezra stiffened beside me.

Laura lent closer to the camera. "What? You never told me that."

Caroline swallowed. "It's not a time in my life I like to revisit."

Ezra's heated glance at me was a mixture of anger and confusion. "What happened?"

"I ended up leaving."

Ezra struggled to contain himself. "And the bastard who was harassing you? What happened to him?"

"He was transferred. And promoted! Can you believe it?

They removed the problem and foisted it on to someone else in another department, and gave the guy a pay rise."

Ezra stared with incredulity at Caroline's troubled image on my laptop.

"I couldn't stay after that. I needed a fresh start." Caroline gathered herself. "Since then, attitudes and procedures have changed to a large degree, although there's still so much room for improvement. I'm convinced that had it occurred now, the outcome would've been so much different."

Laura's voice broke. "I agree with Caroline. You have to expose what these people did and stick by your autobiography."

For a moment, it was as though Caroline had almost forgotten about Laura being present. She widened her eyes in surprise, before they misted over again.

"We're big girls," carried on Laura. "We can get some additional security if we need to."

Caroline sniffed and nodded.

Ezra let out a frustrated sigh. "But these people sound like they won't give up easily."

"Neither will we," insisted Laura. "All the more reason to stand up to them."

I shot Ezra a fleeting smile. Then I turned to glance at Caroline and Laura's images on my laptop. "Determined, wilful, courageous… I can't think for the life of me where they get that from."

Ezra pulled a face. "Very amusing." He leant forward, his brows gathering as he contemplated the situation. "But I want you to take this threat seriously. I want you both to come to Heather Moore where I can arrange protection."

Both Laura and Caroline began to protest. "It's Christmas Eve tomorrow!" stuttered Laura.

"Yes, I'm aware of that, but I can't do this if I'm worried about you. I have great security, and with the people I use, you'll be far safer up here. We can reassess after the holiday." Ezra warmed to his idea. "Will you both come?"

"I'm supposed to be spending Christmas with my girlfriend," said Laura. "I'll have to see if I can persuade Tori to come too because I'm not leaving her on her own."

"Wonderful!" answered Ezra. "Caroline?"

"I'm going with two friends to a cottage in Cornwall. We've had it booked for ages I can't just—"

Ezra arched his brows.

Caroline shrugged helplessly. "Ok, ok. I get the hint. If Laura's in, so am I."

Ezra clapped his ringed hands together in delight. "Excellent. I'll make the necessary arrangements straight away." He paused. "Oh, and before I forget, there's something else. I'm throwing a little get-together on New Year's Eve at Bailey's family home," announced Ezra. "And I'd be honoured to have you both accompany me."

Caroline and Laura both gawped down their screens at their famous father.

"I won't take no for an answer. I insist." He leant forward, looking more intently into the camera. "And if, as seems very possible, we find out through DNA testing that we are related, I'm very happy to go public about our relationship."

Caroline and Laura looked shocked.

"Laura, if you're happy to do this, then so am I," said Caroline a little nervously.

Laura blew out a breath. "In that case, it looks like we'll be coming to Scotland for Christmas!"

Well, well.

Ezra King might just turn out to be a wonderful father after all.

Chapter Twenty

Ezra called his management team as soon as the Zoom call ended and asked for confidential arrangements to be made immediately for Caroline, Laura, and her partner, Tori, to be flown to Glasgow on Christmas Eve morning, collected at the airport and taken straight to Ezra's estate. It sounded like a lovely idea. That way, the three of them could get to know one another and Ezra could ensure their safety.

Ezra also confided in me that he and the two girls were undertaking a fast-track DNA test, to confirm what they suspected – and indeed now hoped.

Meanwhile, I packed up my laptop, thinking how odd life was. If those idiots hadn't threatened Caroline and Laura, perhaps Ezra would never have made contact with them and what a loss that would've been for all three of them.

Ezra snapped shut his phone and observed me. "Thank you, Bailey."

"I haven't done anything."

He snorted. "We both know that's not true."

He followed me to my office door and opened it for me. "It shouldn't have taken something like this to make me think of anyone other than myself. I'm still getting used to possibly being a father, and I know there's a long way to go, but…"

"You want to do what's best for them."

We stepped back into the shop, suddenly surrounded by soft chatter, the scent of Christmas in the air and festive songs buzzing out from the speakers.

"Seems to me that you're already doing very well."

Ezra blushed and stared ahead for a moment, observing Rowan assisting a customer. "If the DNA test confirms what we suspect, I'd like to go public about the girls being my daughters, once all this drama with my book is over." He smiled to himself. "I want to do it properly, Bailey, not like an afterthought, and not rushed into it by these horrid people. I want to get to know them first, and have them get to know me so that we're not strangers when we do meet."

He thrust his hands into his trouser pockets. "I'll talk to them again about that though. It's not up to me. It will have to be *our* decision." He gave a simple shrug of his shoulders. "I admire them so much. How they just handled what I told them." Ezra's face shone. "I realise I don't know them yet, but the way they wanted to do the right thing today made me very proud."

I squeezed his arm. "I have a feeling everything will be ok."

Good grief. The irony! Instead of making Ezra's life implode, the shadowy, blackmailing cretins, terrified about the contents of his autobiography, had brought a family together.

I languished in the bath that evening, mulling over the day's events.

As the warm water lapped against my skin, and my cranberry-scented candle flickered close by, I experienced a glow of satisfaction thinking about Ezra, Caroline, and Laura.

At least the three of them were now in a position where they could start to get to know each other. They could be honest and open with one another, and although there was so much they didn't yet know, there were no lies, no secrets, no bad feelings.

I cringed when I thought about the fact that my identity was still a secret from everyone who was part of my new life. Rowan and Amber, for example, who I saw every day, didn't know who I really was and had been in the past. We'd been rushed off our feet in the shop, and no time had seemed like the right time to speak to them. I was still coming to terms with the fact that I ought to tell them, that I was *ready* to tell them. Now I just had to be brave and come out with it.

Now that Ezra's New Year's Eve celebration was taking place at my parents' home next week, I was running out of time to do it. They knew the event was being held at some posh house, but had no idea I grew up there.

I stared at my waggling toes, slicked with burgundy-coloured polish, under the bubbly water.. I couldn't let Zach's reaction put me off telling other people in my life. I wished he'd given me the same courtesy and been open with me. I wanted to understand why someone like him was grubbing around for a gossip magazine instead of writing important articles that made the world a better place. I didn't like thinking of him as a hypocrite. I knew there must be something else going on.

Realising my bath water was beginning to lose its warmth, I climbed out and swathed myself in a fluffy towel. I would tell Amber and Rowan tomorrow, on Christmas Eve, and they would have a few days to get used to it before we reopened on the 28th. I was very fond of Rowan and Amber, but I couldn't face intense questioning and just wanted to get it over with.

I planned to close Flower Power at lunchtime so opened a little earlier to make sure we had time to get everything organised. I'd pack up the car and head home to Bannock House, crossing my fingers that my brother had changed his mind. He was still ignoring my calls and messages and I wished we could just fast forward to the point in time when he would have forgiven me and got over it. I wished Christmas would work some magic on him!

Chapter Twenty-One

I closed Flower Power at lunchtime on Christmas Eve, posting a festive note on the door, the shop website and on our social media accounts, thanking everybody for their support during the last few months, wishing them a wonderful Christmas and adding that Flower Power would reopen on 28 December.

Earlier that morning, I'd received a phone call from Ezra, quickly followed by texts from Caroline and Laura. The DNA results had come back positive. Ezra was their father.

'Both a shock and what I'd expected,' he'd said, tentatively. 'But they're both lovely young women, which I can take no credit for. I'm rather proud.'

Caroline and Laura had both been sanguine. For them, it was needed confirmation. But I was sure they'd grow to be fond of Ezra in time.

We'd been a bit busier than I'd anticipated for Christmas

Eve morning. There had been some confusion with Mr Snowdon, who had written down the wrong details from his wife about which festive floral dinner centrepiece to collect and then Mrs Hemphill had changed her mind about the colour of ribbon she wanted on her late sister's wreath to take up to the cemetery that afternoon.

Dismissed was the cream satin, and in its place, I weaved a red tartan ribbon.

Once we were officially closed, I insisted on pouring the three of us a glass of Bucks Fizz and gave Amber and Rowan their gifts – fishnet tights and glittery eyeliner for Amber, silver earrings and vanilla-scented hand cream for Rowan.

Then it was my turn to open the lovely gifts they bought me – a pretty mug with a B on it and a new apron which was pink to match the shop and had *Bailey* embroidered across it in sweeping gold lettering.

"Thank you," I laughed, trying it on for size. "I shall wear it with pride."

I watched as the two girls resumed sweeping the floor and tidying. Now would be the perfect time to tell them.

Come on, Bailey. Enough procrastination. It's time.

No more secrets. Look at what damage they can do.

I cleared my throat. "Amber. Rowan. Can you both stop what you're doing for a second, please. I've something to tell you."

My stomach cartwheeled and I placed one hand on it.

Amber's winged eyes grew large. Her attention fell on my tummy. "Oh my God! Are you pregnant?"

I let out a laugh, despite my rattling apprehension. "No. It's nothing like that." I whipped my hand away from my stomach. It would have to be an immaculate conception, if I was. My thoughts zoomed to Zach, but I busied myself with setting up my laptop on the counter.

They both watched me, exchanging questioning looks.

I pulled up images of Bannock House. "I want to show you both something."

The girls came round to stand either side of me at the counter. They gazed at the laptop screen.

Rowan pointed at the photos. "Isn't that the place where Ezra's having his Hogmanay party next week?"

"Yes, that's right."

"And we're both going," squealed Amber, not able to conceal her excitement.

"Of course, you are," I confirmed, my smile shaky. My hands hovered over the mouse.

Rowan frowned. "What is it, Bailey?"

There was a rushing noise in my ears but I carried on. "Do either of you remember a few years back there was that posh girl who was supposed to marry a musician, but he stood her up on their wedding day?"

Rowan furrowed her brow beside me. "Who?"

"You know," I prompted, mentally willing them to remember, so I didn't have to spell it out. "She came from an old Scottish family."

Rowan looked like she was trying to recall her, but was struggling. Then a spark lit up in her eyes. "Oh aye. Now you come to mention it, I think I do remember her. Wasn't she Lady something or other?"

It felt like we were discussing a stranger, and it was such a weird out-of-body experience.

"Oh, I know who you mean," erupted Amber. "Wasn't she the one who was a bit of a party girl?"

Rowan's eyes widened. "Yeah, she was. She was always photographed at wild parties and rolling out of nightclubs at five in the morning."

Amber nodded. "That's right. I think one of the tabloids gave her a nickname. What was it now? Oh yeah! Bollinger Babe, cos she always carried around a bottle of Bollinger champagne. I wonder what happened to her?"

I stood there, cringing into my boots.

Rowan pulled a face. "I bet she hasn't been reduced to flogging some knock-off perfume on the QVC channel right now."

Amber agreed. "No doubt Mummy and Daddy will have seen her right."

This was excruciating, and only served to highlight how far I'd come since then.

"I know what happened to her," I said in a guilty rush.

Amber leant forward, her two plaits trembling on either side of her expectant face. "Do you? Go on, Bailey. Spill. I love a bit of gossip!"

"Oh God! Sorry, I didn't mean to sound dismissive or rude," blushed Rowan. "Do you know her?"

I looked at Rowan and then at Amber. It would be like tearing off a plaster – momentary pain, followed by relief.

The words shot out of my mouth, falling over one another. "You could say that." I studied their expectant faces. "She's me. I'm her." My cheeks zinged with heat. "What I mean is, I am… I *was* her. I'm not Bailey McArthur. Well, I am now, but…" I braced myself. "What I'm trying to say is my full name, my real name, is Lady Anastasia McLaren-Kerr."

They both gawped at me.

Amber made me jump when she took a step closer, to get a better look at my scarlet face. "Sorry?"

I straightened my back and repeated my name.

Rowan and Amber blinked at me like two confused dolls and then at each other. Then Rowan gathered herself. "Are you joking? You're … Lady Anastasia?"

"Yes. I was. I mean, I am. But I don't go by that name any more…"

Amber flicked a disbelieving glance to Rowan and back again. "Are you being serious?"

"Yes."

Amber folded her arms, making her dozens of gold bracelets rattle. "Why didn't you tell us?"

"My fiancé left me at the altar, and I was publicly humiliated. I wanted to move on, to start over without the burden of my past."

Rowan blew out an excited whistle. "We've been working for the Bollinger Babe and didn't know! This is unreal."

I bristled. "Please don't call me that. I hated it then and hate it even more now, although I guess in a way, I did ask for it."

"Well, working for *royalty* then," jumped in Amber.

"I'm no more royalty than either of you," I insisted. "I don't want things to change between the three of us. I'm still just Bailey. End of."

Rowan coloured up. "I'm sorry if what we just said about her … er… I mean, you—"

"No need to apologise. Everything you said was right. It's in the past and it's not who I am anymore."

Amber raised her finger and jabbed it towards the photo of Bannock House on my laptop and its lush, rolling lawns. "And where Ezra's having his party, this is yours?"

I shifted from foot to foot. "It's my parents' home."

Rowan's mouth was popping open with surprise. "I remember reading an interview a while back in one of those glossy magazines about the couple who own the estate. So that's your parents?"

I nodded, beginning to feel relief that this was over.

"So, your mum and dad are Lord and Lady Something?" asked Rowan, intrigued.

I fidgeted with my hands. "Earl and Countess Tweed Muir."

Amber scanned my face, still riven in shock. "Why are you telling us now? Is it because of the party?"

I let out an awkward sigh. "Yes and no. I've worked hard to start afresh, and to build this business – with your help. For a long time, I was running away from what happened, but now I'm ready to face it, to embrace who I used to be, and to know that I'm not that person anymore. I wanted to do something on my own terms and be successful because I'm good at it and not because of the family I was born into and the privileges that came with that. I wanted to know who I am, and to be better than I used to be. And I think… I think I've done that. And that means I'm not afraid of the past anymore. I don't want to be any kind of celebrity, but I also don't want to hide."

They both made sympathetic noises.

Rowan tilted her head to one side. "I wish we'd known."

"I know and I'm sorry. But it was really important to me to know that I could do this on my own and be good at it. Does that make sense?"

They nodded but I could tell they weren't convinced.

"Looking back on it, maybe it wasn't such a big deal, but it felt like a big deal at the time. And maybe it's only because I've done what I set out to do that I've been able to gain some perspective."

"Not a big deal?" repeated Amber, incredulous. "Your house makes Downton Abbey look like a semi-detached."

Embarrassment flared up inside of me.

"Well, now we know we're working for a princess…" grinned Amber, earning a playful scowl from me.

I rolled my eyes. "You're not!" We all laughed.

I closed down my laptop. "As I said, although I want to be honest about who I am, I'd appreciate it if you could keep this to yourselves. It's not a secret exactly, but—"

"We won't tell anyone, will we?" Rowan said.

"I promise," said Amber. "But this is so exciting!"

Chapter Twenty-Two

The journey back home was an odd affair.

Normally, I would've been excited at the prospect of a few days off, relaxing in the warm and cosy festive surroundings of my old family home. But without Marcus, it wouldn't be the same.

As I drove along the network of quiet country roads, which were bursting with holly, ivy, and glistening berries that the blackbirds were busy feasting on, my thoughts flicked from my brother to Zach.

What would he be doing on Christmas Day? Would he be spending the day with someone special? Family members or ... someone else?

I refused to expend any more energy thinking about him. I was sure he wasn't thinking about me half as much as I kept thinking about him. If someone could walk away like that and refuse to talk to me about it... I didn't want to be with someone like that anyway.

And to think I'd started to believe there was something growing between us. *Yeah, fungus,* snorted my head.

The car radio was blaring upbeat Christmas tunes and although I wanted to switch it off, the empty silence would've been even worse. I was just relieved to arrive home before the snow started to coat everything in ethereal dustings of white.

Mum and Dad tried to jolly me along, but we were all upset by the absence of Marcus. When Mum was out of earshot, Dad pulled me aside.

"Marcus definitely isn't coming for Christmas," he said with a grim look. "I managed to get hold of Anthony, that chap he plays squash with."

It wasn't a surprise, but disappointment still kicked me in the stomach. "Marcus won't be on his own, will he, Dad? I couldn't bear it."

"No, he won't be alone. Apparently, he's decided to go away with a couple of friends to a rented cottage up by Inverness."

I began to fiddle with one of the white ribbons on the nearby tree. "But Dad, Marcus doesn't know the whole story. If only—"

Dad gently took my upper arms in his hands. "Marcus is hurting, darling. Give your brother time and he'll come around. Then the three of us can talk to him and explain, ok?"

I gazed up at my dad and sighed. He was like a cooling breeze on a blistering hot day. "Yes. I suppose so."

But the next day, Christmas Day, carried on in the same

anti-climactic way, with me, Mum and Dad sharing tales about past Christmases, Dad regaling us with stories from the golf club and Mum trying to interrogate me about Ezra, while flapping over Ezra's party. I just missed Marcus.

The roast turkey lunch was delicious, but once Mum had indulged in one too many glasses of Moët, her tongue loosened.

"I wish I'd seen through Declan and all that Irish charm. I wish I hadn't taken him at his word. Then you wouldn't have run away from here and your duties."

"I didn't run away, Mum. I wanted a new start, away from everything." I eyed her across the expanse of sitting room. "And as for my duties, I have a duty to myself. To my own happiness."

"What did I do to deserve such feckless nearly-weds for my children?" growled Mum to herself. "Neither of you can be trusted to make good choices."

"Vanessa," warned Dad.

"Oh, it's true, Henry," she scoffed, gulping another mouthful, as the fresh logs in the fire grate spat and crackled amongst the flames. "We knew Anastasia was making a mistake, but we did nothing to stop it."

Dad made us both jump by banging his glass down on the coffee table.

"Just stop this, for Christ's sake! It's upsetting at the best of times, but not on sodding Christmas Day!" My mum stared up at him in shock over the top of her glass. "For heaven's sake, Ness! I thought we were trying to put all that behind us, not drag everything up again. I know our daughter is."

But before Mum could reply, I'd already leapt up from the sofa and strode off to fetch my hat, coat, and scarf from the cloakroom.

I needed to escape into the gardens for a walk.

If Marcus had been here, he would've been my ally. We would've been too busy laughing and gossiping to take any notice of our mother's alcohol-induced psychotherapy.

It was a relief to get away from the family tension. I realised how much I liked the life I had built for myself, on my own terms, out of their sphere of toxic influence.

I huddled deeper into my winter coat and reached inside one of the pockets for my mobile phone. The mid-afternoon light was growing tired already and there was an icy hush.

I attempted to call Marcus, but it went straight to voicemail. I hung up and stared down at my phone, deciding to text him instead, with a few green heart and Christmas tree emojis:

Hi Marcus. Merry Christmas!

I'm at Mum and Dad's. I'm missing you so much.

Hope you're having a lovely time at the cottage.

Love you XXX

I pressed the "send" button and strode on, tugging my

dusty-pink pom-pom winter hat further down over my ears. My long brown leather boots scrunched on the snow and the naked trees had layers of ice dripping from them, like ostentatious Christmas baubles.

I paused, breathing in the tang of winter and relishing the way the bitter cold skimmed its way across my cheeks.

The ping of my phone made me jump.

I scrambled around in my coat pocket to find it again.

It was a reply from Marcus:

Merry Christmas

Not exactly *War and Peace*, but it was a start.

Boxing Day was a test of endurance because Mum had invited some old friends of hers over for afternoon drinks and nibbles. I managed to make polite conversation, but this wasn't the Christmas I was used to or loved. It felt like forced, contrived joviality. I missed my brother and I didn't feel like this was where I belonged anymore. I couldn't wait to head back home to Heather Moore and reopen Flower Power on the 28th.

Home. Yes. Heather Moore was home to me now.

The realisation made me prickle with an independent excitement.

"So that's you setting off then?" Dad said, shuffling from foot to foot as I came down the stairs with my bags.

"Yep. I'm opening the shop tomorrow and I have a lot to do."

Dad pulled me into a hug. "I'm sorry this Christmas hasn't been the one you hoped for, sweetheart."

"It's not your fault, Dad." I planted a kiss on his cheek, just in time for Mum to appear. "Drive carefully, won't you? Please let us know when you get back."

"I will."

My mother gave me a prolonged hug and kiss, before drawing away from me.

"I'll be back in a few days anyway to set up for Ezra's party. I'll let you know when Amber, Rowan, and I will be arriving, Mum. And thanks for insisting they stay here."

My mother's dark blue eyes sparkled with anticipation. "No problem at all. Always glad to accommodate the hired help."

I ground my jaw and Dad rolled his eyes.

"I'll make sure Mrs Bamber has all the guest rooms ready." She studied me from under her lashes. "I hope you have your little flower displays for Ezra well in hand, darling."

I gave my dad a quick glance. "I can assure you, Mum, that Ezra doesn't know the meaning of the word 'little'. These floral arrangements make Kew Gardens look like a tawdry affair." I couldn't resist adding: "Oh, and by the way, Mum, we'll be arriving in my Flower Power delivery van, as we'll have the flower displays with us."

Mum's glossed lips parted in horror. "What? Not that pink and white thing that looks like the van in *Scooby-Doo*?!"

From beside her, Dad was clamping his lips together, trying not to laugh.

"You mean The Dream Machine?" I asked, hiding a smile. "Yes, that's it. See you in a few days!"

I couldn't wait to get back to my real life, and as I drove out through the gates of my parents' home, I wondered when Bailey McArthur, resident of Heather Moore and proud business owner, had become my "real" identity.

Chapter Twenty-Three

All too soon, I was on my way back to Bannock House. The journey was smooth, and the Flower Power van was filled with excited chatter from Amber and Rowan.

They were speculating about which celebrities might appear at Ezra's book launch, and how they might get to meet their favourites. The radio was belting out Scottish reels and optimistic, hopeful songs about fresh starts. I let the joy of their chatter wash over me.

The beginning of a new year was hovering, waiting to be welcomed. I hoped the next year would bring better things for everyone. I wondered what Marcus would be doing tonight and hoped he was surrounded by friends.

As for Zach ... well, he was in my past, I concluded with a painful lurch in my chest. I was determined that when I woke up tomorrow morning, I would look only ahead, not behind.

Excited squeals and gasps escaped from Amber and she shot forward in the passenger seat as we passed through the gates and the tyres scrunched and spun on the gravel.

"It's even more gorgeous than in the photos you showed us, Bailey."

"It's like Cinderella's castle," Rowan chimed in.

"Hardly," I laughed.

They fell into an almost reverent silence as I parked outside the entrance. Mum was going to have a fit! But there were half a dozen other trades vehicles there and what looked like a couple of security people, holding one finger to their ear. I didn't see how my pink-and-white van was out of place.

We clambered out and fetched our three wheelie cases first, which landed on the gravel with a decisive crunch.

"Come on," I said, once we draped our respective evening dresses with a flourish of plastic over our arms. "Let me introduce you to my parents, then we can grab a cuppa and get the flowers out from the back of the van."

Dad bounded down the steps to greet us and proceeded to pump Amber and Rowan's hands up and down in enthusiastic handshakes. Then he gave me a big bear hug and a kiss.

Mum sashayed her way towards them, revelling in their jaws dropping at the sight of her coiffed glamour.

Once introductions had been made, Mrs Bamber furnished the three of us with a pot of tea and slices of her gorgeous cherry and almond stollen, filled with marzipan and Jamaican rum. Then Mum insisted on showing Amber and Rowan their accommodation for the night.

"Rowan, this is your room," announced my mother, sweeping like the grand dame that she was along the corridor and opening the door with a dramatic flourish. "I've allocated you the Rannoch Room."

I mouthed the word *"What?"* at Mum. Since when did we have names for the guest rooms? Her response to me was a narrowed eye, daring me to question it in front of our guests.

Nevertheless, Rowan's delight was evident as she stepped inside. Her room looked out onto a section of the walled garden.

The room interior was a mixture of duck-egg blue walls and mint-green furnishings, with a canopied double bed, small sofa, and an en suite bathroom to the right, fitted out with white and beige marble tiles.

I noticed Mum had replaced the flowery wallpaper that used to be in here.

"It's gorgeous," said Rowan, placing her wheelie case by the sofa and drifting towards the sash window, framed by a set of tie-back emerald-green curtains.

Outside, the walled garden was stippled with hard frost. There were pale pink clouds of heather and glossy ivy snaking up the trellis. In the far corner, sat an ornamental bird table, where a robin and a sparrow were jumping and flitting about for seed.

"I'm so pleased you like it," glowed Mum. "Now, Amber, let's show you to your room."

Amber wobbled behind my mother like an excited baby deer in her platform trainers to the next-door room. Again, Mum placed her manicured hand on the brass handle and paused for dramatic effect. "This is the Katrine Room."

This time, I didn't bother making a questioning face at her. This was obviously a new thing of hers, naming the guest rooms after famous Scottish Lochs. *Whatever floats her boat*, I thought to myself.

Amber erupted in a fit of admiring giggles. She guided her leopard-print wheelie case into the room and was confronted by gold-embossed wallpaper and complimented by burnt-orange fixtures and fittings. The double bed possessed a brass headboard and amber scatter cushions and, similarly to Rowan's room, there was an en suite bathroom, but this one featured biscuit and white tiles.

I recalled this room having previously had that same wallpaper, but the bedding and cushions were new. Poor Dad. Mum had clearly been on a serious spending spree. That must be why she kept steering me away from the guest rooms over Christmas.

The view from the sash window was the same as Rowan's, though you could see more of the lawns and the woodland beyond the walled garden from here. The trees thrust their eager, bare branches up towards the sky. They looked as though they were on fire in the low sun of the late afternoon. Amber fingered the satin curtains.

"It's beautiful. Thank you, Countess Tweed Muir."

Mum preened. "My pleasure. And please do call me Vanessa."

Remembering why we were here, I steered Mum to one side while Amber trotted off to admire the view. "Everything going to plan so far?"

"What a silly question," tinkled Mum, "of course it is."

Once Rowan and Amber had made themselves at home in their rooms and unpacked their belongings, we started ferrying our floral handiwork into the house.

"How on earth could you turn your back on all of this?" Amber asked.

"I haven't," I insisted. "But I'm an adult and I have my own life now. This is my parents' home and my parents' life, not mine."

"I guess," said Rowan. "But it's all so beautiful."

I gave an optimistic smile. "Yes, it is. But it comes with strings attached, and being independent gives me a freedom I never had when I lived at home."

"And what about Marcus?" asked Rowan, squinting. "Does he embrace all this?"

"More than I do," I admitted. "He will inherit it, of course, and he's always known that, so it's different for him."

Amber asked me when Marcus would be arriving.

A pang of sadness struck me. "I don't think he's coming. He's away with friends at the moment."

No need to air our dirty laundry in front of the girls, I thought.

"Right," I announced, changing the subject and

unlocking the doors of the van. "Let's get this lot inside and then we can start setting up for tonight."

My mother was clearly in charge, directing the various teams with an efficiency that spoke of years of hosting parties such as this. She pointed one lacquer-nailed finger here and there to various harassed guys in overalls. They were juggling a huge life-size portrait photograph of Ezra. It was a stunning black-and-white image of him in his younger days, sporting a tux and looking like James Bond. There were also Chinese lanterns, rolls of King Angus tartan supported at either end by puffing, red-faced men, and what looked like a catering company boss speaking to a small group of apprehensive-looking students in smart black trousers, skirts, and shirts.

"Everything all right, Mum?" I asked.

She swept her dark hair back from her made-up face. "It will be, once Ezra and his team get here. I expected them to be here already." Her attention fell on the extravagant pastel-blue wildflowers and Scottish globe thistles I'd arranged in a round cream vase I was cradling in my arms.

Amber was behind me, carrying three frosted navy goblets, which we'd spun with an array of blue roses, cream tea roses, and delicate traces of matching blue ribbon.

Rowan brought up the rear, juggling an arrangement of ice-blue candles surrounded by ivy, frosted cones, and dried twigs.

Mum blinked for several seconds at the displays. "You made these?"

"*We* made them," I said with a smile, nodding at Rowan

and Amber. "We have about a dozen more just like them back in the van to retrieve."

As if on cue, my mobile pinged in my pocket, signalling the arrival of a text. I set down the arrangement on a nearby table to look at my phone. It was from Ezra.

"He's on his way," I assured her. "He and his 'people' left Heather Moore about half an hour ago."

Mum nodded, and I could tell how much she was in her element right now.

"Bailey? How are you? I'm Corrie. Good to meet you at last."

I spun round to see Corrie, the assistant at Ezra's management agency, trundling her wheelie case along the hall floor. "How lovely to see you."

She was pretty in a funky sort of way, with short dark hair and lots of silver jewellery.

"This is going to be a great night," she beamed, nodding at my mum.

"I feel like I know Corrie so well," laughed Mum, lightly grazing her on the cheek with a kiss in greeting. "We've exchanged so many emails and phone calls! Your room is the last one along the upstairs corridor."

Corrie nodded. "Thank you. Ezra, Denise, and the rest of the entourage should be here soon."

"Oh, you didn't travel with them?" asked Mum.

"No," answered Corrie briskly. "I had some things to attend to."

Mum gazed past my shoulder, smiling at Amber and Rowan, who were still hugging the floral displays they were holding while admiring the vaulted ceiling. "Your staff seem like nice girls."

Staff?! "They're my colleagues and friends, Mum."

"Of course they are, darling. Oh, excuse me one moment."

Mum left to direct an anguished-looking man in overalls who clearly hadn't yet benefitted from her precise instructions.

I turned to Amber and Rowan. "Right, ladies. Let's get this show on the road."

Standing in front of the full-length mirror in my old bedroom, I placed one hand on my stomach and gulped with a mixture of excitement and apprehension at the night ahead.

I had piled my waves up into a messy chignon and slipped into a full-length champagne-coloured dress with spaghetti straps, which I'd bought to cheer myself up post-Declan and then never worn.

Although I did feel rather glamorous as I studied my reflection, I couldn't disguise the trepidation in my eyes. I could hear the hum of voices and detect the clinking of cutlery in the Great Hall.

God, I hoped tonight went well. Ezra, Caroline, and Laura had gone through an emotional rollercoaster and from where I was standing, this party of Ezra's was a two-fingered salute to the people who'd been threatening him.

I adjusted one of my dangly earrings and glanced down again at my mobile on the dressing table. I'd made three more attempts this afternoon to reach Marcus, but he still wasn't picking up. I wished I had him here tonight for support.

Checking my appearance again in the mirror, I picked up my mobile and dialled Marcus once more. Still nothing.

I threw the phone onto my bed in frustration. Maybe I should give him some space and wait for him to contact me.

I looked down at my watch. It was approaching 6pm and the party was due to begin in an hour. My stomach swished with nerves. I just hoped everything was going to go smoothly and there were no dramas. Nobody would try to do anything stupid, surely. Ezra had kept his invitee list very selective and there were security people here, to check in the guests as they arrived.

I stood at the window with its brocade cherry-red curtains and rope tie-backs.

It seemed so long ago since this had been my room. I looked out onto the mermaid fountain, which Marcus and I adored so much as kids. It seemed like a lifetime ago.

There was a discreet rap on the door. When I said, "Come in," Amber and Rowan entered, looking gorgeous in all their finery.

Rowan's red waves were intricately styled and she was wearing a stunning electric-blue boat neck dress. Amber, meanwhile, looked equally glamorous in a lemon-coloured knee-length dress which had transparent lacy sleeves caught at the wrists with big buttons. She had undone her usual plaits and opted for a tousled ponytail instead.

We broke into appreciative smiles and gasps and admired each other's outfits. It was obvious how excited they both were about this evening. I wished I could relax and enjoy it the way they were obviously planning to. I wondered when Ezra, Caroline, and Laura were going to arrive.

"Ezra's been looking for you," announced Amber. "He's just arrived with Caroline and Laura and a very glamorous blonde woman who looks like Dolly Parton."

"Ah, I bet that's Denise Gold, his manager."

"Yeah, and he's busy charming the pants off your mum."

"Thanks for that image."

I reached for my clutch bag on the dressing table and popped my phone into it. "You two head downstairs. I'll be right behind you."

I watched the two of them, visions of elegance, negotiate the grand staircase in their heels.

I took one last look at myself in the mirror, then swished down the carpeted corridor, the paintings on the wall of gun dogs and ancestors in sumptuous gowns and brocade and breeches following my every step.

Mum had designated the four bedrooms towards the rear of the house as places where guests could freshen up, and I recalled Mum saying to Corrie she'd been allocated the fourth and last room, which was the one with the claw-footed bath. It also possessed views of the kitchen garden, where our trusted gardeners grew an assortment of fresh vegetables for Mrs Bamber to conjure into delicious meals.

It was at that moment that Mum knocked on my bedroom door and stuck her head round. Her face broke into an admiring smile. "Oh darling! You look beautiful!"

"Thanks, Mum. See? No dirt under my fingernails."

She pulled a face. "I'm sure there isn't."

Then she gave a playful slap to her forehead. "Would you mind checking on that young lady Corrie for me before you come down?"

I started to make my way out of my room. "Of course. Is everything all right?"

"I hope so. She commented to one of the gents in overalls that she seemed to be having a bit of an issue with her shower."

I clicked my door closed behind me. "She can use my bathroom if there's a problem. I'll go and tell her."

"Thank you, sweetheart. I'd better head back down there just to check all's ok, before I get ready myself."

I arrived at Corrie's door and knocked. There was no reply.

Over the banister, I could see people I didn't recognise drifting around below in the Great Hall. There were chimes of laughter and glimpses of sparkles and satin.

I knocked on the door again then reached for the door handle but I didn't need to turn it as the door swung open, making me jump. It hadn't been closed properly. I blinked, not expecting that. I called out again. "Hello? Corrie? It's Bailey. Are you there?"

I poked my head around the side of the door, but the room was empty. All I could hear was the hum of people below and cars arriving outside.

I edged my way in, noticing Corrie's chequered coat lying on top of the satin bedspread and the outfit she'd arrived in draped across the gilt armchair in the corner. It was turning into a chilly, Highland Hogmanay night out there.

"Corrie?" Maybe she was still struggling with the shower in the en suite bathroom.

I knocked on the closed bathroom door, but there was no response. I clicked that open but she wasn't in there either. Oh well. She must be downstairs somewhere and managed to use someone else's bathroom.

I was about to leave and head downstairs, when something on the bed drew my attention. It was poking out from one of Corrie's coat pockets and looked like a typed note, very similar to the one Ezra had received.

I approached the bed.

Glancing over my shoulder to make sure she wasn't standing there; I reached for the piece of paper and eased it out of the pocket. It was a folded-up sheet of A4.

I focused on what it said.

Then gasped.

I wobbled in my heels.

It couldn't be.

My eyes scanned the bold black capital letters on the note in disbelief. It said:

YOU ARE PUTTING YOUR DAUGHTERS IN DANGER. RETRACT CONTENTS OF YOUR BOOK. YOU'VE BEEN WARNED.

My head was racing. What was Corrie doing with a threatening note? It was identical to the last one Ezra received.

My breathing came out in a series of fast and furious gulps. Why did Corrie—?

A dark thought erupted.

No.

My imagination was running riot. She wouldn't have anything to do with this. She was part of Ezra's management team.

I sank down on the corner of the bed. This didn't make any sense.

I could hear more tinkling laughter wafting its way up the grand staircase from the Great Hall. Maybe Corrie had discovered the note and didn't want Ezra to see it right before the party? She would tell Ezra about it, but hadn't had an opportunity yet. Or perhaps someone had sent it to her, for Ezra's attention?

I got up, absently smoothing my dress and still clutching the note. I made a move to push it back into her coat pocket, when my fingers brushed against something else. It was another piece of paper.

My heart hammered in my ears. I tugged it out. This too was folded up. I opened up the second sheet of paper. This one contained scribbled, personal notes about Caroline and

Laura, as well as small photos of them – and scribbled beside them, was written *Ezra's weakness,* in messy handwriting.

What the hell?! My heart raced. It was too much of a coincidence. What was Corrie doing with all these strange notes?

With my head still fizzing with confusion, I stuffed both notes back into her coat pocket where I found them. Should I mention those notes to her? No. I couldn't. She would know I'd been snooping around. There could be an innocent explanation. But the thought festered with me; why hadn't she said anything?

It didn't look good.

I began to back away from the bed. Was she in league with someone? Perhaps someone that Ezra was naming and shaming in his book? Maybe they were in this together and were intending to split the proceeds of any blackmail money?

"Can I help?"

My blood froze.

I swung around. Corrie was framed in the doorway. There was a harsh angle to her feline features.

"I-I was looking for you."

Her light, cool eyes travelled to the bed and her coat. "Well, here I am."

I felt my hands tumble over each other as I stood there.

"What for?" she asked.

"Sorry?"

"Why were you looking for me?"

My stomach rolled over and over, but somehow, I managed to find my voice. "To discuss final arrangements for this evening."

Corrie's gaze became flinty. She looked powerful and capable in her pillar-box red dress, with its slashed neckline and matching jacket. "Everything's in hand." Her eyes flickered over me. "So, what are you doing in my room?"

I could feel a lump sticking at the base of my throat. It felt like my dress was clinging to my suddenly damp skin. "Why do you have those threatening notes?"

A glimpse of resignation settled on her face. "Ah. That's a pity."

"What is?"

"You finding them."

Corrie turned and in one swift move locked the guest room door.

My legs jittered against my dress. Oh no. I'd put my clutch bag down on top of the bed. It was too far away to reach it. My mobile was inside.

I folded my arms, my heart pumping crazily against my ribs. Would someone even hear me if I cried out? There was a lot of noise and gaiety to contend with from downstairs. "Why?" I croaked. "Why have you got those notes and details about Caroline and Laura?"

She rolled her made-up eyes. "Isn't it obvious?" She gestured to her coat on the bed. "I'm sure I don't have to tell you how explosive King's autobiography is. There are a number of influential people not very happy about its release."

I took an unsteady step backwards in my heels. I could feel the bedframe digging into the backs of my knees. "But what do you get out of it?"

A self-satisfied smirk spread over her features. "Oh, don't be gauche, Bailey – *Lady Anastasia*. It doesn't suit you. Money. What else?" She slid me a triumphant smirk. "My initial plan had been to tell the press about you and where you were now, but that money would've been small fry, compared to what I can get if I help these people force old man King to retract that book of his." She performed a sarcastic tutting noise. "I'd hoped that drunken waste of space of an ex of yours might keep your nose out of everything, but I underestimated you."

I stood there, blinking at Corrie, trying to take it in. "So, that's how Declan knew about me? You found him and told him where I was?"

Growing fear reared up inside me.

"Yep. A bit of detective work on your Irish rover proved to be very valuable. He likes a drink, does your Declan. I hoped he'd make more of an inroad with that trashy *Stargazer*, magazine, but he was too pissed half the time to be of any value. Never mind. Things are going just as I hoped."

I studied her, my chest heaving with adrenalin. "So how and why did this all start?"

She appraised me from top to toe. "I was contacted by a 'concerned party' who said they'd reward me if I could get some dirt on our friend Ezra and shut him up." She cocked her head to one side. "I was racking my brains, trying to think how I could do it. Then the arrival of those two bimbo daughters of his changed everything."

I shook my head, disgusted. "How could you do something like this? Ezra's only telling the truth in his autobiography. These people deserve to be outed."

Corrie gestured around the guest room. "Oh, I know he is. But come on! That's rich coming from you lot!"

"What do you mean?"

"You landed gentry have been taking what isn't yours since time began."

"You can't justify what you did."

Corrie's temper flared. "I don't have to justify anything to you, you stuck-up bitch!"

I couldn't take any more steps backwards. I was pinned against the frame of the bed. The air in the room was cloying and oppressive. It smelled of flowers and Corrie's dark, fruity perfume.

I couldn't equate the ever helpful and charming Corrie on the phone with the avaricious, sinister version I was confronted with now. My head was struggling to accept it. "And so, you came up with the idea of threatening Ezra's daughters?"

She performed a sarcastic, slow-hand clap. "Well done! They were a gift, those two. It was tricky at first, trying to think of his Achilles heel. We did wonder about going for some of his former lovers, but there's quite a list, I can tell you. So, when those two women came along, we gambled on him feeling protective towards them, so we threatened them and the old bugger went for it. It was perfect. And of course, working for Ezra's management team, meant I had all the knowledge about them at my fingertips." She grinned, displaying white, but slightly uneven teeth. "At first, these people named in Ezra's autobiography investigated the legal route, but unfortunately, what King wrote was legally watertight and all true. That wasn't ideal." She gave a shrug. "So, alternative methods to persuade him to reconsider his actions had to be deployed. And that's where Caroline and Laura fit in. The best Christmas present I could've wished for."

My clutch bag, containing my mobile, glittered on top of the bedspread. I took a couple of steps to the side.

Corrie glanced at my bag and back at me. She shook her head. "I wouldn't, if I were you." There was a deep element of threat in her voice. What was she capable of? A lot, going by the situation she'd got herself into, just for money.

I could hear my breathing escaping from my chest in a loud, ragged rush. Should I scream? Would anyone even hear me? The noise from the party was growing louder and more enthusiastic.

I had to do something. Anything.

I opened my mouth and prepared to yell for help.

"Bailey? Bailey! Where are you?"

My head whipped towards the locked bedroom door.

That voice… It sounded like Zach!

No. I must have imagined it.

"Bailey! Are you ok?"

Oh God. It *was* Zach! *What was he doing here?*

"Zach," I managed, rising fear in my voice. "Oh God, Zach! Help me! I'm in here!"

Corrie swore and rushed towards me, a blur of incensed red satin.

Panic rose up in my throat. In desperation, I lunged across the bed, snatched up one of the heavy glass table lamps and hurled it at her with all the force I could muster.

As the lamp connected with her arm, Corrie yelped in pain and staggered backwards.

I scrambled to right myself on top of the bed, as loud, desperate kicks pounded against the door.

Another male voice rang out this time. "Sis! Move! Get away from the door!"

Marcus?!

I sprang onto the carpet, my heels dangling half off my feet and my hair escaping out of its up-do.

"Anastasia!"

Marcus called out again from outside the room.

"Marcus! Help!"

Corrie was sprawled on the teal carpet, still clutching at her upper arm and trying to right herself in her spikey, crimson heels.

There was another heavy-footed bang against the door, before it splintered away from its hinges with a giant crack.

I watched open-mouthed as Zach and Marcus bundled in. My big brother swooped me into his arms. "Christ! Are you all right? Are you hurt?"

I let out a grateful sob and managed to shake my head as I clung to him. "What are you doing here?"

Zach hoisted one arm under Corrie and yanked her roughly to her feet.

He gestured out to the corridor and two of the burly security guards, who had been recruited by Ezra's management team, entered the room and hauled Corrie away. "Can you keep an eye on her please?" asked Zach.

One of the towering guards, who was sporting a hipster-style beard, glowered down at Corrie, who jutted her chin out in defiance. "We'll take her down to the service entrance, sir."

The two security guards hoisted her away, and I could hear her protesting all the way down the hall.

Zach smoothed back his sweep of dark hair. His white shirt sleeves were rolled up to his elbows.

Bewildered, I stared from Zach to Marcus, who was still holding me in his arms. I felt as though I was dreaming underwater. "Will someone please tell me what the hell's going on?"

Zach glanced at my brother, before focusing on me. "So, you know about Corrie then, Bailey?"

I suddenly felt very vulnerable, standing there with my messy hair and crumpled dress.

"Yes," I faltered, "but only because I found two threatening notes in her coat pocket." I pointed to the coat still lying on top of the rumpled covers. "And details about Caroline and Laura." My head was swimming. "How did you find out what she was up to?"

"I'm a journalist, remember?" Zach said, smirking at me across the room.

Marcus gave my arm a comforting squeeze.

Zach thrust both hands into his trouser pockets. "This was the development I hinted at before. I got a tip-off from one of Corrie's colleagues at Sublime Entertainment, who I know from when I worked with him on one of the London papers. He told me she seemed very interested in Caroline and Laura – unhealthily so. He also started to notice her splashing cash she always claimed she never had."

Zach eyed Marcus and me. "This colleague of Corrie's began feeding me information and kept watching her. He said she started working late when she never used to before, and was forever disappearing from her desk with her mobile, taking a variety of frequent calls." He went on to explain that Corrie had been acting suspiciously around her PC at work, looking up information on Ezra's former partners, as well as trying to find out about his general movements, the hotel accommodation for his book tour, and looking into his inner circle of close friends.

"She'd seemed unnaturally interested in him," explained Zach. "They've got other clients at the agency of course, but anything to do with Ezra and she was always volunteering to deal with it. I suppose she was hoping to stumble across something juicy from his past and wanted to be in a position where she was able to use it on behalf of the shady individuals who were paying her."

My breath quickened again. Thank goodness Zach and Marcus showed up when they did. Lord knows what Corrie was capable of.

"So, when did you find out about Corrie and what she was up to?"

Zach shot me a charged look. "I got confirmation just after … I last saw you in Heather Moore and that was when I returned to Glasgow. It seems Corrie has a tendency to hang around with the wrong sort of company; people you wouldn't want to upset." Zach gave his brow a wipe with the back of his hand. "Corrie and her boyfriend are rumoured to have been involved in a number of unpleasant online blackmailing scams."

My mouth dropped open. "But why didn't you tell me as soon as you found out about her?"

He took a few steps towards me and caressed the top of my arm. Marcus was observing both of us. "I'll speak to you in a minute." He offered Zach a small, grateful smile and vanished out into the corridor.

Zach's expression was etched with concern. "I wanted to take as few risks as possible. I thought the less you knew, the safer you'd be."

"And that's the only reason? Why you disappeared?"

Zach dropped his gaze. "No, it wasn't the only reason."

I heard the sound of chattering and clinking glasses travelling up from downstairs.

His deep, dark eyes locked with mine. "I knew I was beginning to fall for you, Bailey. But I didn't want to put you in danger."

"Danger? What do you mean?"

Zach sighed as he gazed down into my eyes. "That's why I lost my job a couple of years ago at the *London*

Inquirer. I got too close to a high-profile media mogul who was taking backhanders from a political party."

I stared up into his face. "What?"

Zach rubbed at his stubble. "You've heard of Sir Clifford Bain?"

I frowned up at him. "Of course. Always wears a cravat and smokes a cigar. Didn't I read recently that he's invested a lot of money in boxing?"

"Yes. That's him. I've learnt that the cash he's pumped into it comes from the party he's been pushing in his newspapers." Zach eyed me. "Bain's name has been attached to a few other dodgy deals as well, which I'm also looking into."

Zach explained further. "Bain has majority shares in the *London Inquirer* and when he found out one of its reporters – namely, me – had been sniffing around his business affairs, he leant on the board and my editor had me sacked."

His handsome face took on a pensive look. "He also made sure no other newspaper title would touch me."

I let out a stunned gasp. "That's awful. Having your job taken away from you just because you were doing the right thing and trying to expose corruption..."

His eyes never left my face. "Not only that, but Bain also had his people threaten me and anyone close to me. Said I'd regret it if I persisted with my investigation."

Zach stroked my cheek. "I swore to myself that I wouldn't get you caught up in anything. I knew I was falling for you, but no matter how hard I tried to keep you at arm's length, my feelings started getting in the way." He hesitated, before carrying on. "Then when I found out who you were, I knew I definitely couldn't put you in the firing line of anything risky. It was bad enough when I didn't know you were Lady Anastasia, but then when you told me that, I decided I was taking too much of a chance." He gave a small smile. "I didn't want you splashed across the papers again and seeing as you do come from a high-profile family, I wasn't prepared to take the risk that you, your parents or Marcus could come to harm." He pinned me to the spot with his earnest gaze. "I almost told you a couple of times about this and what I was involved in." Zach performed a small smile. "I didn't want to keep any secrets from you, but the thought of putting you in potential danger was too much of a risk that I wasn't prepared to take."

Zach examined my face. "See what you've done to me? I was beginning to let my heart rule my head and I was so worried in case Bain's cohorts discovered you too."

I searched his face. "Believe me, there have been plenty of times when I wished I didn't have a title! After Declan made such a fool of me, I knew I had to get away from everything. I wasn't trying to deceive you, but I learnt the hard way that I can't trust my instincts when it comes to knowing who to trust." I let out a sigh. "It was so important to me to know that I could do it on my own, and that my success is because I'm good at what I do and not because of who my parents are."

Zach nodded. "I know that now." He continued to trace his hand down my cheek. My stomach swirled at his touch. "I was trying to convince myself that I didn't have feelings for you and also trying to protect you at the same time. I thought that if I kept you at a distance, I could control my feelings for you but it didn't work that way. Quite the opposite." Zach gave me a rueful smile." I've been so pig-headed and stupid."

"We've both been stupid and pig-headed." My heart was pumping in my ears.

Zach's lips morphed into a grin. "I can't argue with that."

"I just wish you'd told me before you left. It hurt that I opened up and trusted you but you didn't do the same."

"I know, and I'm sorry. I never meant to hurt you. I hated the thought of anyone else hurting you – I wasn't prepared to risk that. I would never have forgiven myself. That's why I've been keeping tabs on you from a distance."

My stomach flipped.

"You thought I'd abandoned you, but in fact, I was never far away." Zach's voice was earnest. "When you said you weren't going to back away from all of this with Ezra and you were still going to try and help, I realised why I was falling in love with you."

My legs wobbled.

"When I got offered the *Stargazer* position by Adam, I knew it wasn't what I wanted to do." Zach eyed me, willing me to understand. "But it was the only opportunity I was offered to keep me investigating, reporting, and writing – and the way I saw it, exposing those who deserve it."

I studied his lips. I thought he'd abandoned me, but Zach had been there all along.

"Yes, I've been writing the trashy celeb stuff, but that's been more like a smokescreen. I've been investigating *Stargazer* magazine over a mass phone hacking controversy, involving so many celebrities. I'm still gathering the information."

"Really?"

Zach nodded his dark head. "There have been rumours about them for a while with the phone hacking thing. When I got offered the job with them, it was the perfect way in – and of course, the money came in handy when the *London Inquirer* got rid of me, just for doing my job."

I stared at this wonderful, moral man who I'd doubted.

An excited rush travelled through my whole body. I wanted Zach to kiss me. I couldn't think of anything else. I didn't want anything else. Or anyone.

Zach's intense brows gathered. "All the while, I've been investigating Bain's shenanigans, the phone hacking allegations against *Stargazer*, what Corrie's been up to, and also trying to look out for you."

He let out an infectious laugh. "You could say I've had rather a busy in-tray."

I felt my shoulders slump under my strappy dress. "I'm so sorry, Zach. I've been such an idiot." I threw my hands up in the air. "But now I don't care who knows about me. Not anymore." I shot him a dreamy smile. "All I care about is you."

Zach's fingers brushed my shoulders. His touch made my skin prickle. "You're a wonderful, gorgeous, brave woman with a kind heart." His expression softened even more as he gazed down at me. I could hear the ceilidh band firing up downstairs and there were hoots of excitement from the guests.

An involuntary gasp escaped from my throat as Zach placed one hand at the base of my back and pulled me to him. "Lovely dress."

We were hypnotised by each other, reading every detail of each other's faces. I admired the arch of his dark brows and the deep curve of his mouth.

Our lips moved closer until they were inches apart. At last, they met, before I reached my arms around his neck and our kiss deepened. After what seemed like ten minutes, we parted.

Zach grinned against my mouth. "I'll have to kick more doors down if that's the response I get."

Now it was my turn to grin at him. Then my mind turned over everything Zach had just told me. "So, what happens now with your Bain investigations?"

"The proverbial is about to hit the fan," admitted Zach with a twinkle. "Just got to get a lawyer to go over the details and then it'll all get published."

Zach gave me a wink. "Working for *Stargazer* and reporting on Z-list celebrities gave me the cover I needed, not only to check out Bain and his misdemeanours, but also this phone hacking scandal." Another smile toyed with his lips. "Could you see me giving up on a good story?"

We took each other's hands and moved out of the guest room. Marcus was standing outside gazing down over the banister. He turned and looked at me. A watery smile spread across his face. "I was so worried about you."

I held out my hand and he took it. "I'm so sorry, Marcus. I should've told you straight away when Mum revealed she'd given Samuel money to vanish out of your life with Jabob, but you don't know the whole story. She begged me not to tell you."

"I know," he smiled softly.

I gawped at him. "You know?"

"Mum collared me when I arrived. Told me all about that snake asking her for money, otherwise he'd go to the press." Marcus nodded. "He put Mum in a difficult position and she did what she thought was best."

I gripped my brother's hand. "I was just worried that after Finn Coulter, Mum might've been up to her old tricks again."

Marcus was puzzled. "What's Finn got to do with it? "

"Let's just say Mum encouraged him to find employment elsewhere."

My brother looked appalled. "Are you being serious?"

"I'm afraid so."

I squeezed his hand and promised to tell him about it another time.

Marcus rubbed my fingers. "God. I'd no idea." He searched my face. "Perhaps in an odd way, she did me a favour with Jacob. I was just so hurt when I thought Mum was interfering behind my back."

"I know she loves us both, but she has to stop with the incessant meddling," I said.

Marcus sighed and shook his head in disbelief. "When I found out about what she'd done, I thought Mum had offered Samuel the money and paid him off. I didn't know Samuel had bloody blackmailed her for it in the first place!" He blushed. "Siobhan tried to tell me as much, but I was so shocked, I pretended I wasn't feeling well and left the meeting." My brother snatched up my other hand. "When Ezra called me…"

My mouth dropped open. "Ezra?"

"Who's talking about me?" A deep, crumbly voice travelled to us from the top of the stairs. "I say, it's all kicking off tonight! I just saw Corrie being manhandled by two security guards."

Ezra was dressed in his tux and accompanied by Denise, Caroline, and Laura and a couple of harassed-looking young ladies in glittery frocks, who I presumed were from his management team. And behind them, was Joshua in a very similar suit to Ezra.

My mouth sprang open. "Joshua?"

Joshua gave me a wink. "Och, Ezra thought it might be a good idea to bring me along as a decoy, if things got a bit tasty." He let out a chuckle. "I did wonder why that dark-haired young woman kept bobbing up wherever I was."

Ezra grinned. "So, your doppelganger idea wasn't so crazy after all, Bailey." He looked from me to Marcus. "Ah. Splendid! So, you took my advice then, young man?"

Marcus blushed. "I did."

I marvelled at Ezra. "What did you say to him?"

"Let's just say I reminded your brother how important it

is to surround yourself with family. I've just spent the most wonderful Christmas with my daughters and I can't tell you what joy they have brought to my life. I never imagined…"

I could tell he was getting emotional, and I was so glad he was getting to have the experience of fatherhood at last.

"Writing the book felt like a way to confront the ghosts of my past, and I'm so glad I did. But the girls are my future, and I want to go into the new year with them by my side."

Chapter Twenty-Four

Ezra stood halfway up the staircase and addressed his guests, thanking my mother for the party in a way that made her glow and preen. I watched him charm the crowd, ever the entertainer. They laughed and clapped and it was clear he had them in the palm of his hand.

Looking like a suave Bond villain, Ezra raised one hand and indicated towards the drawing room. "Please, ladies and gentlemen, do avail yourselves of the wonderful hospitality and let's celebrate the start of a new year and the release of my autobiography. Here's to free speech!"

He winked at me and scooped a fresh glass of champagne from a passing waiter. There was a loud ripple of applause and calls of "Hear, hear!"

Ezra caught my eye and I smiled. I hoped he could read in my expression my gratitude for all he had done and my admiration for how far he had come. I turned my gaze to Caroline and Laura, who were standing discreetly off to one side. I turned back to Ezra, and he seemed to catch the question in my look. *Now?* it seemed to say. I nodded.

He looked over at his daughters and they both smiled.

"Excuse me, ladies and gents. If I could just have your attention again for a few minutes more, please, before we engage in an evening of debauchery on this wonderful Hogmanay night…"

Lusty cheers and laughter rose up from the assembled throng.

"I would like to introduce to everyone here two very beautiful and special young women."

Caroline and Laura exchanged a glance, and I could see that they now held hands; supportive sisters who would never be alone so long as they had each other. Family indeed.

Ezra beckoned to Laura and Caroline to stand in front of him on our spiralling, grand staircase. The partygoers gazed back up at them, bemused. "I would like to introduce Caroline and Laura … my daughters."

There was an excited hum that swept through the assembled guests.

"Yes, you all thought this handsome old goat never had any children. Well, it transpires that I did, but I only discovered that recently." Ezra's expression was shyly proud. "I must give full credit for these two wonderful young women to their mothers." Ezra broke off and gestured towards the back of the crowd. "Toni? Jules? Where are you both?"

Stunned heads, including mine, turned to see the two

elegant women clutching champagne flutes. Toni was glamorous in a long, flared, silver dress and Jules looked classy in a pale pink, long-sleeved number. "Ah. There they are. The beautiful mothers of my two beautiful daughters."

Caroline and Laura gawped at one another and then at their mothers. If their shocked expressions were any indication, they had not been aware that their mothers would be here tonight.

"They've made me realise what's important in life. It hasn't been an easy few months for me, as some of you might know. My reputation was called into disrepute."

There were tuts and murmurs of agreement. "But though I've missed out on my daughters' formative years, I want them both to know that I won't miss a single second of the rest of their lives and intend to make a bloody nuisance of myself from now on!"

Ezra hugged the girls and they all exchanged teary smiles as there were enthusiastic shouts and applause.

"So, let's raise our glasses to the only thing that really matters. Here's to family!"

Glasses clinked, there were more exclamations and shouts of "Hear, hear" and a round of applause, before the guests milled past us, eager to sample the generous spread of Scottish fayre that my mother had organised. The swirl of bagpipes started up again and there was a thump of joyous, tapping feet along to the music.

Mum and Dad nodded and smiled at the sea of faces.

I watched them gliding through the crowd, Ezra in the middle and proudly linking arms with his two lovely daughters receiving the congratulations and greetings of the guests. Laura beckoned to her partner, Tori, who was looking ravishing in a gorgeous ice-blue frock, and they too linked arms. Ezra gave Tori a dazzling smile. "Have I told you three girls about the time I sailed the Med with Richard Harris?"

I rolled my eyes. Goodness knows if any of these tales were true, but they were certainly entertaining. Then my attention fell on my pale and distracted mother.

As soon as the remainder of Ezra's guests spread themselves out between the drawing room and the library, Mum moved towards Zach. Her expression was haunted.

"Marcus just told me what you did. You were looking out for Anastasia."

I noticed two smears of colour appear in Mum's cheeks.

"Yes. At least I tried to."

She swallowed, an odd look rearing up in her eyes. "More than I ever did, and I'm her mother."

"What?"

Mum gave her dark, shiny cloud of hair a shake. "What Ezra just said is true, but I haven't been doing that for either of you. I've been far too busy judging my son and daughter, because I didn't want you to make the same stupid mistake I did."

"Marrying Dad wasn't a stupid mistake," grinned Marcus. His smile vanished when he saw Mum wasn't smiling.

I shot my brother a puzzled look. "Mum, what is it? Is there something you're not telling us?"

Dad smiled at Mum. "Come on, Ness," cajoled Dad. "You know you can tell us anything."

"I'm not perfect. Far from it," she blurted out. "But I just wanted to make sure our children stayed on the right path. I didn't want either of you doing what I did. Risking everything for somebody who wasn't worth it."

I glanced at Dad, as if to say, "What on earth is she talking about?"

Mum carried on. "I still feel so wretched over that Declan Rooney. I should've known what he was like from the off. He reminded me so much of him."

Mum's pensive stare carried across the grand hall, through the sea of bodies. She appeared lost in her own thoughts for a few moments.

"Mum?" I asked, concerned. "Talk to us. What is it? Who are you talking about?"

Mum steadied herself. "I was eighteen at the time and had fallen for someone who I thought loved me back. His name was Ace Watson." She hesitated, gathered her thoughts, and continued. "He told me he needed money; that he'd got himself into a spot of bother and, like a fool, I agreed to help him. So, I stole your grandmother's trinket box and gave it to him to sell."

"Mum!" I exclaimed. I was stunned.

"Your grandmother spotted me in the garden, giving the trinket box to Ace and demanded he hand it back. But he threatened me with a knife, so your grandmother let him have it. I never saw him again."

"Sounds like a real charmer," ground out Marcus.

I stood there, shocked, my sympathy for my mother rising. It was starting to make sense now. The constant protection and need to look out for us; the judgemental way Mum viewed our relationships; the helicopter parenting, even now we were adults.

That was why she'd always been so judgemental about Marcus and me and our futures. She'd been carrying this guilty secret around for years. She'd fallen for a bad boy who'd betrayed her and she didn't want either me or Marcus going through the same thing.

Mum took a gulp of champagne. "Ace's family moved away shortly after."

"What happened to the jewellery box?" I asked. "Was there anything valuable or sentimental in it? Was Grandma cross?"

"I don't know," she confessed with visible embarrassment as she took another mouthful of her champagne. "No doubt he sold it and pocketed the money. My mother was furious, but I think overall she felt I'd had a lucky escape. She was glad he had shown his true colours before anything more … significant happened. I did think about recruiting a private investigator to try and find the pieces, but there was nothing of any real value – just costume jewellery. I felt wretched about it. Still do." She rolled her eyes upwards. "So now you know. That's why I was always so tough on both of you. I didn't want you to echo the mistake I made." Her eyes filled up again. "I love you both so much. I'm sorry." Her voice tailed off into a whisper.

"Excuse me," I smiled to one of the waitresses. "Could I have a glass of water for my mother please?"

The young woman nodded her dark plait. "Of course, madam."

When she returned with a glass of water, Mum took it with grateful thanks and savoured one long gulp.

Dad, meanwhile, pulled Mum tighter to him in a visible act of support.

"Why didn't you tell us any of this, Mum? Why have you kept it to yourself all this time?"

Dad agreed. "This is the first I've heard of any of it."

Mum's tear-sprigged eyes shone. "I was so ashamed. I stole from my mother for a rat who didn't deserve my loyalty. It was a terrible thing to do and my mother was so disappointed in me. I was disappointed in myself, and that feeling never left me."

That sounds very familiar, I thought to myself. We were much more alike than I'd ever imagined.

She blushed deeper, her bottom lip wobbling. "I didn't want either of you to go through what I did. There are so many untrustworthy men—"

Dad pretended to gasp in shock. Mum managed to laugh, despite a tear sliding down her cheek. She gave the lapel of his dinner jacket a playful slap. "You're the exception, Henry."

"Thank goodness for that!"

Her expression became earnest again. "I know I haven't handled things well. I should've talked to you instead of trying to interfere in your relationships." Mum gripped her glass of water. "But it felt like the past was repeating itself and I realised what I should have done is teach you how to spot grifters and cheats and liars instead of just paying them to go away." She flicked us both pleading looks. "Can you forgive me?"

Marcus scooped Mum into his arms. "Yes, Mum. Of course we can."

They hugged.

Then Mum gestured to me and I hurried over to be gathered into her arms. We held each other for what seemed like the longest time. "I'm not going to interfere anymore," she croaked into my hair.

"Well let's not make too many rash promises," I laughed, planting a kiss on her cheek.

Mum bit back a sob and laughed. "I mean it. In a few hours, it'll be midnight, so that's my New Year's resolution. I'm so proud of both of you."

I dropped my eyes. "I'm sorry too, Mum."

"For what?"

"For partying like that and always getting splashed across the tabloids."

She shrugged. "It's all in the past, and anyway, there are far worse things." Her gaze was soft and appealing. "And look what you've achieved! Your business is thriving … and you're so good at it, darling." She looked over at Zach who was talking to my father. "Something tells me you and that handsome young man are going to be very happy together."

Suddenly, Ezra's theatrical burr rang out and

interrupted us again. Ezra was standing in the doorway of the drawing room, with his party guests arrayed behind him. "I think we need to see our fabulous hostess on the dance floor. Please give a warm round of applause for the wonderful Countess Tweed Muir."

Mum protested, going pink. "Oh God! I can't! Not after all this!" she hissed to the four of us. "I must look an absolute fright."

I reached over and dashed a bit of stray mascara away from under Mum's right eye. "Yes, you can. You're good to go."

Dad agreed. "Come on, Ness. When have you ever let your audience down?"

Mum looked doubtful, but after more cajoling from me, Marcus, and Dad, she adjusted her dress and strode towards the drawing room.

There were cheers and thunderous applause.

Zach grinned across at me and a smile broke out across my face.

"Ezra was right, you know. The show must go on." He gave me a mouthwatering smile. "So will Lady Anastasia therefore do me the honour of dancing with me this evening?"

I smiled against his mouth as his lips came down to meet mine. "Bailey will do, thank you very much. And yes, I'd be delighted. Just give me two seconds." I winced as my toes let out a howl of disapproval. "I just need to take these bloody shoes off!"

Epilogue

12 months later, New Year's Eve, Bannock House

It does come in very handy, having a talented and tenacious journalist as my husband.

In the court case for Corrie, he helped prove that three high-profile names in the entertainment and fashion industry recruited her to blackmail Ezra, in order to prevent their dubious activities from the past being exposed. These were individuals who Ezra had named and shamed in his autobiography, for failing to provide safe and sanitary working conditions in the fashion business, as well as a sleazy casting couch producer and a predatory film director.

Brad Janson was also proved to have arranged for the movie script to have been "stolen" and Ezra implicated. Brad's reputation in Hollywood was now in tatters.

As soon as Zach got signed off from the legal

department, he published his story about Sir Clifford Bain and then handed over all his evidence to the police, which led to Sir Clifford being arrested, charged, and eventually convicted.

And the phone hacking scandal at *Stargazer*, which Zach was investigating, hit the headlines six months ago. The magazine faces closure and there will be prosecutions of certain members of staff, as well as management who knew about the unsavoury practices but did nothing to stop it.

Ezra gave Zach an exclusive interview earlier this year, talking about his career and becoming a father later on in life. Gorgeous photos of a proud Ezra with Caroline and Laura accompanied the piece.

Zach felt like he'd turned a corner and got his life and reputation back.

I glowed as my husband's warm, dark eyes glittered my way in the Great Hall, which was decorated with two Christmas trees and an extravagant ribboned garland wound around the ornate stair banister.

"Here's the thing," he started, pulling me back to the present. "There's an Italian family in Glasgow who've got in contact with me." He lowered his voice. "They were in possession of a sketch book, which it's claimed belonged to Sandro Botticelli."

"THE Botticelli?" I gasped. "As in *The Birth of Venus*?"

"The very one."

"So where is it?"

Zach looked excited. "That's the question. They believe a

rival business associate has managed to acquire it and has taken it back to Florence, where Botticelli is from."

"Oh," I exclaimed, clasping my hands together in front of my cream woollen shift dress. "That sounds like a juicy story for you."

Zach grinned down at me. "It is. The Bianchi family are desperate for the sketch book to be found. Mrs Bianchi's elderly mother's health isn't at its best."

I frowned. "Oh, I'm very sorry to hear that."

There was a dramatic pause. "Bailey, the family would like me to travel to Florence and find the sketchbook on their behalf. It would make a great story for *The Glasgow Independent*, especially now I've been promoted to News Editor."

I gave a brief, small smile in my brother's direction, but he was too preoccupied flirting with Mrs Bamber's attractive, redheaded nephew. When Marcus saw me looking over at him, he flashed me the widest smile. Thank goodness he was moving forward with his life.

I turned back to look up at Zach. To my surprise, he was shaking his head.

"No, forget I said anything."

"What? It sounds like a great story."

He squeezed my hand. I could feel the gentle coolness of his gold wedding band press against my skin.

"No. Forget it. It's a wonderful human-interest story, but I'll send one of the team." His smile softened further at me. "I think we need to concentrate on each other for a while, and there will always be another story to chase. I keep forgetting I'm an editor now, not a roving reporter." He pulled a sarcastic face. "Sorry. I can't switch off, can I?"

I stroked Zach's hand. "You're a wonderful journalist and I wouldn't have you any other way." I eyed him again. "Are you sure you don't want to follow up this story?"

"One hundred per cent sure."

Zach had done some digging on Declan and discovered he'd checked himself into rehab after finally hitting rock bottom. I was glad he was getting help, and hopefully some therapy too. It seemed like he was trying to turn his life around, and I found I was glad about this. I really had moved on, and just wanted to look to the future, not the past.

I rubbed Zach's hand. I could still see the excitement about the Italian story mirrored in his melting, dark eyes.

"Well, I think you should go for it. For this story in Italy."

Zach opened his mouth to protest, but I silenced him with a kiss.

"Perhaps we could spend some time in Italy. We could call it a babymoon…" I said, my hand drifting down to my stomach.

"What's a babymoon?"

Zach's attention shot from where my hand was resting on my belly to my face. He broke into a huge, lopsided grin. "Are you…?"

I leant up and planted a kiss on his mouth. "Yep. One

last adventure, before we book some ante-natal classes. What do you think?"

"I think, Lady Bailey, that I have the best wife in the world."

"I think you do too..." I laughed and kissed him again.

Finally, I felt like I could trust in the future. Our future.

Acknowledgments

I'm so lucky to have the most wonderful editor in Jennie Rothwell.

Thank you, Jennie for your patience, understanding and your legendary editing skills! Huge thanks also to all the rest of the fab team at One More Chapter and HarperCollins, to Emily Thomas for her line edits, to Caroline Scott-Bowden for her copy-editing talents and Janet Marie Adkins for her proofreading. Much appreciated!

Grateful thanks as always to my amazing literary agent, Selwa Anthony and to Linda Anthony – you are both incredible women and I feel honoured to know you.

Love to my boys.

And finally, to the NHS nurses, doctors, and staff – you're incredible.

I wrote the majority of this novel while being treated for breast cancer. It was discovered early during a routine mammogram, thank goodness, and the care, attention, and compassion I received during my lumpectomy and radiotherapy, was second to none.

Huge thanks to everyone at Gartnavel Hospital in Glasgow, especially all staff at the Breast Care Unit and in

The Beatson, for your excellent support, kindness, sympathy, and humour!

Please keep your routine screening appointments – and enjoy every minute of life.

When ambitious city girl, **Darcie Freeman** is sent to the Isle of Skye to conduct research for a travel guide, she's horrified. The prospect of having to travel to a remote island in the Scottish Highlands leaves her wondering what she'll do. Step in **Logan Burns**. Gorgeous and adventurous, he lives and breathes the island, and along with his sister Iona, who owns a rather haphazard PR company, they're going to show Darcie everything she needs to know about Skye.

As Darcie swaps her designer shoes for her walking boots, will she learn there's more to life than the picture-perfect presence she shares on social media, or will it be the case that Skye is the limit...

Extract: A Scottish Island Summer

Chapter 1

Criminal thoughts about Justine, my agent, whirled through my head as I glowered out of the coach window.

There was an eerie mist swallowing everything up; rickety fences, fields and craggy mountains. It was supposed to be Easter in a few weeks. Maybe the weather memo hadn't got this far yet, I thought with a stab of sarcasm.

Where the hell were we? I couldn't feel my arse. It had gone to sleep.

The coach driver had let out a bellow of laughter, when I'd asked if we'd arrive in Skye in a couple of hours. He'd hoisted my Louis Vuitton wheelie case into the luggage compartment at Glasgow's Buchanan Street bus station alongside the other passengers' belongings and shook his shiny head at me. 'Och no, lass. Takes about six and half hours, more or less.'

Six and a half hours?! Where in God's name was this place? New Guinea?!

The coach trundled on. This Monday morning at the beginning of March the landscape was shrouded in grey, with only the occasional peak of a hillside visible. I peered out at the dancing mist, swirling over everything. Any moment now, I expected Dracula or a werewolf to emerge – or both.

Actually, come to think of it, being bitten by a vampire or savaged by a werewolf might be preferable to what I was about to put myself through.

I ground my teeth. Bloody Justine Carew!

Here I was, Darcie Freeman, luxury travel influencer—someone who'd built up an impressive following on social media, due to my varied and exotic jaunts around the world—rattling along in a coach to the Highlands of Scotland!

My lip curled in horror as I took in my travel surroundings.

The coach consisted of bottle green and navy-blue tartan seats, with matching curtains tied back at the windows.

One of my hands reached up to stroke my long, conker-brown hair. Thank goodness I'd brought my rose-gold GHD straighteners. If the weather continued like this, I ran the risk of ending up like Curly Sue in no time.

I pushed out my feet, encased in my wedged, claret suede boots and fired an icy look around myself at the other half a dozen or so passengers. Thankfully, the seat beside me was empty.

The other people I was travelling with appeared to be lost in books and newspapers.

I let out a grunt. I should've been flying out to Paphos now, not on my way to some remote Scottish island to freeze my knickers off for three weeks. I gave an inward shudder. Three sodding weeks!

I folded my arms and huddled deeper into my belted, checked coat. This was all bloody River Banks's fault. Like me, River (real name Emma Jones from Caerphilly) was a luxury travel influencer. However, where my number of followers had stagnated, she was hoovering up social media fans faster than a supersonic Dyson. That was why River had been awarded the partnership with Techno, the hot new mobile phone brand, instead of me. Its USP was its global plan that made it easier for travellers to stay in contact with those back home, and it would have been perfect for my audience.

So here I was, travelling to Skye, instead of jetting off to Paphos to promote Techno.

The good news was that Justine had secured me a book deal with Caldwell Publishing, and they were huge. I had been commissioned to compile a *Spring into Skye* travel guide, the first in a series of seasonal travel books set around parts of the UK. *Summer in Sutherland, Autumn in Alnwick* and *Winter in Windermere* were the other three titles that were to follow and would be written by a well-known breakfast TV presenter, a famous character actor, and an assertive, blonde radio journalist who all the politicians were terrified of, respectively.

The bad news was that yours truly had been commissioned to write the spring edition, about Skye. Now, don't get me wrong, I was very flattered to be included amongst such esteemed company, but I had very quickly grown used to staying in sumptuous accommodation, surrounded by fluttering palm trees and sharing my blog posts and pictures from sun-drenched locations with solid gold taps.

Normally, I would've been able to sweet-talk Justine into suggesting one of her other clients for this, by buying her a few cocktails and telling her how amazing she was, but not this time. Over lunch in Strattan's sumptuous restaurant in South Kengsinton just last month, she'd informed me that I had to branch out into the 'unexpectedly exotic', which she felt would open up new opportunities for me. 'We're talking UK-based tourism boards and agencies, darling. You'll appeal to all those new followers who want to live the same wanderlust life as you, but on a more realistic budget.'

She gave me one of her gimlet glints. 'Caldwell Publishing are very keen to have you on board with this, Darcie, especially with your photographic credentials. It makes things simpler for them, not having to recruit a professional photographer to accompany you.' She offered a winning smile. 'And you've always said you wanted to produce a beautiful photography book, anyway.'

'Yes, that's true. But I imagined it'd feature my work from somewhere like Casablanca or Mexico.'

She'd twinkled across the dining table at me, all coiffed, bouncy dark hair and ringed hands. 'But think of your carbon footprint.'

Her persuasion gathered momentum. 'You've got to be seen to be more in touch with the masses. Writing a book like this will go a long way in doing that. You'll be producing your own guide about a place here in the UK, that's accessible to more people, rather than another unattainable five-star, sun-soaked country.' She eyed me. 'You're coming across as too high maintenance.'

'That's because I am! And anyway, that's no bad thing,' I'd insisted with a swish of my hair.

'It can be.' Justine had propped her pointed chin on one hand. 'River's follower numbers are rapidly going up. I don't have to tell you that. That's why she's currently a more attractive prospect to brands that you've worked with before.' She'd picked up her wine glass and waggled it in her manicured fingers. 'You need to up your game; get out there and show there's more to you than designer sunglasses and heels. Show the public you're far more approachable than you appear.'

'I am approachable.'

Justin's eyebrows had threatened to take off. 'You can be. When you let your guard down.'

I'd bristled. 'What do you mean?'

'I mean, when you allow yourself to trust people.'

I knew what Justine was talking about. She was

referring to my previous relationship with good-looking acting bad boy, Nile Munroe. I fell for him big-time, thought he felt the same about me, but then he decided to publicly cheat on me with his sexy, red-headed soap producer.

Since then, I'd closed myself down to men. I didn't want the hassle or the risk of putting myself through hurt again. My career came first.

I deliberately changed the subject. 'I just don't see how catching the flu in the middle of nowhere is going to help my career.'

I'd chewed my lip as I listened to her over the hum of the other diners.

'I've been in this game a long, long time, Darcie. Take my advice: you need to diversify your offering if you want to reach a wider demographic.'

And so here I was, having my senses tortured by Ceilidh music blasting from the coach driver's digital radio.

More Scottish towns slid past my passenger side window, together with toffee coloured Highland cattle, blobs of sheep and soaring hills, studded in heather; Inverbeg, Crianlarich, Tyndrum… They weren't real place names, surely? They sounded more like the noise you made when you cleared your throat.

Desperation clutched at my insides. I was going to die on this coach. I'd be discovered in a year's time, frozen to death in my seat and with the waviest explosion of hair sprouting from my tragic head.

My aunt Sandra had been no better than Justine, when I'd told her about this trip. Four years ago, my parents had passed away within a matter of months of one another, and Aunt Sandra and Uncle Vernon had been the only family I had left.

'Oooh Skye!' she'd sighed down the phone into my ear earlier in the week. 'Beautiful.'

'Have you ever been to Scotland, auntie?'

'No.'

'At all?'

'No.'

'Then how do you know it's beautiful?'

'It sounds it in all my historical romances.'

Pictures of her bedtime book covers, with swooning damsels and topless Highland warriors, danced in front of my unimpressed eyes.

Uncle Vernon had been positive too. 'Never driven the lorry as far as Scotland,' he'd admitted to me during the same phone call. 'But some of the other lads have and they said it's a stunning country, even in awful weather.'

I could hear him smiling down the line, trying to inject me with some enthusiasm. 'Old Marky's wife comes from Scotland and he said when the weather up there's good, there's no finer place to visit.'

'Yes, there is,' I ground out to myself as the coach glided past a crumbling castle ruin. 'The poor woman's obviously been brain-washed.'

I tried to dismiss images of River Banks's freckled, smug face and reached into my bag in the vacant, tartan seat beside me, to root for my mobile. I decided to have a scroll through social media to keep an eye on what the competition was doing. Plus, there was nothing else to do on this tartan biscuit tin with wheels, except be assaulted by the sound of bagpipes.

Then I would make notes on my phone about my ideas for my travel guide.

My plan was to write a funky, informative but visually artistic travel guide, instead of the usual, run-of-the-mill versions out there, and the publishers were all for it. There could be a mix of selfies and landscape shots, together with close ups of flowers and fauna.

And I'd decided to list the information in an easy to read, A-Z format, so readers could dip in and out at their leisure and find what they were looking for more easily.

Even though being sent to the Scottish wilds was not top of my agenda, I was determined to produce a travel guide that was glossy, modern, snazzy and comprehensive.

For my birthday last year, my beloved aunt and uncle had insisted on buying me the latest, top of the range Nikon and my treasured camera was with me, ready to take photographs for the book. I'd tried to dissuade them from making such an expensive purchase, but they were adamant that after what I'd done for them financially (I'd made a significant amount of money from my partnerships and ad revenue streams) it was the least they could do.

I thought of them and my mouth broke into an involuntary smile. Thank goodness I had both of them in my life.

Focusing back on my phone, I tried to access my social

media channels and attempted to pull up my Instagram account first. Nothing. I then tried TikTok.

I jabbed at my phone again and again with increasing frustration. Why couldn't I get on the internet? What was going on with the Wi-Fi?

'Excuse me?'

I snapped my head up to see the middle-aged man who was sitting across from me trying to catch my attention. He'd set down his thick brick of a paperback in his lap. 'You'll not have much luck using that on here. It's the atmospherics.'

His voice was warm and sing-song Scottish.

'Of course not,' I ground out through a rictus smile. 'Thanks for letting me know. Foolish of me to think otherwise.'

I folded my arms and scowled out at the rain. Sod it! I'd do some work instead.

So, I pulled up my notes app on my phone and rattled down some brainstorming ideas for my travel guide, which included teasers I could post on my social media, to give followers a flavour of what would be in the book. I also needed a co-ordinated, complimentary series of posts to promote it. Pics of me on a beach, clutching unusual shells; close-ups of thistles and heather maybe… My heart deflated as I looked out of the coach window at the raindrops whizzing down the pane.

I let out a grumpy harumph noise.

I thumped my phone back into my bag and thudded my head against my seat.

The days when I worked in public relations for a radio station in North London seemed like a world away now. I'd been there for about three years when I started posting articles and interviews on the radio station website.

My 'Ten Random Questions With…' slot with various guests soon gained momentum when a couple of well-known singers re-tweeted my posts, and I found I was beginning to get a big increase in followers on my personal social media accounts. That was when I decided to launch my own website.

I began blogging on it, talking about news stories and people I was meeting at the station, and companies began sending me their products to review: everything from hairbrushes and nail polish to notebooks and mascara.

I would write up short, snappy reviews under the moniker *Darcie's Delights* and it went down a storm.

Soon after, I found myself approached by news programmes to talk about and give my opinion on topics such as the influence of social media on people in the twenty-first century and can modern women really have it all?

Then came the offers from travel companies to review their hotels and accommodation abroad. I couldn't believe what was happening. I was caught up in this sudden whirlwind of opportunity and things snowballed from there, the travel review requests coming in harder and faster. And then Justine contacted me, to offer representation, and I ended up resigning from the radio station to do my blogging and travel social influencer role full-time.

Sometimes, it felt like the whirlwind had happened to someone else. There I was, an ordinary girl from Clerkenwell, with two hard-working, amazing parents, thrust into this world that was completely at odds with what I'd grown up with. I still experienced tidal waves of imposter syndrome from time to time.

I guess in a weird way though, it had come at a good time as it helped me focus on something else, when I lost Mum and Dad in quick succession. It even spurred me to enrol on a home study diploma course in photography with the British Academy of Photography, which helped to keep me occupied and focused on something other than my grief, but also improved the quality of my content, which led to more opportunities with brands. On the course, I learnt everything from lighting and perspective to using multiple angles for the most creative shots and not being afraid of monochrome. I realised that with my photography, I could use my initiative—follow my creative gut, which I loved. I also liked that photography allowed me to use my imagination and create memories that lasted. Pictures remained forever. Unlike people and relationships.

I also threw myself even deeper into my social media and blogging, determined to make a success of what I was doing and raise my profile. I knew it was the only way I could try and deal with the shock and pain of my parents no longer being there.

We passed a sign for a place called 'Kyle of Lochalsh' and it pulled me out of my meandering thoughts.

More fields, rock faces and swooping mountain ranges emerged. They began to melt together in front of my eyes.

Was there just sheep and Highland cattle round here? What about actual people?

I could feel my eyelids drooping and before I knew it, I was slipping into a disgruntled sleep.

Available to pre-order now!

The author and One More Chapter would like to thank everyone who contributed to the publication of this story...

Analytics
James Brackin
Abigail Fryer
Maria Osa

Audio
Fionnuala Barrett
Ciara Briggs

Contracts
Sasha Duszynska Lewis

Design
Lucy Bennett
Fiona Greenway
Liane Payne
Dean Russell

Digital Sales
Lydia Grainge
Hannah Lismore
Emily Scorer

Editorial
Arsalan Isa
Charlotte Ledger
Bonnie Macleod
Janet Marie Adkins
Jennie Rothwell
Caroline Scott-Bowden
Emily Thomas

Harper360
Emily Gerbner
Jean Marie Kelly
emma sullivan
Sophia Wilhelm

International Sales
Peter Borcsok
Bethan Moore

Marketing & Publicity
Chloe Cummings
Emma Petfield

Operations
Melissa Okusanya
Hannah Stamp

Production
Denis Manson
Simon Moore
Francesca Tuzzeo

Rights
Vasiliki Machaira
Rachel McCarron
Hany Sheikh
Mohamed
Zoe Shine

The HarperCollins Distribution Team

The HarperCollins Finance & Royalties Team

The HarperCollins Legal Team

The HarperCollins Technology Team

Trade Marketing
Ben Hurd

UK Sales
Laura Carpenter
Isabel Coburn
Jay Cochrane
Sabina Lewis
Holly Martin
Erin White
Harriet Williams
Leah Woods

And every other essential link in the chain from delivery drivers to booksellers to librarians and beyond!